Every Man's
Brother

NORMAN LEWIS

Every Man's Brother

HEINEMANN : LONDON

William Heinemann Ltd

LONDON   MELBOURNE   TORONTO
CAPE TOWN   AUCKLAND

First published 1967

Printed in Great Britain by
Cox & Wyman Ltd, London, Fakenham and Reading

To
KINNIE

'At the hand of every man's brother will I require the life of man.'

GENESIS IX, 5

1

In the first week in May Bron Owen was discharged from Hayhurst Gaol, Cheshire, having completed, without any remission of time for good conduct, sentences totalling five years.

At nine in the morning, after a breakfast of liver which the nervous spasms in his throat and chest had forced him to leave largely untouched, Bron was taken by a warder to see the Chief Medical Officer.

The warder pressed the bell and the door was released from the inside by an electric catch. He put his head through the opening.

'Owen asks to see Dr Dallas, sir.'

Dr Jedder frowned with the impatience that had become a habit.

'Dr Dallas is not here today.'

'Ask him if he'll see me,' Bron said in a low voice to the warder.

'Owen requests an interview with you, sir.'

Jedder waved his hand as if trying to disperse a small cloud of smoke. 'Oh, very well, then. Tell him to come in.'

Owen came through the door, a short, stocky Welshman with a handsome, southern face who had retained the offensive ability to look a prison officer in the eye. He was dressed in a stiff, grotesquely fitting prison-issue suit, tight white cotton shirt with a tie patterned with diamonds, and black, thick-soled shoes. His own clothing had been lost in the shift from Wandsworth to Hayhurst after being sentenced to an additional two years for assaulting a warder. In the records office his card had already been transferred to the discharged file. It was a card marked with a blue band which meant that he was regarded as dangerous and intractable to discipline. Prisoners like Bron, until a mild reform had overtaken the prison, had been kept in a special refractory block, where the warders' motto had been, 'Hit them first. Ask questions afterwards'. Jedder studied him with contempt but his contempt was weakened by hatred, bearing with it, as ever, its faint undertones of respect.

'What is it, Owen?' Jedder said. 'I'm busy.'

'I'm going out today, sir.'

'So I observe.' By comparison, Jedder thought, prison uniform had flattered the man. One sleeve of his jacket was noticeably longer than the other.

'Dr Dallas particularly asked me to see him before I left.'

'There's nothing I can do about it, Owen. I've already said he's not here.'

'Could you tell me if he's likely at all to be back today, sir?'

'No, I could not,' Jedder said, studying a small damp patch on the wall between two sporting prints slightly to the left of Bron's head. 'I really haven't the faintest idea of his movements.'

There was nothing for it but to take a chance. Bron passed the tip of his tongue over his lips. 'I'm sorry to bother you, sir, but I wonder if he could possibly have left anything for me, with you or with Mr Armitage?' Mr Armitage was the prison pharmacist.

Jedder shifted his eyes to Bron's face, his expression charged with theatrical astonishment. 'And what, may I ask, do you expect Dr Dallas to have left for you?'

2

Bron shrugged his shoulders, uneasy at the turn things were taking, anxious to avoid any possible difficulties for Dallas, the psychiatrist, with the man who was nominally his superior.

'Don't waste my time, Owen.'

'I understood it was to be a continuation of the treatment I was receiving.'

'Your treatment? Oh yes, I remember now. Lobal epilepsy, wasn't it?' He suddenly threw back his head and released a macaw-like cackle of high-pitched, angry laughter. 'Temporal lobe epilepsy, eh, Owen? Not very original perhaps – but never mind. Whatever treatment Dr Dallas may have felt persuaded to order, one thing I can quite definitely assure you, there's no question whatever of its continuation when you leave here. It would be a breach of the regulations, and I know Dr Dallas wouldn't countenance that.'

There had been a trial of strength between the psychiatrist and the chief M.O. over Owen and Dallas had won, so that Owen had passed out of Jedder's care into Dallas's, and Dallas took what Jedder saw as Owen's malingering seriously. Jedder had never forgiven Owen for his defeat.

'Would it be possible to see Mr Armitage, sir?' Owen asked.

'It would not; and I may as well tell you I don't believe your story. You knew perfectly well that Dr Dallas wouldn't be here today, so you thought you'd come and see if you couldn't hoodwink me into supplying you with drugs. Isn't that the fact of the matter?'

'I suggest you ask Dr Dallas himself, sir.'

'You've been pretty successful on the whole, Owen, in pulling the wool over Dr Dallas's eyes, but in my case you've failed completely. I saw through you from the beginning.' Jedder pressed the bell on his desk and the warder came in.

'You're an impostor, Owen,' Jedder said. 'Now get out, and don't let me see your face again.'

The warder tapped Bron on the arm and jerked his head and Bron turned and went through the door with the warder behind him.

Jedder went to see Dallas in his office on the Monday morning. Dallas was just back from a conference.

'Owen went out on Saturday.'

'I know he did. Pity. I particularly wanted to see him before he left.'

'Did you?' Jedder sat down, hands in pockets and legs out-thrust, staring straight ahead, purposefully ignoring his surroundings. Dallas's office was the brightest room in the prison. Dallas had convinced the Governor of the psychological value of a temporary escape from the grimness of the penal environment and he had been allowed to buy the furniture and in particular a carpet. It was this carpet which had aroused Jedder's jealousy and made him Dallas's enemy.

'He had the effrontery to come and see me with some cock-and-bull story about your giving him treatment to take out with him. I think he was trying to get barbiturates out of me.'

'I left some largactil with Armitage for him.'

'But that's against the regulations.' Jedder was unable to suppress a bitter little smile of satisfaction. One move to me, he thought. Fourteen feet by nine feet of olive-green Wilton carpet had divided Hayhurst into two camps. In the end it became a dispute in which nobody managed to sit on the fence although most of the pro-Dallas or the pro-Jedder factions hardly realized how the feud had started. The carpet had convinced Jedder, who once had regarded himself as a man of liberal views, that psychiatry was largely an

4

imposture. It had won him over to the M'Naghten Rules, made him see the 40 per cent mentally subnormal of the Hayhurst population as clever shammers and put him on the side of the prison officer in the argument about the reintroduction of the cat. These days the formerly easy-going Jedder always found a man in good enough physical condition to stand restricted diet or cellular confinement. One hundred and twenty-six square feet of carpet had transformed error and the cruelty of destiny into sin. The sins of the fathers shall be visited upon the children for the third and fourth generation, and punishment was all part of the visitation. You didn't cure sin, you punished it.

Dallas showed no signs of discomfiture. 'Regulations are meant to be broken when necessary. Owen's a sick man. Personally I would like to have kept him until the cure was as nearly as possible complete.'

'Until the cure was complete! Surely you're being a trifle over-optimistic. You'll never cure a hoaxer with barbiturates. Anything you might have given this man would simply have been flogged for a couple of packets of cigarettes.'

'Just a moment,' Dallas said. 'Am I to understand that he never got the treatment?'

'Of course he didn't. You said nothing to me about it, and in any case I couldn't have allowed myself to be party to a breach of regulations.'

Dallas flushed like a girl. It was a slow, deliberate spread of pigmentation that left pale circles round the eyes like those produced by constantly-worn dark glasses in a suntan. He was twenty-eight years of age. The youngest man in his profession in the prison service and, as Jedder saw him, horribly callow, yet commanding, it seemed, almost superstitious awe and respect as a practitioner of his brand of insolent mumbo-jumbo.

Dallas fought for control of himself as the flush paled away. He got up and went to a metal filing cabinet, took out a folder and handed it to Jedder. 'I wonder if you'd care to look at that, Doctor.'

Jedder held the folder which had metal edges where it clipped into the expensive system Dallas had been permitted to buy. On the cover had been carefully printed in ink in large round capitals: OWEN BRON. B. MORFA 1938. There was a faint trace under the name of ruling in pencil which had been rubbed out. He opened the folder and glanced at the top sheet of the sheaf of papers it contained, his interest momentarily caught not so much by the information it presented but by the even, meticulous typing, the exact spacing, the formality of the punctuation, the underlining in red. It was a report laid out for the eye of a second person, perhaps an examiner who could be induced to allot a certain number of marks for neatness alone. Everything Dallas touched seemed to become infected with this model-schoolboy priggishness of his.

He read a few words of the case history, written in self-conscious textbook style, then skipped to the heading, SYMPTOMS. 'Patient complains,' Dallas had written, 'of headaches in an early stage of the attack, frequently accompanied by visual and auditory hallucinations. Phobic symptoms about real or imaginary odours are particularly marked. There are personality changes, moods fluctuating abruptly from docility to violence, acute increase in libido together with impaired judgement and incapacity to understand the possible consequences of anti-social acts. These, when committed, are characterized by lack of apparent motivation, planning, or attempt at concealment, and are followed by complete or partial amnesia.'

Dallas, watching Jedder's face, saw him smile almost tenderly and a dimple appeared in each cheek. Jedder took

6

the top immaculate sheet and laid it aside. Underneath was a paper headed 'Transcript of tape-recorded interview 1.1.66'. There were a lot more of these, and he flicked through the sheets and picked one at random.

Q. Now let's go back to those cases of the boys you attacked, at your first school. Do you remember experiencing any strong feelings of hostility towards them?

A. None at all.

Q. You were expelled from this particular school for knocking a boy unconscious with a brick. Do you recall the incident?'

A. Not the incident itself. Only the fuss it caused.

Q. I believe you were taken away from the next school after smashing all the lavatory wash-basins. Any idea what made you do it?

A. The place had a very bad smell. I remember that I always had a horror of bad smells. That probably had something to do with it. I know I smashed the hand-basins but don't remember doing it.

It was almost incredible to Jedder that any medical man could allow himself to be led by the nose in this way, and yet seemingly enough it was the normal thing in this most gullible of all branches of the profession. The kindest thing one could say for these chaps was that they were pioneers in hardly explored territory, equipped with little more than guesswork and intuition. Psychiatrists would believe anything, and you could never find two of them to agree over a particular case. Jedder himself had seen two so-called distinguished psychiatrists, one for the prosecution and one for the defence, stand up in court and practically call each other liars.

'And what was the treatment in this case?' Jedder asked.

'Sedation and tranquillizers. No more than that. I tried straight barbiturates for the first three months. After that I decided to switch to largactil. A hundred and fifty milli-grams of largactil worked wonders. The attacks were diminishing in frequency and violence. I think we were on the point of breaking the cycle.' Dallas was determined to make Jedder understand the importance of his struggle to reclaim Owen, and the tragedy of its frustration when victory had been in sight.

Jedder hardly heard him. He was looking through the window where spring had splashed a granite wall with sun-shine, and a pair of sparrows carried on sprightly and inces-sant copulations on a ledge. It had been a long winter, and he would have liked to drop everything and go fishing. Dallas's last sentence registered, however, and he considered it.

'You'd never have broken the cycle, Dallas, because Owen would have seen to it that you didn't. If you'd been in this wretched business as long as I have you'd realize that nothing's easier for a cunning and persuasive criminal like Owen than to simulate all the symptoms of a mental illness, and extract whatever benefit he can from it. I've seen it happen a hundred times. If this man's picked up next week for rape or murder it's useful to be able to say he's been having psychi-atric treatment at Hayhurst. No, I'm sorry, Dallas – I don't mean to be offensive about this – but to employ the ver-nacular, you've been taken for a ride.'

Dallas felt himself colour again. 'I don't agree with you at all.'

'You're bound not to. Our outlook's quite different. You believe that most of these people could be put right by psychiatric treatment.'

'All of them, if you had the staff to cope,' Dallas said.

'I'd say one in a thousand. If that. As for the rest –' Jedder shook his head, the corners of his mouth turned

8

down. 'You might as well try to turn a wolf into a sheep-dog.'

Dallas took his problem to the Welfare Officer, a man whose originally religious views had been undermined and hollowed out by the constant seepage of experience and doubt.

'John, I've got a rotten conscience over Owen.'

'I don't see why you should have. You've done all you could.'

'Have I? I wonder. Apart from any question of one's duty to the public, he was such a likeable and engaging chap most of the time.'

'So often the case. One sometimes gets the impression that chaps like Owen seem to be able to purge the vice from their systems with these unpredictable outbursts they go in for.'

Dallas said, 'This is another case where I've broken the first rule of no emotional involvement with a patient. Isn't there anything that can be done? By my reckoning he'll have another seizure in a week or ten days.'

'Not really. Nothing at all. The man's served his sentence, he's been released and our responsibility's at an end. Let's hope he does get in touch with you, as you say he possibly will.'

'He should have been sent to Broadmoor or Northfields in the first instance,' Dallas said. 'He could have been kept inside until he was safe to be released. It's a crime to turn a man in his condition loose on society.'

'I couldn't agree with you more, old boy, but what can you do? Judges happen to prefer punishing criminals to treating the insane. And that's the way it's going to stay in our lifetime.'

9

2

He found no caution in people's faces. Everything that moved, moved more quickly than before, and with ceaseless noise. It was May and the grass between the grey buildings was green fire. The earth, stones and a trickle of gutter rain had their smells. The pink blood could be seen under the skin of all the free men and women, and the aroma of their lives leaked out through open windows. People came and went aimlessly with brusque changes of mind and direction. He was invisible. No-one stared. Half was the purest pleasure, and the other half a kind of fear bred in the consciousness of weakness in this state of being reborn as an adult. Habit had begun to mark him like a faint pattern left by a rough surface pressed into the skin. Here I am, but where will I go? Where will I sleep tonight?

Two young married women on their way to a point to point gave Bron a lift in their sports car for the first few miles. They were coquettish and ready to be amused, but when spoken to he could hardly reply. Something in his brain that commanded the power of speech had stiffened.

His senses were soon dazzled by their restless, bustling movements and the perfumed air in which they were encased. Light skipped back at him from eyes and teeth seen in the driving mirror, and from fair shining hair. Openness – everything was openness. Landscape and sky emptied away into the infinite distance. Openness and unlimited time. Time, after two thousand days chopped into segments, had no end.

The young women were accustomed to being besieged for their love and felt the subconscious challenge of his aloofness, of their instinctive recognition that in some way he was not to be reached. One of them traced her thoughts in the air as she talked, drawing angels and swans with a cigarette that burned slowly towards two curved-back fingers. An impulse urged him to touch the curling white porcelain of her ear. Then a bad patch in the road set the sun jogging in the sky and knocked the sparrows out of the trees. His mind changed gear with the car.

'When the time comes,' Dallas had said, 'I should put myself as far as humanly possible beyond the reach of women. Just to be on the safe side. See how things go for a while at least. Potentially you've been a rapist as well as a killer.'

After that a lorry driver with a load of furniture stopped for him. The lorry driver was a quiet man who liked company on the long, monotonous roads. Bron, who had recovered by this time from the nervous silence imposed by the presence of the two young women, bombarded him with questions. He was interested in all the facts of the driver's life and occupation and the problems of long-distance driving, and after that in the lorry's age and performance, the political situation and the rising cost of living.

He was a man who didn't seem to be able to stop talking, and the driver defended himself by replying, whenever he could, with a non-committal grunt. There was something about Bron that he couldn't place, couldn't put his finger on, much as he prided himself on his knowledge of men and their motives. He was abnormally squeamish for one thing, because once when a hare came through the hedge into the road ahead and the driver accelerated in the hope of running it down, Bron leant across him to press the horn, explaining that he had a 'thing about animals'. In the end the driver concluded that he must be a sailor.

They stopped at a pull-in and had cakes and tea for which Bron paid with one of the five brand-new pound notes they had given him. He left the waitress a half-crown tip and she smiled with delight, lifted his cup and saucer, polished the table under it and put it down. Flush, eh? the driver thought. Well, anyway, seamen were like that. Bron was examining the appointments of the café as well as its customers with pleasure and interest. For him it was a gay and exciting place, on the crossroads of adventure. He found himself rubbing his forehead. A tapping had started at the back of the left eye.

He was subject to headaches, and it might or might not mean anything, but to be on the safe side he decided to phone Dallas, who had given him his private number to be used in any such emergency. The lorry driver showed him how to use the new automatic phone but there was no reply. Dallas was evidently still away, and Bron decided to try again that evening. Two motorcycle policemen were standing at the counter munching currant cake when he came back, and one of them turned his head to watch Bron go to his table.

Back on the road again they soon plunged into the cold tropic of Wales, the hills around them furred with pine forests and indeterminate rain; waterlogged valleys, a sullen panoply of black shadow of forest and mould-green fields. May was left behind.

The lorry driver dropped him at Conway, where Bron's road turned off into the hills, and here, at The White Hart Hotel, Bron drank his first pint of beer for five years. The experience was disappointing. He was saddened to find that beer seemed to have lost its flavour for him. He found that he had to force himself to finish the pint. Immediately afterwards, the headache, which had been absent for a while, returned.

Bron stayed in the saloon lounge for a half-hour, holding the empty glass, rocked in a warm tide of alcoholic sociability. The room was awash with companionable boisterousness and laughter. He trod softly backwards and forwards over the carpet, his first filter-tip cigarette hanging from his lip, ran a finger admiringly over the moist, dimpled leather upholstery of a bar stool, read all the humorous notices about the denial of credit, even made an attempt to edge his way into a loosely knit conversation at the bar. Lack of success here made him understand that intangible barriers still separated him from men who had always been free. It's the prison smell on me, he thought. They pick it up subconsciously: the reaction of the skin and glands to perpetual half-light, and the improperly metabolized starch in the pores. In a few days it will be gone, he assured himself. But I must get rid of these clothes.

Bron took a bus from Conway to Morfa, the small market town, unchanging as Jerusalem, where he had been born. In Morfa, he hoped to kill two birds with one stone by a visit to the family's doctor of old.

Dr Emlyn Griffiths saw him immediately in his consulting room that smelt as ever of incense cones, and was as crammed as an antique dealer's with period furniture.

The doctor was a bear of a man, rugged and timeless, overbrimming with passion and charm, but mined through and through with secret sorrows.

Griffiths had been embittered by near-success. His hard climb into the foothills of affluence only revealed the inaccessible peaks of prosperity and prestige, and the sight saddened him. There were always richer and more successful men than he a rung higher up on the social ladder. Lonely old women died and left the handsome doctor their houses, furniture and blue-chip shares but he took these minor pieces of good fortune for granted and, surrounded by Chinese vases and Chippendale, he longed for Impressionist paintings. The turning point of his career came as a result of a quarrel with Bron's brother Evan, who had threatened to report Griffiths to the General Medical Council for improper association with his mother, then in middle age. Griffiths, roaring with angry laughter, had taken Evan by the shoulders and pushed him out of the door, but the walls of the consulting room had had ears, and his practice began to fade away. That year he was defeated in the County Council elections and a subscription to the Conservative Party's funds that should have gained him recognition in the Birthday Honours failed to do so.

'In me you see a man,' Griffiths was ready to say, 'who could have done anything. I had the kingdom of heaven within my grasp. It wasn't to be. What I've become I owe to one man alone. Incredible that a single human being can have so much influence in one's life.'

In the days when Griffiths had retained any capacity for love he had come close to loving Bron. There had been some doubt in his mind about Bron's paternity. Now the thing no longer mattered one way or other. He could still maintain an outward show of bluff kindliness and charm, but there was no room in his heart for anything but imaginary moves and countermoves in the battle against the world.

'My boy, I can't tell you how happy I am to see you again. You haven't changed in the slightest. Not a day older. I wish I could say the same for myself. You must have been through a dreadful time. I've often thought about you and your predicament.'

14

'It wasn't as bad as all that,' Bron said. 'I've always tried hard to accept things, and it helps. Some kids are born without arms and legs. If you can bring yourself to accept what comes it's more bearable. Anyway, I was always a bit of a bookworm, so they put me in the library. I tried my hand out at writing. It wasn't nearly so bad as you'd have expected.'

'You never were one to indulge in self-pity,' the doctor said. 'It's the thing I've most admired about you. A great pity that more of us can't possess such an admirable personal philosophy. No one knows better than I do how difficult it is to maintain one's serenity when every man's hand is against one.'

He poured Bron two enormous whiskies in quick succession, and then told him some of his recent troubles.

'To start with,' he said, 'they're building a high wall across the bottom of my garden. Why? Simply to demolish my view. This is part of the main offensive. The other things like cutting off the water and refusing to collect the waste bins, I regard as pinpricks. I have a neighbour who uses some form of diabolical chemical spray on his weeds and always waits until the wind is in my direction. Consequently, I shan't have any roses this year. I defeated him on the Council in '54, and this is the way he gets his own back. You wouldn't believe it humanly possible, would you, that a man could descend to such depths of paltry spite?'

Bron sympathized and wondered. He remembered the doctor's complaints of persecution of old, but what had once been a cloud the size of a man's hand now filled the whole sky.

'And what are your plans now?' Griffiths wanted to know.

'I was thinking I might try and see my brother. Do you happen to have any idea where the family moved to?'

'Down South, near Brynaron. Don't tell me you didn't know?'

'I knew they moved away, and I heard Evan finally got married. Someone sent me a newspaper cutting about Mother's death. That's all.'

Griffiths shook his head. 'I must confess I find it all very extraordinary. You'll forgive me for saying this, but I suppose it was no more than one might have expected of your brother.'

'I don't blame him. I expect he'd reached a point where he couldn't take any more.'

'Nevertheless, blood is thicker than water. Or it should be. You probably remember that Evan and I severed diplomatic relations a number of years ago. Your mother, I'm glad to say, remained a dear friend until the end.'

So Griffiths had succeeded in hanging on in the teeth of all opposition. Bron supposed that the sexual attraction of many years past had transformed itself into a mercenary one of equal strength. He could never remember his home in childhood without the doctor's presence. His father had never been more than an ineffectual figure in the background, while the household revolved round the dynamic, even formidable doctor. Bron had been told so often by his mother that Griffiths was devoted to him and he to Griffiths, that he had accepted her assurances, but now he believed that he had felt nothing for the doctor, any more than he did at this minute.

'Your mother passed on,' Griffiths said. 'God rest her soul. And your brother married a young woman half his age. A shop-assistant, so they tell me. And that, I'm afraid, is the end of the story so far as I'm concerned. One learns in the end to expect very little of this life. It's you I'm sorry for, my boy. There was a fair sum of money left, and half of it should have been yours. I happen to be in a position to tell you this because your mother asked me to advise her when she was drawing up the original will. Unfortunately there was a last-moment change. In the nature of things there was bound to be. At your mother's time of life she couldn't be expected to stand up to the continual pressure. You've been treated shamefully, my boy. There's no doubt in my mind at all about that.'

'Whatever Evan may have got, let him have it. I'm not acquisitive by nature.'

'That I perfectly realize, but it distresses me to see you taken advantage of.'

The telephone began to ring and the doctor sighed. He reached out and took off the receiver. 'I never bother to answer it except in surgery hours, because I know that whoever it is will only hang up. It's a war of nerves.'

He returned to Bron, coaxingly, scenting the remote possibility of vengeance that could be accomplished through him. 'Well anyway, my boy, should you ever decide to claim your birthright, you can count on me. That's all I can say. Speaking as a medical man and one who knew all the circumstances, I would say that there's no doubt in my mind that undue suasion was used.'

'He's welcome to it, whatever he got.'

Dr Griffiths suspended the attack. 'And how have things been otherwise since I saw you last? You know what I mean. Any improvement?'

'As far as I know I'm cured. I've been put on some new drug. No trouble at all for the last two or three months.'

'Splendid,' Griffiths said. 'I'm delighted to hear it. It was a most curious case. A baffling one in many ways. I sometimes thought of writing it up for one of the journals. Those unaccountable aggressive tendencies.'

'They got me into trouble at Wandsworth. I was sent up

for another two years. It turned out a blessing in disguise because they moved me to Hayhurst where they give psychiatric treatment.'

'And they finally managed to cure you.'

'So the psychiatrist seemed to think.'

'That's wonderful news. Wonderful news.'

It was at this very moment that Bron noticed that the pains in his head were back again. 'As far as possible,' Dallas had said, 'don't talk about the thing. There seems to be some mysterious mechanism that tends to trigger itself off.' The pain was spiralling up from the base of his ear to his temple. With it came a dizziness. The doctor's big head, with its sad, solemn, unblinking eyes had become puffed up and seemed to be jerking slightly against the background of marquetry and ormolu, as if on a spring. The doctor leaned forward, his face floating in from a great distance, to lay his hand on Bron's knee. 'Are you sure you're all right, my dear boy?'

And then they were in Griffiths' surgery in the dark with a machine whirring faintly and light flickering on and off through a shutter into Bron's eyes. 'Keep the eyes open,' Griffiths said. 'Try to count the flashes. How do you feel now?'

'A tightness in my head, that's all. The circulation in my fingers seems to have gone.'

They went back into the living-room. 'It's nothing,' Griffiths said. 'Tiredness. When are you planning to go to Brynaron?'

'Tomorrow,' Bron said. 'I'll get a room at the pub tonight and push off tomorrow morning.'

Griffiths went into the surgery again, filled a small carton with lime-green-coloured aspirins, specially prepared for the deception of hypochondriac patients, and came back.

'You will do nothing of the kind. You will stay with me.

I should be most offended if you went to the pub. In the meanwhile take one of these. Hayhurst hasn't got a monopoly of the latest medicines. This isn't even on the market yet. One to be taken three times a day for the next four days. If there's even the remotest chance of trouble these will take care of it.'

3

'Here we specialize in murder,' Inspector Fenn said. 'Half a dozen sure-fire cases in three years and not a single arrest. I'm saying nothing about missing persons.'

He had called his subordinates for an urgent conference in his Brynaron office following a headline in the local newspaper, 'Unsolved Crimes – What is the Remedy?', and an unhappy conversation this had provoked with the Divisional Superintendent. Fenn was a Londoner with a bony, urban face and an urban economy of mind, who had reluctantly allowed himself to be exiled to this place because it had been the first inspectorship going. He realized that he was out of his depth, floundering in a foreign land, among people who concealed their secret thoughts in terrible verbosity; too dependent upon his men's willingness to break through the local conspiracy of silence on his behalf.

'From now on,' Fenn said with mechanical fierceness, 'we pull out the finger, get off our backsides and go out and get results. Less talk, cut down on the reports – action, in fact.'

His two sergeants and seven constables had nothing to say. Jones, the one Fenn despaired most of, was classifying the passers-by through the office's fake-Tudor leaded windows on the basis of their heights. The short were the miners, virtuous but damned; those who reached the window's second row of panes were farmers, also good chaps; the tall were English bastards, managers and top employees of the local factories.

Even when a big man turns up among these pigmies, he's weedy, like a child who's outgrown his strength. Trips over his own feet. No blood in his shins. We're all survivors. We escaped with our lives and our limbs intact from the black battlefield of the mine. That's the best you can say for us.

'Pay attention for Christ's sake, Jones. What's the news, if any, about the Roberts case?'

'The man and woman are somewhere under thirty acres of swedes, sir. We'd have to dig the whole area to six feet to find them.'

Sergeant Harris broke in. 'Constable Jones put in a month on the case, sir. After that he suspended his activities on my instructions. The only hope was to use a bulldozer, but the Police Solicitor advised against it.'

Fenn, who had served two years in Aden in the M.P.s, recalled the Sergeant-Major's warning definition of a native: 'He likes you. He's your friend. He wants to shake your hand. Anything you want you can have. Cold beer, his sister – you name it, he's got it. He's the chap who always says yes. Don't let him get behind you on a dark night.' These men weren't English. They were natives. Jones and Harris had bazaar faces. One of the lost tribes? His imagination dressed them in caftans and had them squatting behind trays of disgusting fruit. 'Have a loquat, Mr Fenn. No money, please, from an old friend like you.'

'We're undermanned,' Jones explained.

'I realize that, without your telling me.'

Fenn turned his attack on another of the men and Jones went back to the view through the window. He was happy for an excuse to come in to headquarters after the long night of winter and early spring. Brynaron was a town that captivated by its ugliness. Jones was enchanted by the mists that smelt of beer, the distant sounds of wheezing harmoniums and shunting trains, the seagulls lamenting on the public buildings, the pregnant women lined up to buy chips – fog-softened figures by Blake although dressed by Marks and Spencer's. The river almost encircled the town, ready at any moment to spill its floods as far as the doorsteps of the houses built at the lowest levels. There were mists at all seasons, and the lungs here drew in soft Celtic air laced with minute drops of water.

The Inspector came back to him. 'No suggestions to offer then, Jones? You were born and bred in this neck of the woods.'

Jones said, 'A hundred-acre farm offers infinite possibilities for concealment. Especially when there are old mine-shafts everywhere. It's like a rabbit warren.'

'We've moved on from the Roberts case now,' Fenn said. 'We wrote it off while you were asleep.'

'The sea is even worse,' Jones went on, 'and it's only a half-hour away. There have been several cases of bodies weighted in an intelligent manner and disposed of in this way. Shortly before you came we had a lobster fisherman who did away with his partner. Didn't even trouble to clean the bloodstains off the boat. Nothing we could do.'

'From now on we're taking a different line,' Fenn said. 'There is something we can do, and we're going to do it. The next case we have, we're going to work on it until we crack it. All of us. Someone is going to be sent up the steps, however much work has to be put in. Is that understood?'

He surveyed the semi-circle of mute faces that concealed, he was beginning to suspect, a sly contempt, besides a stubborn will to smother all his efforts in passive resistance.

They're like a lot of natives, he thought.

After the conference Fenn took Jones round to the Dragon and found a quiet corner in the comfortless saloon bar that smelt of metal polish and varnish. The Superintendent had asked him for a confidential report on Jones's work and attitudes. 'I'm simply interested to know,' the Superintendent had said, 'what he does with his time.'

'For instance,' Fenn asked him, 'do you ever book a Welshman?'

Jones, mild and professional-looking, and nearly bald at thirty-eight, looked hurt. 'So far as I know, Mr Fenn, I've no racial prejudices.'

'I've been checking up on the names and addresses of your victims and they're all from places like Wrexham or Stoke. Let's take a look at some of the charges. Last June you had a breaking and entering – chap from Macclesfield – and a wilful damage to public property – that was a Whitchurch lad. In July you charged an Englishman with grievous bodily harm for slogging a Welshman with a broken bottle in the pub at the Cross Hands. August was your peak month. You brought two cases of wounding sheep with firearms, one of disorderly conduct on a caravan site, and five of poaching. All the accused were visitors from over the border. You seem to have a mania about poaching.'

'I'm very much against it when it's conducted in an unsporting manner,' Jones said. 'Shooting at salmon with a shotgun, for example.'

'Am I to understand that all crimes are the work of summer visitors? Don't the Welsh at Cross Hands break the law?'

'Very rarely,' Jones said.

'How's that then?'

'They haven't got the spirit. It's been a depressed area for a hundred years. Only good for cheap labour. Five generations of crawling about under the ground produces a man that keeps out of trouble.'

Fenn was staring moodily into his beer, watching the particles in suspension – tiny pieces of what appeared to be fungus, or brownish fur. 'This beer is terrible. It's absolute piss.'

'It's specially made for the mining market,' Jones said. 'They can't take anything stronger, and when your mouth and throat are coated with mineral dust you don't notice that the beer's sour.'

'Have you ever considered the possibility that you may be a square peg in a round hole?' Fenn asked.

'Yes,' Jones said, 'many times, and I probably am.'

'You write poetry, don't you?' Fenn asked, mustering all his reserves of tolerance and self-control to receive the answer.

'I don't write it, I translate it.'

'Don't you find yourself a bit up-stage for this job?' Fenn remembered some of Jones's scholarly and interminable reports, one of which had included a Latin quotation.

'I wouldn't exactly say that. Education may sometimes appear to be thrown away, but it never is. Being a police- man gives one an insight into the workings of the human mind. It increases one's knowledge of humanity and of oneself.'

'And that's all there is to it, eh?'

'Taking a purely selfish viewpoint – yes,' Jones said. 'A policeman has the time to be alone with his thoughts.'

'I'd agree with you there,' Fenn said. 'Unfortunately we happen to have the Divisional Superintendent breathing down our necks, and he's beginning to wonder if you don't spend too much time alone with your thoughts. Now take yesterday, for instance, what did you do with yourself?'

'To be precise I walked eight miles over the mountain to Penlan.'

Fenn couldn't help being impressed. Penlan came under their jurisdiction but the road that reached it round the back of the mountain was in the next divisional area. Every year or two someone got lost in the mists up those slopes and died from exposure.

'What was the trouble, then?'

'Couple of boys said they'd seen a ghost. There was a bit of a panic about it.'

God give me patience, Fenn said to himself.

Their corner of the saloon filled up with farmers, talking beery platitudes in high-pitched, excited voices. They had bright red cheeks as if daubed with rouge. Fenn waited to speak until they moved away, slapping each others' backs, and gesticulating like Greeks.

'What do you know about Evan Owen of New Mill?'

'He's from the North. Strong chapel man. Very hard-working.'

'Any money?' Fenn asked.

'Not much. They twisted his arm when he bought New Mill about five years back. The farm's under the floods most of the spring and autumn. Only land that stays dry is up the mountain, and that's covered with bracken.'

'Anything else?' Fenn said.

Jones thought. 'There's a bit of a mystery about what he did before he came down here. The rumour is the family was in some trouble. Never mentions his past. He married a girl much younger than himself. Used to work in C. & A., just down the road from here.'

'Is he the kind of man to have enemies?'

'They all have. They live in a kind of vacuum up in these hill farms. Hating somebody is an emotional outlet.'

'We've had an anonymous letter about him.'

'It's the form of literary composition locally,' Jones said. 'I've had up to three in one day.'

Fenn took a folded paper from his pocket and handed it to Jones who unfolded it, smoothed it out on the table and read:

25

Ask Evan Owen what happened to the 2 cows with the foot-and-mouth and to whom was disposed the meat WICKED-NESS PROCEEDETH FROM THE WICKED.

He studied the careful round handwriting. 'A kid wrote this.'

'Perhaps,' Fenn said. 'Or perhaps it's someone trying to write like a kid. What's the wife like?'

'Pretty,' Jones said.

'How pretty?'

'Very pretty; in a chocolate-box sort of way, if you understand me.'

'Does she go in for the chapel stuff too?'

'Well, not before she was married, certainly. She used to hang about the street corners on Sunday nights.'

'And now?'

'There's an apparent reformation. Joins in all the religious activities.'

'And you don't imagine she's giving her old man the run-around on the quiet?'

'I doubt it. New Mill is a very isolated place. Not much on in the way of temptation up there.' Jones folded the paper again and held it out to Fenn.

'You'd better keep that,' Fenn said. 'Let me know who wrote it and why?'

Jones said, 'Excuse me, Mr Fenn, but do you think it's worth the trouble? There's no foot-and-mouth up on New Mill. There never has been. You don't get it on that kind of farm.'

'I'm not only interested in the foot-and-mouth. I want to know about the motives of the writer.'

Jones put the paper in his pocket. 'If we put a stop to anonymous letter-writing in this country we'd halve the postal revenues.'

26

'Investigate it all the same. It'll be good practice,' Fenn said.

Back in his office an hour later he had finished typing his report to the Divisional Superintendent. His findings on P.C. Jones were summed up in the last sentence. *Although not conspicuously energetic in the performance of his duties, his special knowledge of the area and its inhabitants is such that he might not be easy to replace.*

All the problems of Cross Hands, now that the last of the mines had closed, arose from two outstanding facts in the lives of the people. One was the factory of British Metal Investments, known as 'The Metal', which owned every building in the village, employed the whole population and supplied all their needs. The other was the mountain of Pen Gof – 'The Mountain'. Pen Gof fell short of Snowdon in height by several hundred feet, but at its base it was enormous. Throughout human history a doomed class of farmers had fought to tear a living from its slopes, driven upwards by some mysterious and suicidal urge towards the land that was practically theirs for the taking, but was quite valueless when it had been occupied and scratched with a plough. Under the spell of their environment the farmers of Pen Gof had turned into a special race. They had become so inured to hardship as almost to ignore physical pain. They kept to themselves, married late, bred few children, spoke like lighthouse keepers by signs and in monosyllables, and dreamed of heaven. A few painters had tried and failed to capture the forbidding beauty of The Mountain in water colours. It was un-Welsh – almost Chinese – in silhouette and atmosphere, drawn on cloud and mist in quick brush strokes with a minimum of detail: a few pines and wind-flattened oaks, a jagged pinnacle, a precipice, a waterfall, and a Fuji-like summit, scrubbed and polished by blizzards. Those whom The Mountain defeated decisively, The Metal awaited below. An official of The Metal had measured Cross Hands by a novel yardstick: the egg test. He had always found in any country he had visited that the higher the degree of civilization, the worse the eggs tasted. The only eggs he had ever found to compare with those of Cross Hands were those of a miserable Central American Republic where half the population was dying of starvation.

Jones's attitude to his job was a fatalistic one. He saw himself as the spectator of human processes he could do little to influence. He spent the next morning comfortably, devoting much of it to a polished report on the parking problems of Cross Hands, a village with a population of eight hundred, and five streets. A colleague who had been working with Jones on the Roberts case called over to ask for his advice. Hounded on by Inspector Fenn he had examined the contents of several dry wells in the vicinity, and in one had discovered some bones, which even if human were too old to belong to the missing man and woman.

'Let sleeping dogs lie,' Jones said. 'Emphatically. The Roberts business has died a natural death. Fenn won't thank you for starting up something new.'

In the early afternoon Jones went down to meet the bus from Brynaron to see if there were any parcels for him. He noticed a stranger get out. Jones turned to study him, making a brief mental catalogue of all that was memorable in his appearance. A stranger in the village was a rare enough event to be registered by all who saw him. There was nothing to bring anyone there until the summer visitors began to drift in from the caravan sites, and even they were recognized and remembered.

No parcels had come by that afternoon's bus, and as soon as Jones got back the operator put through an urgent telephone call. This was from a public box near the Elan caravan park, and was made by a slightly hysterical woman who had a caravan there and who complained of being disturbed by a prowler.

Jones made arrangements to meet the woman outside the park, got on his bicycle, and rode over there.

There were thousands of caravans at Elan, parked in long, sweeping lines along the curve of the river just beyond the reach of the floods and all of them belonged to the English summer visitors. The first English invasion of the valley had been in search of minerals, and now they had come back to seize and demolish its peace. By August, Elan – now only coming to life – would be a raucous town on wheels, full of strident music and wild laughter, discharging its litter into the green fields all round, and filling the neighbouring villages with gangs of youths and girls on the lookout for mischief and adventures.

The woman was waiting for Jones, as agreed, in her Austin-Mini just outside the entrance to the park, a South Midlander with a screeching voice and pink satin slacks. She directed Jones to her caravan and gave him the key, and Jones, seeing nothing unusual on the way, found it and let himself in.

He waited for an hour watching from behind the curtains, and was on the point of giving up when a lanky youth of about seventeen, unkempt and in jeans, and answering to the woman's description of the prowler, came into view. He went round the back of a caravan and looked in at the window.

Jones slipped out, keeping a row of caravans between him and the boy, and came up suddenly behind him. He turned round at the last moment, saw Jones, started to run, then stopped. He had an ugly, pimpled face framed in long, fair hair and, grinning in a kind of terror, he showed broken teeth in bluish, swollen gums that were puffy with infection.

'What's going on here?' Jones asked, trying to force his absurdly mild face into an expression of sternness.

'I'm not doing anything.'

'What's your name?'

'Dickie Beynon.'

'Have you been in any of the caravans? Turn out your pockets.'

The pockets produced a filthy handkerchief, one screwed-up ten-shilling note and a series of photographs taken by an automatic machine of the boy's ugly, oafish face in varying poses.

'You're a peeping Tom, aren't you?' Jones said. 'You're one of those dirty-minded individuals.'

'No, I'm not.'

'How many windows have you been looking into?'

'Only a couple.'

'You realize that's a serious offence?'

The boy shook his head.

'Loitering with intent, and insulting conduct,' Jones said, trying to make it sound like attempted murder. 'I've seen you before somewhere, but you look different. What happened to your teeth?'

'I got in a fight and somebody put in the boot.'

'You deserved it. They probably caught you up to some of your tricks. You work for Evan Owen, don't you?'

'I look after the cows.'

'Do you live in the farmhouse, then?'

'I used to. Got a shack along the river now.'

'Let's go and take a look at it,' Jones said.

The shack had been put up near the river's bank below the caravan site. It had been made of the wreckage of old poultry sheds and caravans that had been neatly patched together and freshly painted cream and green. A few yards beneath, the night's high tide had slobbered the new spring grass with its jetsam: a seabird's carcase, slimy driftwood, several plastic bottles.

'Where did you get the bits and pieces to make this?' Jones asked.

'Out of the river.'

'You'll lose it the next flood we get.'

Jones strolled down to the river's bank. The river had filled with inert yellow tide water. Across the valley the Nayland Express crawled at 80 m.p.h. through the patched sunshine and rain showers, scattering seagulls and galloping sheep. The sky was spread like a dirty cloth, with the rain building up again. It only wanted twelve hours of rain plus a westerly gale in the mouth of the estuary to float Beynon's shack away to sea plus half a dozen more of the same kind built on the unclaimed land all along the river.

'Let's go inside,' Jones said.

Beynon produced a key, unlocked the door and they went in.

The interior of the shack, too, had been freshly painted. There were pieces of new deal furniture, two chairs, a table, a chest of drawers – Jones examined the details of the carpentry with admiration.

'Did you make all this yourself?'

Beynon nodded.

The table was piled up with magazines and there were more on top of the drawers. Jones went through them. *Dude Man. Sex Confessions. Stripper. Bad Girls. Sex Fun.* The magazines were neatly arranged under their titles and in date order.

'You read this stuff?' Jones asked.

'I look at the pictures. Sometimes I read a bit when I feel like it.'

Jones picked up a number of *Stripper*, flipped through its

pages and put it down. He found an envelope in his pocket and handed it to Beynon with a ball-point pen.

'Write your name on that.'

Beynon held the pen between his thumb and three fingers to write his name. Jones had never seen anybody hold a pen like that before. When Beynon had finished he examined the result.

'Now write "wicked".'

He watched Beynon's face for change of expression, but there was none. The end of the pen trembled slightly as Beynon wrote. Jones looked over his shoulder. 'You read the Bible, don't you, as well as all that muck? What was the idea of writing that letter?'

'I don't know anything about any letter,' Beynon said.

'You wrote a letter to Inspector Fenn, but you forgot to sign it. We happen to have a handwriting expert at headquarters. I don't want to have to put him to a lot of trouble, because if I do it won't be funny for you. Now what made you write it? What have you got against Mr Owen?'

Beynon had automatically tidied away the copy of *Stripper*; now he was staring down at his feet.

'Come on,' Jones said. 'Let's have it.'

'It's just that I don't like him too much. That's all.'

'You ought to be ashamed of yourself. Has he ever done anything to you?'

'Not intentionally, I suppose.'

'What's it all about then?'

'It's Cathy – his wife.'

Jones was astonished to observe that Beynon's eyelids had reddened behind the long, sandy lashes.

'Well what about her?'

'I'm in love with her.'

'At your age? A pimply kid like you. And what does she have to say about it?'

'She doesn't know.'

'And you sent Inspector Fenn a letter accusing Mr Owen who's never done you any harm of flogging diseased meat. You ought to be shot.'

'I can't help it,' Beynon said. 'It's Cathy. I'm mad about her.'

'What do you do with yourself when you're not milking cows?'

'I come down here and work on the place a bit.'

'Yes, and read sex magazines. Have you got any friends?'

'Not here. I don't know anybody here. I got friends back in Swansea.'

'Your people live there?'

'Only my Auntie Florrie.'

'How did you come to land up in a dump like this?'

'Evan Owen's my Auntie's cousin. He told her to send me down here. She wanted to get me off her hands.'

'You're solitary,' Jones said. 'That's your trouble. You need to get out and see people. Let some fresh air into that dirty mind of yours. Why don't you be like other kids of your age – buy yourself a ton-up motorbike and all the gear, and have fun? You ought to go back to Swansea.'

Beynon, scratching the top of the table with a broken fingernail, had nothing to say.

'Well, what about it? Maybe we could find you some sort of job in Swansea.'

'I couldn't go away and leave her. I couldn't leave her with him.'

Life's paradoxes never ceased to amaze Jones. For instance, this sad and lonely outsider gorging pornography in his brightly painted cell. 'You could be sent away for what you've done. You know that as well as I do. Wasting the police's time by making grave allegations against your employer, knowing them to be untrue. How would you like to spend a month or two in a remand home?'

'Not much.'

'Very well then, this is your last chance. I'm going to hold up taking action for one week. You can come and see me at the station next Monday morning and tell me what you've decided to do. If you want to go back to Swansea voluntarily I may be able to persuade the Inspector to let the matter drop. Otherwise I'm afraid we shall have to see what can be done about getting you into an institution.'

4

The bus put Bron down at the end of the narrow lane leading up to New Mill, and the conductress stood for a minute looking after him with her finger on the bell. She was a dumpy figure like an awkward army recruit in her long greatcoat with brass buttons. Bron walked towards the farmhouse concealed in the trees at the end of the lane, still joined to her by a fine thread of hope. Among the ten thousand chances buried in the lucky dip of the future was the chance that he might travel again on her bus. A daydream faded, she sighed, pressed the bell and began to forget.

Bron walked on towards the house. He had had no difficulty in tracking his brother down. In fact the first inquiry he had made – in the Dragon, Brynaron – had not only produced Evan's address but significant information about his sister-in-law: 'We used to see a good bit of his wife in here in the old days.' Rain spattered on the thin raincoat buttoned over the suit that felt as if cardboard had been sewn into it, the white cotton shirt with the collar half a size too small sawing into his neck. Around him spring displayed a handsome, sopping landscape, the river in spate flinging its suds into the meadows, below, the ranks of caravans, mist patches caught up like lambswool in the gorse, sodden blackthorn blossom in the puddles, rain blown from leaf to leaf, the new bracken sending up its curled shoots everywhere like question marks through the brown wreckage of winter. He examined all the components of this scene with delight.

Freedom was still new and painted in vivid colours. He had travelled down from Morfa by easy stages in a day, and the tiredness, and with it the headaches of the day before had left him. By this time he had taken four of the tablets given him by Griffiths.

New Mill farmhouse when it came into sight was unimpressive. This was the country of ugly buildings and New Mill was uglier than average; a squat grey house with mean windows and a door with a ramshackle porch wearing an untidy creeper like a shroud. Bron was just going through the gate when something he had at first taken to be a scarecrow left propped against a wall moved, and became an untidy, dirty-looking youth who gave him a vacant yet ferocious stare before slinking out of sight behind an outhouse. A beatnik, Bron thought. He'd seen pictures of the breed in the newspaper they were given at Hayhurst every Sunday, but this was the first he'd run into in the flesh, and being a man almost with a craving for neatness and order, he didn't like what he saw.

Bron opened the gate and passed through into a yard littered with the familiar bric-a-brac of such places. An abandoned tractor-tyre here, a battered oil drum there. He stopped, took out his handkerchief and pressed it to his nose. The sensation of nausea passed. It was the smell of any farmyard – the odour of dung and of the ammonia released from urine-soaked earth. I'll get used to it, he thought. This is the way the whole country smells. He rapped twice on the door, then as there was no reply, pushed it gently open and went in.

The room was empty. A black cat, curled up on a table, opened yellow eye-slits, and stretched out its forepaws lazily, displaying its claws. Bron crossed the room to stroke it. A nice cat. A nice furry, well-kept cat. He drew his fingers gently across the fur over the muscles of the neck, and the cat rolled over on its side, beginning a tremendous, chesty rumble of content.

Bron summed the place up, making a catalogue of the furniture and fittings. The general impression he got was one of a fight against poverty. There were no signs of his mother's prized antique cabinets, chairs and tables. Most of the furniture was new and of poor quality; cheap woods with an overbold grain, and hideously varnished. The move from Morfa had clearly been for the worse. The farmyard puffed its bad breath at him through an open window, and Bron closed it to. He went to the foot of the staircase and whistled up it. A door creaked behind him, and he turned and saw Evan standing there.

At first Evan didn't seem to recognize him. His mouth opened and closed, then a muscular contortion pulled his face into an expression that was almost one of horror.

'Bron,' he said. 'Bron.' Without moving, he seemed to retreat.

Bron went to him, and grabbed his hand, laughing. 'Evan, old boy. I'm sorry. I should have let you know, but I didn't know your exact address until an hour or two ago.'

Evan stammered something inaudible through an agonized smile. Bron was shocked now by his appearance. In five years age had overtaken him. It was on him like a mould. He was a shrunken parody of his old self. His eyes appeared to have been pressed back into his head. The half-exposed muscles and sinews of his neck and chin reminded Bron of an anatomical diagram. He was sorry for him. 'Work is another form of praise,' their father had been fond of saying, and Evan's devotion to work was clearly killing him. He forgave him for whatever there was to forgive.

Evan, a fluent man, found himself for the first time in his life without a word. There was no excuse, no motive for an utterance of any kind, no way out, nothing to be said to heal the huge wrong of the years of repudiation. All he craved was to escape from this moment, and everything about him seemed the prey of this impulse to take to flight. His hands, hanging at his sides, fluttered like moths trapped behind a pane of glass. Even the skin on his scalp wriggled in agitated waves under the stubbly white hair.

'Old Evan,' Bron laughed. 'Good old Evan.'

'We didn't hear anything from you,' Evan finally managed.

Bron laughed again. 'Didn't you? Well that doesn't surprise me, considering I had no address to write to. I knew that you decided to pull out and that Mother died. The rest was silence.'

Evan raised a hand to his eyes, and sighed.

'Well, anyway, that's all over and done with,' Bron said. He clapped his brother on the shoulder. 'I can understand now what you and Mother went through. Few people know more about the pangs of remorse than I do. Why don't we forget about it?'

'You were never far from our thoughts,' Evan said. 'We prayed for you continually. Thank God you're back, Bron boy. You must have had a terrible time.'

'I survived,' Bron said. 'That's the main thing. I pulled through. I don't think I'm any the worse.'

Bron was conscious in a moment of silence of the eavesdropping of ticking clocks. This was a sound salvaged from the old home in Morfa – the sound of life and time bleeding softly away. The clocks that he had detested of old had survived, but little else remained. Everything in the room was brightly polished. Bluebells wilted in a vase that might have been won at a fair. A plastic humming-bird had been clipped to a branch of a potted plant. 'We Ask Thee Lord to Bless This Our Home', in a bamboo frame. The place was full of honest endeavour and ugliness.

38

'Have you made any plans for the future yet, Bron, boy?'

'No plans. Not yet, anyway. All I want to do is to settle down for a day or two in a quiet place and think about things. Get my bearings.'

'Bron, I'm more than happy – I'm thankful that you decided to come straight here. This is your home. Your home to come and go as you please. Cathy will be very happy you've come to us. She's gone to Brynaron to do her shopping today. Back on the evening bus. You knew I got married, Bron, didn't you?'

'Dr Griffiths told me.'

Bron noticed Evan's face tighten.

'Cathy is a very wonderful woman,' Evan said. 'One in a million. Marriage has enriched both our lives. Our one regret is that we have no children. You'll find that Cathy has a warm and generous disposition. She'll be very very happy to have you with us.'

Evan thought that the time had come for tea. He went out to the kitchen and came back in a few minutes carrying the cups on a cheap brass tray stamped out with a muddled oriental design.

'Bron boy, I'm afraid you won't find this a comfortable house. We haven't felt that we could afford to spend much money on it as yet. Have to plough everything back into the land. It's been an uphill struggle. Still, it's a house. Our home and yours.'

'The house is fine. There's nothing wrong with the house. I'm worried about you, though. You've lost a lot of weight. You've been overworking.'

'We've not been as lucky as I could have hoped,' Evan said. 'Still, the worst is over now. We try to think of it as an adventure.' He broke out into a fit of coughing, winced and put his hand over his heart.

Thunder crashed overhead with the sound of a house

falling, and rain slashed on the window-pane. 'Let's hope this doesn't last,' Evan said. 'The floods have been the worst ever this year. Three bad seasons in a row. We've decided to abandon most of the land at the bottom of the valley. It's hopeless to go on.'

'Just the way it used to be with Dad,' Bron said. 'I remember some of those winters we used to get.'

'Except that it's much worse in these days. The weather seems to be more unpredictable. This March we lost half our lambs in the blizzards. Fifteen-foot-deep snowdrifts. In March. I expect you read about it.'

Bron shook his head. 'We led a very cloistered existence at Hayhurst. Very little access to the problems of real life.'

'Farming in this part of the world offers a challenge,' Evan said. 'That's the best thing you can say for it. The high ground's infested with bracken. You have to clear it before the grass will grow. And now the rabbits are back again. Twice as many as before. Graze more than the sheep.'

Beyond the window the day had darkened to a false twilight. Lightning flared through the rain and the thunder boomed again.

'If this keeps up I'll have to go down and see what's happening to the sheep,' Evan said. 'The river changed its course the first year we came, and it's been floods ever since. The sheep are liable to get cut off when the water comes up. Last time we had a flood we lost fifteen ewes.'

A look almost of pleasure had come into Evan's face. In a perverse sort of way, he had actually come to enjoy disasters, Bron thought. Apart from his wife, the only thing that had ever happened to him was a calamity. He was like the pathological gambler, infatuated with the savage emotion of loss.

'If it's not trial by water it's fire,' Evan said. 'Last year a maniac burned down the hayricks. I found that the insurance had run out only the week before.'

'It sounds as though you picked a pretty tough spot to farm.'

'On paper it sounded all right. The real trouble was I was in too much of a hurry to get away from Morfa. You can probably guess why.'

'I've always supposed I had something to do with it.'

'You're wrong, Bron. You're quite wrong. There was no question of running away, and in any case all our neighbours and friends couldn't have been more understanding and sympathetic. I simply decided that it was the only way to break the unfortunate influence Dr Griffiths had over Mother.'

'Wasn't it a bit like taking a sledge-hammer to crack a nut?'

'You've no idea of the strength of his hold over her, Bron. And she wasn't the only one. I took legal advice but there was nothing I could do. It was simply a matter of selling up and moving out of the district. Under the pretence of caring for the sick Dr Griffiths wormed his way into people's homes and into their lives. He was the evil genius of our family.'

'I should have described him as slightly mad. He put me up for the night. Couldn't stop talking about the people who were persecuting him. It was a bit of a relief to get away in the morning.'

'This is the man that was never out of our house for thirty years. I've often suspected that half Mother's trouble was mental. He convinced her that she was a sick woman so as to make himself indispensable,' Evan said.

'From what I gathered, he was after her money, and he nearly got a good slice of it. I had to listen to an endless rigmarole about changed wills. You're one of a number of people who are out to ruin him. He talks like a raving lunatic half the time. I wonder he gets anybody to take him seriously.'

Evan seemed to break away. He reached the window to stare out at the boiling clouds through the water twisting and cascading down from a broken gutter. The thing was to escape if only for half an hour for the last solitary struggle with his conscience which he already knew could only result in one decision.

'I'm getting worried about the sheep, Bron. Perhaps I ought to run down and see if everything's all right.'

'You carry on,' Bron said. 'Don't let me hold up the work.'

'It all depends if it's raining higher up the valley. If it's not raining higher up, we'll be all right.'

'Better be on the safe side. Don't mind me.'

'I'll get the car out and just pop down and see how things are. After that we'll go and pick Cathy up at the bus-stop. We'll give her a wonderful surprise.'

Bron waited an hour, and the rain stopped and the sunshine broke through, diluted but warm. He found a scrap of paper and wrote on it, 'Gone for a walk. Back soon,' and put it under the vase with the bluebells.

Outside the rain had sharpened the air and filled it with earthy odours. Bron, trudging down the lane, stopped once at a gap in the hedge to look down over the river, snaking through a marsh tinselled with flood water. At the bottom of the hill the river roared just under the road, the water curling and leaping, carrying with it what it had snatched from the farms higher up and the fragments of a butter-coloured sunset.

At the edge of the waters the caravans, row after row, awaited the summer.

The Salutation was just beyond the crossroads, an uninviting public house built squarely in the local greystone, with dead flowers in yellow window boxes. Bron went into the saloon. There were two self-contained conspiratorial semi-circles of regulars at the bar, and a handsome and opulent barmaid moved between the two. She served Bron, eyes averted, with a pint of beer. He said it was a pleasant evening, and she said it was nice to see the sun for a change, if only for a few minutes, and left him. Bron felt excluded. This was a closed society united on a common front by a narrow range of shared interests, shared prejudices and shared suspicions. He knew that if he came to drink beer here every night for a year the barmaid might turn her smile in his direction and these men might open their ranks to receive him as a member. In the meanwhile friendly overtures would be treated with distrust. And this was exactly the kind of semi-oblivion he needed. It filled most of the requirements of the rules he had laid down for his survival. All I have to do is to lie low. *All I have to do is to lead a quiet life. Keep clear of trouble. Keep off the drink. Keep clear of the women. Learn to vegetate.* As Dallas, still a little uncertain of himself in matters of diagnosis, prognosis and treatment of his elusive complaint, had said, 'We have to learn to live with our limitations. When you get out why not look round for a really quiet place, and bury yourself? A nice Hebridean island would be just right.'

This wasn't exactly a Hebridean island; it was certainly the next best thing. The heavy damp air you took in with every breath was a sedative in itself. Perhaps I'll give Evan a hand on the farm. Look after the sheep or something. Do a bit of fishing. Go for long walks. Just the place for long, lonely walks. Good thing he didn't object to his own company.

Bron took his beer and backed away to stand by an empty fireplace under a case containing a stuffed pike. A short, scarlet-faced man he took to be the landlord came out of a

43

room behind the bar, nodded and flashed his teeth in response to greetings from several of the regulars, stood behind the barmaid to let a proprietorial hand slip down on to her hip, and went off. Bron gave himself ten minutes to finish his beer and go back to the farm. Evan's reception had come as a surprise and a great relief. He was clearly suffering from a bad conscience, and Bron suspected that there had been a grain of truth in Griffiths' paranoiac ravings about his mother's will. But what did it matter, after all, if Evan had persuaded the old lady to leave all her worldly goods to him? Hadn't he worked for them all his life? Hadn't the old farm at Morfa taken away from him his youth and strength – and wouldn't the new enterprise at Cross Hands finish him off in the end?

He went to the counter to put down his empty glass and was going when the door opened with a bang and two outlandishly dressed youths came in. More beatniks, Bron thought, but these were of a different brand from the skulking boy he had seen up at the farm. The two newcomers drifted in dribbling an imaginary football towards the bar, shoving and charging each other, shouting mock protests and laughing violently. Bron felt rather than saw the nervous shrinking of the regulars away from them.

One beatnik was tall, with thick feminine features – the features almost of a negress – and wore a balaclava, and the other, shorter, was dressed in a long black jacket and denim trousers thrust into tall boots. The short beatnik was sad-faced, but laughed continually without any basic change in his sorrowful expression.

They reached the bar and the tall one rapped on it five or six times with a huge, bony fist. 'O.K. then, how about some service?' he said. Long black hair curled from under the balaclava on his shoulders. The regulars began to back away along both sides of the bar.

44

The sad beatnik, arms, legs and shoulders continually on the move, began to sing.

'Baby, I got that feeling.

Want you to go along.'

'Do we get service or don't we?' the tall beatnik asked. He struck the counter again and the regulars jerked a little farther away, shifted by the impact of the fist rather than by their own volition.

'Want you to hold my hand, baby.'

The sad beatnik danced and jigged at his friend's side, striking him playfully in the ribs.

'Hey, cut it out.'

'Maybe I got you wrong.'

'Let's have some service, eh?'

Urged on by the landlord, the barmaid came.

'We got service at last – any coffee?'

'I'm afraid we don't serve coffee here.'

'Seven-Up, then? Got any Seven-Up?'

'Coca Cola,' she said. 'Only Coca Cola.'

'O.K. then, but pull the finger out.'

'Maybe you got me wrong, baby.

Don't say I got you wrong.'

The barmaid came back with the Coca Cola and the sad beatnik leaned across the bar and took her by the elbow.

'How's about you and me going case, baby?'

She twisted away to free herself. A shout of indignation from the landlord. A small man wagged a finger under the nose of the sad beatnik and found himself on the floor. A friend came to his aid and was pushed away. A couple of bar stools crashed down. Bron had the not unfamiliar feeling of having participated in this scene before, of standing on the edge of a preview of events to come. The sensation was an unpleasant one. The sound had been cut off and now for a fraction of a second the action stopped. In a last instant of general agitation a beer glass had gone over, and suds of beer, held by a high-speed camera, hung like a lace teacloth over the counter's edge. A mouth had been opened to sing and others to shout. The landlord, a finger in his ear, reached for a telephone enshrined in bottles. The barmaid, flouncing away, had been caught with one hip back-thrust and so much lower than the other as to verge on deformity. A caged goldfinch, leaping from top to bottom perch, remained in mid-air. The tall beatnik's head came close for inspection, a tiny triangle of saliva uniting top and bottom lip in the corner of his mouth.

Sound and action came on, and a voice with a range of four musical notes sang in Bron's ear, 'Trouble they give and that incessant smash the place up as soon as look at it, by damn, telephoning for the police constable might as well telephone the prime minister absent on duty elsewhere for certain he is when he's most wanted prefers to sit quietly on his arse and wait for promotion.'

Bron remembered his tablets. He took two, washed them down with a glass of water and turned to go out.

The tall beatnik cut him off, his crudely carved African idol's face fallen into a loose grin.

'Where are you going then, Taffy?'

'Home.'

'Can you sing, Taffy?'

'When I'm in the mood.'

'Give us song then.'

'I'm not in the mood now.'

'If you can't sing, what can you do?'

His hand dropped on Bron's left arm.

'Come outside,' Bron said. 'I'm going to let you into a secret.' He took the youth's forearm in his fingers and felt muscles separate as he squeezed. The big, clumsy face knotted in anguish. Bron let his arm drop.

'You've outgrown your strength, boy. Too tall for your weight. Call your friend and let's go out.'

Bron closed the door gently behind them. They began to walk towards a bar of blue night sky squeezed between rising and falling shutters of mist. The first of the weak smeared lights of Cross Hands were ahead. An invisible curlew whined and yapped like a lost puppy dog.

'Not much of a place, is it?' Bron said.

'Dead loss,' the sad beatnik said. 'Nothing to do with yourself.'

'Where are you boys from?'

'Bristol. We got a loan of a caravan up here.'

'Thinking of staying around much longer.'

'Not a chance of it. Nothing to stay here for, is there?'

Bron said, 'I wouldn't like it to get around, that's why I ask. As you're on the move I may as well tell you. I just got out from doing five years. Grievous Bodily Harm. Too much form to want to get into more trouble. You know what I mean.'

He went back because he couldn't remember paying for his beer.

The barmaid, haloed by a semicircle of spotted mirror, awaited him with a smile. A little to one side, the landlord, flushed and short of breath from the emergency, was still jiggling the receiver hook of the phone.

'What can I get you, sir?'

'Nothing more, thanks.'

'This is on the house. Won't you have a drink with me?'

'In that case I can't very well refuse.'

She was a pretty woman, a little past her prime, softening everywhere towards middle age, with diffused features projecting soft shadows like a portrait photograph made with a soft-focus lens. Bron found that her hair style was too fanciful, and her lipstick too bright and that there were too many rings on her fingers, but her perfume reached out and enveloped him and he forgave her.

'Whisky?' she asked, arching her brilliant lips in a wide smile.

'Very nice of you,' Bron said.

'Lucky it was for us you happened to be here. Probably have smashed the place up like they did last year. Thirty-eight pounds' worth of damage. Started a fight in the Dragon in Brynaron last week. They say the girls are worse than the boys.'

The landlord had given up his attempts to reach P.C. Jones on the phone. 'No answer as usual. Waste of time trying. No bloody use to anyone. I don't see why we pay the rates.'

'What was all the trouble about?' Bron asked. 'What do they go in for this kind of thing for?'

'Don't ask me. I know what they bloody want, though. They want a good hiding. They want a taste of the bloody birch. That's the only kind of argument those louts from the caravan site understand.'

The barmaid brought the whisky. When Bron took the glass she held it for a moment in such a way that her pink fingertips with their silvered nails touched his.

'And what happens,' the landlord said, 'even if one of them does get picked up by some bloody accident? A five-quid fine. Ten at the most. They want a taste of the bloody cat. That would make them think twice next time.'

The barmaid rolled her eyes, showing impatience and contempt. She leaned forward slightly and Bron caught sight of the lower half of her body mirrored among the beer bottles at the back of the bar. In his imagination he curved the palm of his hand over each buttock. The landlord had carried his grumbles out of hearing into his private room. As the barmaid's face, imprinted with its radiant smile, came closer, Bron picked out the details under the layer of powder, the fine lines, the downy hair and the mole on the cheek. An enormous gold locket bobbed gently on the upper slopes of her bosom.

'What's your name?' Bron asked.

'Wendy.'

'Have a drink with me, Wendy.'

'All right.'

'And I'll have another one at the same time.'

She measured out two trebles, and Bron put down a pound note. Wendy pushed it away, and Bron took her hand and put the note in it, and closed her fingers over it.

'Any chance of taking you home?' Bron asked.

She shook her head, and seemed to glance back towards the private room with its glass door. 'I live in.'

'What do you do when you close up for the night?'

'Plenty of cleaning up to be done. After that I go to bed.'

With him, I suppose, Bron thought. While considering his next move he became aware of a slight thumping sensation at the base of his skull. He put down his glass. He hoped the tablets weren't losing their effect.

'What about Sunday, then?'

'I don't know. Have you got a car?' She lowered her voice almost to a whisper. The door opened and three customers came in. 'Excuse me,' she said.

Wendy drew three beers and came back. She looked worried.

'What do you say?'

'It's a bit difficult,' she said. 'I'd have to think about it. Let you know.'

'When?' he asked, putting his hand over hers.

A door handle clicked and an instant of alarm fluttered in her features. She pulled her hand away. Bron saw the landlord in the doorway of his room.

'Wendy, may I have a word with you?'

'Coming, Mr Oakes.'

She drew two glasses of beer for the customers and went towards the private room, taking her time.

Oakes backed into the room, his jacket off and sleeves rolled up. His fists were doubled.

'All right,' he said. 'You can cut the innocent stuff I happened to be watching.'

'I don't know what you mean.'

'I saw that fellow mauling you. I saw him mess you about.'

'I wasn't aware he was messing me about.'

'He was taking bloody liberties then. Get rid of him.'

'Get rid of him yourself.'

'I will too, by God,' Oakes said. He threw out his chest, marched two steps towards the door, and stopped.

He came back and she laughed. Oakes lifted his hand ready to smack her face.

'I shouldn't,' she said. 'And you'd better close the door if you want to make a scene.'

'Always someone hanging about the place. Always someone after you, eh?'

'It's good for business, isn't it?'

'You slut.'

'Don't call me names,' she said. 'I won't stand for it.'

'Why can't you show a bit more self-respect?' He was whining now. 'Why do I have to keep telling you how to behave yourself?'

'Especially as it happens to be none of your business anyway. I'm a free agent. You're not my husband. I can do what I like.'

50

'I don't know what I'd do if I was. I swear to God I don't. I wouldn't be responsible for my actions.'

'You're not anyway half the time. More like a great big kid than a grown man.'

'I know what I'm going to do one of these days. I'll tell you that.'

'You're going to do nothing. And another thing, the next time you raise your hand to me I'm going to leave you. I'm going to walk right out of here and I'm not coming back.'

She turned to go back to the bar, and he followed, anxious and ready to plead with her. This made things worse.

In the bar Bron had found an ally and adviser in the small farmer who had been knocked over by the beatnik, and who had now ventured back. He was full of confidential information.

'As good as a film any day. Jealous of her and won't let her out of his sight. This kind of thing goes on all the time. Some of the chaps pretend to make up to her to get him going. We always get a big laugh out of it.'

'But if she's not his wife, why does she stand for it?'

'She wants to marry him, and she will in the end. He's loaded. Rich man. Half interest in a cinema. House property and God only knows what else.'

'Not much hope in that direction in that case.'

'Oh, I don't know. I wouldn't say that. It can be done, and it has been done. He goes away on business trips sometimes. Can't very well chain her up, can he?'

'No, he can't chain her up.'

'She has to be a bit careful, but where there's a will there's a way.'

Bron moved along the bar away from the farmers to catch Wendy's eye as she passed. 'Sunday then?' he said.

She smiled and shrugged her shoulders.

'Where is he now?' Cathy said.

She was still wearing her coat, an acid-green, hairy garment with a thousand minute raindrops clinging to the hairs, and a handkerchief over her head to keep the rain out of the tight new curls the hairdresser had put in earlier in the day.

'He went for a walk, dear. I can't think where he can have got to. He said in the note he would be back in a few minutes. I really shouldn't have gone out, I suppose. But it looked as though we might be in for another bad flood.'

He helped her off with her coat. 'You must be tired out,' he said. 'Sit down and rest yourself, and I'll go and make some tea.'

'I really think I ought to tidy up a bit first,' Cathy said. 'The rugs get in such a mess in this weather. And what are we going to do about the laying on of hands tonight?'

'I'm afraid we shall have to call it off. I'll ring up Mr Bowen and explain. It won't be necessary to go into details. I'm sure our friends will be very understanding. The main thing is not to miss tomorrow's Investment in God, as it's the most important day.'

'Yes,' she said. 'We mustn't miss that whatever we do. What's your brother like?'

'In appearance, do you mean? Well I don't suppose you'd find him particularly prepossessing. I suppose it's not to be wondered at when one considers the unfortunate life he's led. Other than that I should describe him as rather quiet and reserved. Much more so now than ever before. To be frank, after not seeing him for five years his manner came as the greatest possible surprise. I have a feeling, deep down, that he may be a changed man. Perhaps our prayers have been answered.'

'Perhaps they have,' she said. 'We were always praying for him.'

'Prayer can be a very mysterious thing,' Evan said.

'Will he be staying with us?'

'I shall do my best to persuade him to.'

'What are we going to do about telling our friends?'

'You mean that Bron's been in prison? If the occasion arises we shall tell the truth.'

'Yes,' she said. 'That's the only thing to do.'

He patted her arm affectionately.

'Will we put him in the back bedroom?'

'We could,' Evan said, 'but I think perhaps we should make a little sacrifice and move into the back bedroom ourselves. Would you mind very much, my dear?'

'Of course I don't mind.'

'The back room does rather need repainting. I think that's the next thing we ought to attend to as soon as we can afford it.'

'The view from the front bedroom is much nicer,' she said. 'I'd better go up and change the bed and move the things out of the wardrobe.' She got up.

'Before you go, dear, I think there's one other thing we ought to discuss while we're by ourselves.'

Cathy sat down again and waited. Evan occasionally conducted an internal struggle before coming to some major decision. The existence of this conflict was betrayed, as she observed, by a certain interplay of the muscles at the corners of the mouth, which was to be seen at this moment.

Evan said, 'I've been giving a good deal of thought to this business of Bron, not only since I've seen him again, but in the past few months. You may not have been aware of it, but I've experienced moments of self-questioning and depression. I regard his arrival today as providential. I may as well admit quite frankly that I feel very badly about my treatment of my brother. I turned my back on him in his hour of need.'

'What could you have done?' she said.

'Materially very little perhaps, but I could have kept in touch with him while he was in prison and made him understand I still believed in him. As it was I failed him, and I regard this as a heaven-sent opportunity to do everything I possibly can to make up for my cowardice and neglect.'

'You must do what you think best, dear.'

'I'm always encouraged by the knowledge that you're at my back,' he said. 'I'm a very lucky man.' He took her hand and pressed it.

'I believe the thing I've worried most about was that trouble over Mother's will. Bron's already been told about it by Griffiths. I can't tell you how much I wish that it had not been left for him to find out from that evil old man.'

'You've nothing to blame yourself with,' she said. 'Your mother did as she pleased. You didn't try to influence her one way or the other.'

'That's just the point. I didn't influence her when it was my duty as a Christian to do so. When Mother cut Bron out of her will and told me she'd done so, I should have insisted she was doing wrong, and I didn't. I had no right to allow her to do what she did. Don't you agree with me that I ought to do everything that it's in my power to do, to put right what I now see as a wrong?'

'Yes, I do,' Cathy said. 'Knowing you, I know you'll never be happy if you don't.'

'My intention,' Evan said, 'is to ask Bron to come into partnership with me. It's tantamount to giving him half my worldly possessions, but I don't think anything short of that would meet the case.'

'Well you must do just that, dear.' Cathy said.

She felt no special surprise at the abrupt turn of events.

54

After marrying Evan she had soon picked up a kind of resigned, submissive patter that was part of the game of life played in this way. She possessed a quiet unspectacular fortitude that was the strength of all her family, passed down to them by forgotten generations of miners who had learned to construct uncomplaining existences round the minutest grain of hope. She accepted the small satisfactions of her married life's security, offsetting them calmly against her physical and emotional isolation. Her stoicism was effortless, just as was the stoicism of her sister Linda who had married a Persian student in Cardiff, had gone to live in the mountains of Khorasan, and had written once mentioning in the most casual way that she now wore a veil. Whether life meant prayer meetings or a yashmak in an Iranian village it was all the same to the Thomas girls. They built a plain version of happiness with whatever bricks happened to be available.

It was a quarter of eleven when Bron got back, and Evan awaited him, full of misgivings.

'Sorry,' Bron said. 'I rather fell by the wayside. Popped into the Salutation for a drink and got talking, and then one thing led to another.'

Evan could smell the liquor on his breath, but other than that there was nothing to justify his fears. There was still nothing about Bron to remind him of the moods and violences of the years of early manhood.

'We were beginning to worry that something had happened to you,' Evan said. 'I persuaded Cathy to go to bed. She was very tired after her day in town. She asked you to excuse her. Well, anyway, sit down and have your supper. Nothing very exciting, I'm afraid. Cold beef and pickles. We can talk while you're eating.'

Bron sat down at the table and Evan pulled up a chair to face him.

'They tell me the Salutation's a very comfortable place now, under the new management. You probably saw some of my neighbours there. I rarely visit a public house myself.'

'There was a spot of bother with a couple of beatniks. However, they agreed to go quietly in the end.'

'Young people from the caravan site, I suppose. It's becoming quite a problem. They tell me it's dangerous for a girl to go out alone in Brynaron.'

'How were the sheep?' Bron said. For an instant Evan thought he detected a note of derision in his voice. He dismissed the thought.

'As it turned out they were perfectly all right. I got a soaking for nothing. They've usually got the sense to make for the higher ground when the meadows start flooding. Sometimes I wonder if we don't underestimate a sheep's intelligence.'

'I'm sure we do,' Bron said.

Evan looked at him closely again, but Bron's eyes were on his plate, and his expression unrevealing.

'They tend to entrust the decisions of the flock to its most intelligent member,' Evan said, 'but I seem to remember that humans are liable to do the same.' This was a favourite theme, and slight encouragement would have been needed from Bron to set him moralizing on the foolishness of mankind in contrast with the comparative sagacity of the animal kingdom.

Bron was about to add his comment when he had an upsetting experience. Evan filled a tumbler of water and put it in front of him, and Bron reached out to pick up the tumbler to find that his fingers closed on nothing. This failure to pick up a glass provoked a twinge of panic, and for some obscure reason he remembered an electric fan he had once been watching, which had appeared to stop. He reached out again, warily, hooking round his hand, took the tumbler from the rear and picked it up, then felt obliged to glance at Evan to see if he had noticed.

Evan said, 'Bron, boy, I had another reason for sending Cathy off to bed. I wanted to have a quiet chat with you, and I always feel that even the best of women can be in the way when men want to talk business. I may as well come straight to the point. What would you say to the idea of staying on here and coming into partnership with me?'

Bron put down his knife and fork. 'There's nothing I'd like better than to stay, Evan, and I must admit I was hoping you might suggest it, but any question of a partnership is out. I've got nothing to put into it. All I've got are the clothes I stand up in. If I stay here I'd expect to work for my keep. Not much I know about farming, but I suppose I could pick it up.'

'You don't quite understand what I mean. You wouldn't be expected to put anything into the partnership. I realize perfectly well that you haven't got anything to put in – well, that is, nothing but your enthusiasm and your youth. Cathy and I discussed this while we were waiting for you. This farm isn't much of an enterprise, but such as it is we both believe that you're entitled to an equal share in it.'

Bron's first moment of dazed unbelief vanished. Can he mean it? Yes—of course he does. Evan, a slow, cautious and narrow man, was capable of sudden sweeping gestures and almost violent decisions. Just as in the case of Dr Griffiths. There had been no way of ridding himself of the man except by leaving the area, and Evan had calmly sold up, uprooted himself, and gone.

'Bron – the motive's not entirely free from self-interest. We won't go into details now but I need your help every bit as much as you need mine. We could do wonders with this place, working together as a team. Up till now I've been on my own, and we've managed to keep our heads above water, but that's about all. If we got together and put five years hard work into this farm we could turn it into the best small farm in the county.'

'The only trouble is,' Bron said, 'that you've got more faith in me than I have in myself. In its strange, twisted way I've led a protected life for the past five years. Prison deprives you of the right to use your initiative. There aren't any problems except toeing the line. It's all worked out for you. I just don't know how good I am at anything yet, or if I can stick at anything, or do anything worth doing. I'd be afraid of letting you down.'

'It's a risk I am quite prepared to take,' Evan said.

He had done the right thing. In a life preoccupied with the theory of faith and immersed in mechanical pieties, he had at last been faced with the test of a practical issue. He felt the incredulous joy of an ungifted schoolboy who has somehow scraped through an examination he believed he could never pass.

Bron found the breakfast-table conversation next morning a little strained; see-sawing between Evan's eager geniality and Cathy's reserve. In between nervous silences Cathy treated him with a kind of twittering kindness, and the over-consideration well-meaning people were always inclined to use towards a man who had been in prison. For her he might have suffered some cruel bereavement.

Her ordinariness came as a surprise after the report he had had of her. He would have been prepared to admit that she was good-looking but it was a local type of beauty that would never have turned a head in the street. She was tiny, and inconspicuous in face, manner and voice, with the reddish hair you often saw in these waterlogged and forgotten valleys, belonging, Bron supposed, to the descendants of ancient Celtic tribes whose blood had survived because of a talent for self-effacement, for acceptance in silence, without revolt or protest, whatever slaveries the centuries had laid upon them. Evan didn't seem to be able to take his eyes off her. He was full of small attentions and gallantries.

Evan carved his salt mountain bacon and babbled on in his enthusiasm. They would buckle down together, buy derelict hill-pasture, dismantle the ruined buildings of defunct mining companies, clear the bracken, and stock up with black-faced sheep. The sheep would increase and multiply like the flocks of the Hebrews of old approved of by the Lord, and with the profits ploughed back, they would drain the meadows and marshes at the bottom of the valley, and frustrate the baleful power of the river. The depressed factory workers of Cross Hands, chronically on part-time work, would be somehow reclaimed for the righteous struggle with nature, covering the barren, exhausted hilltops with green fields. Sometimes Evan halted the flow of his vision for a smile and nod of agreement from Cathy, which was never withheld.

Listening to him with a growing sense of withdrawal, Bron realized that Evan's strength lay in his enthusiasm. He looks old. He looks worn out. But he can't be. He's like an old volcano with the fire still bubbling about deep inside. Oh, to have fire in the guts. Bron feared he was without fire, and that he had suffered all his life from a terrible debilitating detachment. At this very moment he was aware of the sensation of not being wholly a component of this scene. He was outside his body, watching his own movements and listening to his own voice when he spoke. He was a ghost, and Cathy was a ghost, and Evan was a ghost too. Three ghosts

c

round a table, a detached ghost, a nervously twittering ghost, and an enthusiastic ghost. Bron ordered his hand to pick up his coffee cup, watched the hand convey it to his lips, and drank. His palate assured him by a kind of remote control that it was hot and sweet.

Cathy was twittering and smiling at his elbow as his ghost and body were reunited. 'Have some more coffee, Bron. Do help yourself to more toast. I'll go and get you another rasher of bacon.' On the other side Evan, too, urged him to eat and drink.

'Cathy and I will be attending the prayer festival tonight,' Evan said. He raised a reassuring hand. 'Don't be alarmed, we don't expect you to come. Tonight's the last meeting but one, and we feel that we ought to be there. The theme for today is "Investment in God". By the by, Cathy dear, did you remember to pick up the tracts at the printer's?'

'They were the "Cast Thy Burden Upon the Lord" ones, weren't they, with Morgan the pork-butcher's advertisement on the back? Yes, I did.'

'I think it might be a good idea if they were handed out after the meeting this time, instead of before, don't you?' Evan said.

She agreed. 'Otherwise they have a habit of getting overlooked in the general excitement. Quite a lot seem to have been left behind on Saturday.'

'Cathy is a wonderful organizer,' Evan said. 'She's a very active worker. It was her idea to appeal to local tradesmen to assist in the cost of our printed literature by their advertisements. We were lucky enough to find a backer for every day of the festival.'

5

Up on the slopes of Pen Gof, the mist was still streaming up in all directions like the smoke from numerous fires. Behind the mists were dark rain-sodden colours, blacks, bronzes and blues, and a violent green that lay on the lower fields like synthetic dye. The polished dome of Pen Gof itself had lifted clear of the mists in the sky, and it dominated the whole landscape. Evan, with his back to the mountain, could see through to the bottom of the valley where the water that had slopped over the riverbank at high tide had drained away to leave a creamy encrustation with the seagulls circling over it. Thin, echoless sounds, trapped in the mist, reached him: a church bell chiming the half-hour, a distant car hooter.

Evan had divided the lower slopes into rough geometrical shapes to be cleared of bracken and sown with grass, and he was coming to the end of the clearing that could be done in time for the spring sowing. The ancient covering of bracken that had begun to reach slowly up the mountainside as soon as the forest had been cut down in the remote past was immensely resistant. The bracken could be killed by spraying but the root clumps had to be dug out before the grass would grow, and Evan, with or without help, had been working his way slowly up the mountainside for three and a half years at an average rate of twelve feet a week on a front of three hundred and fifty yards. It was the kind of elemental struggle, producing its meagre but visible day-by-day result, that provided a deep satisfaction.

By ten o'clock the freezing mist patches had torn themselves to tatters and cleared entirely, and a little mangled sunshine struck through the clouds here and there. Evan, sweat-soaked, stopped to open his shirt at the neck. Straightening himself, he felt a twinge under the ribs somewhere in the region of the heart. This he supposed to be no more than the rheumatism which was the universal ailment in this climate. He put down his spade and waited for the small pain to pass. He noticed with pleasure that the threat of rain was receding. Far above him in a pocket of meadow where the bracken had never taken hold a row of minute sheep climbed out of a low cloud that stuck to the mountainside like cotton wool, to pass into the indigo shadow of an outcrop of rock. Below the sheep he could see the carrion crows chasing one another. Evan picked up his spade and started to dig again.

A few moments later he heard a sound behind him and looked up to see Beynon standing there. Beynon's first job was to take the cows to the fields and after that he came up to help with the clearing. Evan found him an enigma. He had a background of family trouble, had been abandoned by his mother and passed on from relation to relation, and eventually banished to New Mill, and Evan, taking all the grim circumstances into account, and making all the allowances he could, found Beynon hard to understand. For the first few months Beynon had occupied the back bedroom of the farmhouse, and then, without a word of any kind, he had gone off to live in his shack, repaying Evan's kindnesses with increasing rudeness and taciturnity. Cathy had on more than one occasion asked Evan to send the boy back to his aunt. This he was loth to do, believing that Beynon would eventually go on his own account and without warning – simply failing one day to put in an appearance.

Beynon, as usual, had nothing to say, grunted something

inaudible in reply to Evan's 'Good morning', and got on with his work. He had recently bought on his own account a very expensive new spade with a tungsten steel blade as sharp as a knife, more of a weapon than an agricultural tool, Evan thought. Evan listened to the smooth hissing chop as Beynon's new spade went into the massive root clumps, and smelt the acid aroma of the bracken exuding raw sap through its gashes. This morning Beynon seemed to be working with something like ferocity. The strange thing about the boy was that in spite of his sullenness and taciturnity he seemed to dislike working alone. All that morning Beynon kept very close, always there at his back, and in between the chop of his spade Evan could hear him taking in breath through his open mouth. Once Evan heard him stop work and something made him turn to find Beynon watching him, the spade held like an axe.

Eleven o'clock was the earliest time when Evan felt sure of finding his solicitor in his office, and just before this he left Beynon and walked down the mountain slope to the place where he had left the tractor and drove it back to the farmhouse. He was in tremendous spirits. In the lane separating his property from the next farm he ran into his neighbour, Hughie Phillips, also at the wheel of a tractor.

A cone-shaped segment of land owned by Phillips towards the summit of Pen Gof separated Evan's land from the larger farm owned by the Roberts family, and it had been assumed locally that Robert Roberts, the only man on Pen Gof who had been able to get together a bit of money, would soon take over Phillips's ruined holding. But Roberts and his wife had disappeared, and were supposed by rumour to have been done away with by their nephew and buried somewhere under their own land. Now, with the Roberts

63

competition apparently out of the way, a favourable moment had come for a move by Evan.

'I've decided I might do a deal with you for that land on Pen Gof after all.'

'I knew you would if I waited long enough,' Phillips said.

'Can't say anything now for certain, but I may come and see you next week.'

'No hurry. Any time. Any time.' Phillips was a religious man, a member of Moriah who lived in hope of promotion one day to Hebron, and he was happy now that Evan looked like getting the land rather than a pagan Roberts.

Cathy came down from the front bedroom where she had been polishing the windows and scrubbing up the paint. The many light tasks she found to do about the farm kept Cathy from doing as much work in the house as she would have liked to do.

'A man called Jenkins phoned you. He said he was the manager of Penfold Motors, Brynaron. He thought he'd found the car you'd been looking for.'

'News to me I've been looking for a car. What I may have said to Mr Jenkins was that I'd have to change the Austin sooner or later.'

'Anyway, he'd got this car which he was sure you'd like and the idea was that Bron would leave the Austin with him and run it over to show it to you.'

'Just a moment, dear. Where does Bron come into this?'

'He called at the garage to get petrol and Mr Jenkins saw him.'

'And what did you say?'

'What could I say? I said it would be all right.'

Cathy went for his slippers and came back.

'It seems rather a waste of everybody's time,' Evan said.

'I suppose they're prepared to go to almost any lengths to make a sale. What kind of car was it, by the way? Did he say?'

'Some sort of Jaguar,' she said. 'A Jaguar saloon.'

'Good heavens.'

'He said it was a few years old, but had only had one owner and was in very good condition.'

'I feel like ringing him up and telling him I haven't the faintest intention of buying a car at present. How long ago was this?'

'Half an hour. Perhaps more. I doubt if you'd catch Bron now.'

'Was he coming straight back here in this car?'

'He was going to do his shopping first.' After breakfast Evan had given Bron £30 and told him to go into Brynaron to buy a new outfit of clothes. 'Can't let people see you in these things. You can call it a loan. Pay me back out of the profits.'

'Bron spoke on the phone too,' Cathy said. She hesitated. 'He sounded strange.'

'Strange? In what way?'

'His voice sounded thick. Slurred.'

'Perhaps it was the phone.'

'Mr Jenkins' voice was quite clear. Do you think Bron can have been drinking?'

'It's very unlikely. Especially at this time of the morning.'

'I suppose it could have been my imagination,' she said.

'Let's hope it was, dear.' A most disturbing thought struck him. 'I've just remembered he couldn't possibly have had a valid driving licence. I'm afraid it's my fault. It went right out of my head.'

'It's hardly likely that he would have any trouble with the police just driving into Brynaron and back.'

'Apart from any question of that, he *is* breaking the law.

It was very remiss of Jenkins not to check up as to whether he held a licence. But still, there it is, I suppose. Anything for a sale.'

On the second attempt Evan reached his solicitor.

'I'd like you to make it as simple as possible. A straight-forward partnership, with an equal share in everything. I'll leave it to you. Stock, equipment and the lot. You can date it as from tomorrow, and I'll look in sometime in the morning to pick it up.'

'I don't think I'll bother to go up the mountain again this morning,' he told Cathy, 'it's hardly worth it. I can find plenty to do in the cowsheds to keep myself occupied.'

They waited until two-thirty for Bron before sitting down to eat. 'I can't think what's holding him up,' Evan said. 'Allow half an hour each way, and an hour to buy whatever he wanted to buy. Two hours at the most.' He tried over and over again to telephone Penfold Motors, but the number seemed to be permanently engaged.

It was three o'clock, and he was just going out to the mountain again when the phone rang.

'This is Jenkins of Penfold Motors, Brynaron, Mr Owen. I hope you don't mind my bothering you. I just rang to inquire whether you'd been able to make up your mind about the car.'

'Mr Jenkins, in the first place I don't want a car. This car or any other car. Apart from that I've tried to get through to you several times to tell you there's been no sign of the car or my brother here. Shouldn't he have been here long ago?'

'An hour or two at least, I should have said, Mr Owen.'

'At what time did he pick this car up?'

'It must have been around about eleven.'

'It's most extraordinary,' Evan said. 'Could he have run out of petrol on some lonely road?'

'These things do happen, sir, but it's rather unlikely. There was a fair reserve in the tank. Well, anyway, Mr Owen, perhaps you'd ring us, or ask your brother to give us a ring as soon as you know anything.'

'I'm sorry I can't be of more help,' Evan said.

Cathy was upstairs again, polishing floorboards.

'He seems to have vanished into thin air,' Evan said.

'Do you think he could have had a smash?' Cathy said.

'I don't know. Anything could have happened. We can only hope he's all right. It all seems so extraordinary. It's four hours since he took the car. Even if he were in a ditch somewhere you'd think we'd have heard by now. The road from Brynaron to Cross Hands isn't as quiet as all that.'

They waited in silence another half-hour, and Evan said, 'I'll have to go up and do something about Beynon. I've just remembered he hasn't had anything to eat today unless he brought sandwiches with him, which is unlikely.'

'I'll come up as soon as there's any news,' Cathy said. 'Or I'll send Bron up himself.'

Beynon didn't look up when Evan got back. He appeared to have been hard at work and had cleared far more land than Evan would have expected.

'Sorry I got held up. Have you had anything to eat?' Evan asked.

'No.'

'I've brought some ham sandwiches.'

Beynon didn't reply.

'I said I've brought some sandwiches for you.'

'I don't want any food.'

'Why not?'

'I'm not hungry. Food sticks in my throat.'

'You can't carry on like that. Not when you're expending

energy all the time. Anyway, you'd better pack up and go and bring the cattle in.'

Beynon picked up his spade, carefully wiped off the blade, shouldered it and went off, and Evan set to work. He made slow progress. A heaviness of spirit, and vague forebodings had translated themselves into physical lethargy. With the onset of evening the colours of the landscape had lost their identity and merged to form an inert and muddy green. Clouds sagged all along the horizon under a puffy sky, blunting the edges of the hills, and to the west a shutter of rain had unrolled. The birds of the marsh and moorland, curlews and redshanks, calling morosely – another element of loneliness. Phillips's land on the grey flanks of Pen Gof which that morning had been almost his for the taking was as inaccessible now as the moon. At seven o'clock, having accomplished very little, he went back to the farm.

'What news?'

'None yet, dear, I'm afraid,' Cathy said.

'I think we must get in touch with the police,' Evan said. 'Something serious may have happened.'

The Station Sergeant at Brynaron had nothing to tell them except that Penfold Motors had reported their missing car. He asked Evan for Bron's particulars and Evan could hear him typing them out.

'Would you describe your brother as a man of regular habits?'

'Most certainly.'

'Well, we'll pass this information on to the other stations in the locality and ask them to keep a look-out. Should your brother turn up in the meanwhile you'll let us know, of course.'

They sat and faced each other across the table, gave up the idea of supper, drank coffee, played three distracted hands of rummy, and Cathy flipped through old magazines while

Evan started a small carpentering job in the kitchen and gave it up.

At eleven-fifteen they heard a car coming up the lane and headlight beams flattened themselves on the window panes and swung away as the car turned to draw up by the gate. Evan went to the window and saw, edge on, the blue-lit panel of a police car. 'The police are here, dear,' he said to Cathy. 'I think you'd better go to bed.'

There were two policemen, one the mild and affable Constable Jones, who gave Evan a funereal smile and then did his best to sink into the background, and the other Sergeant Hankin of the Swansea City Constabulary. Bron was with them. He was still in his badly fitting prison clothes, and something heavy filled in a space in Evan's chest and began to press against his stomach and lungs at the sight of that too-familiar smile that he believed was linked to no emotion.

Hankin was remote and non-committal, a policeman with a face made by his profession, eyeless until he removed the pulled-down peaked cap to come into the house.

'This gentleman tells us that he is your brother, Mr Owen.'

'He is,' Evan said.

'He wasn't known to Constable Jones who's been in these parts for a considerable number of years, so we were obliged to check up.'

'My brother has been away for some time,' Evan said. 'He only got home yesterday.'

'I take it you are the owner of Austin number DOP377?'

'I am.'

'And did your brother have your authority to drive this vehicle?'

'He did,' Evan said. 'To be exact he wanted to do some shopping in Brynaron, and I told him to take the car.'

'Were you aware of the fact that he was not in possession of a current driving licence?'

'I'm afraid it was a possibility that never occurred to me. It completely went out of my head. I'm sure it was no more than a slip of the memory in my brother's case too.'

'I see, sir. And do I understand that you were quite agreeable to your brother offering this car in part-exchange for another vehicle at Penfold Motors of Brynaron?'

'Actually I think you'll find there's some mistake there. Penfold Motors seem to have been under the quite mistaken idea that I wanted to buy a car. There was no question at all of a part-exchange. You didn't say anything to Mr Jenkins about a part-exchange, did you Bron?'

Bron, the blunted smile unchanged, shook his head. He was sitting bolt upright on the chair, arms hanging down, eyes exploring the space between Evan and Constable Jones.

'Very surprising that a firm of their standing should make that kind of mistake,' Hankin said.

'Forgive me,' Evan said. 'You said you were from Swansea, didn't you? Is there any special reason why you should have been called in?'

'The vehicle in question was found by colleagues of mine in a Swansea street earlier this evening,' Hankin said.

'Why Swansea, Bron?' Evan said.

Bron's lips moved. He shook his head again.

'We may want to see Mr Owen again,' Hankin said, 'when certain investigations have been carried out. Is this likely to be his permanent address.'

'Oh yes. This will be his address from now on.'

'I take it we can be quite sure of that?'

'Quite sure.'

'Very good, sir. I think I should make it clear that there may be other charges than the charge of driving a vehicle without being in possession of a driving licence contrary to the Road Act of 1960, and this being the case we're obliged to satisfy ourselves that Mr Owen will be available if required.'

'Could you give me any idea at all of what these charges – should they be brought – are likely to be?'

Hankin, collecting Constable Jones and moving towards the door, shook his head. 'I'm afraid I can't say any more than I have done. The whole matter's under investigation. You may or may not be hearing from headquarters in the next day or two. I can't tell you more than that.'

'What on earth happened, Bron?'

Evan knew by the infinitely repeated pattern of the past that he would be faced with a flawless half-truth. Every action would have its reasonable explanation, delivered in that gentle, absent monotone.

'What on earth happened?'

'Well there it was. I went into Penfold's to fill up, and they told me you'd be interested in this car.'

'Weren't you supposed to be coming straight back here with it?'

'The actual words used were "keep it as long as you like".'

'But what was the idea of going off to Swansea?'

'Burton's couldn't fit me up with what I wanted. They said I'd find it at the Swansea branch.'

'They kept you a long time, Bron.'

'The trousers had to be shortened.'

'The whole afternoon and evening to shorten a pair of trousers? Do they work at night, then?'

'They were only going to take a couple of hours to do the job. I went into a cinema to pass the time while I was waiting and dropped off to sleep. When I came out again the shops were shut.'

'So you didn't collect the suit after all?'

'No, it was too late. It had gone eight. Nearly dark. They can post it.'

'But how do the police come into this? What's this talk about the possibility of other charges?'

'Someone ran into the car. I left it in the street outside the cinema, and someone must have hit it.'

'Was it in a no-waiting area, then? Was that the trouble?'

'I believe the constable thought I was drunk. I had to go to the station. They gave me some sort of test.'

'Are you sure you're well, Bron? Can it have been the old trouble again?'

He shook his head, the face still completely emptied of expression, eyes inert, meaningless smile, replies obediently muttered through almost motionless lips at the promptings of a hypnotist.

'I think there must have been oil fumes in the car. Made me sleepy. I could smell the fumes all the time.'

There may be other charges. There may be other charges. The words tolled in Evan's brain. He had to know the worst whatever it might be. However unpleasant the news anything was better than suspense and sleepless nights.

'I think it might be as well if I ran over to Brynaron in the morning and had a word with the police inspector. May do good. I certainly can't do any harm.'

Evan left the house at 7.30 a.m., to catch the first bus into Brynaron. Bron had not yet appeared on the scene.

Cathy went with him as far as the gate. Evan said, 'I've given a good deal of thought to it, and I'm sure everything is going to be all right. I admit I was really frightened by the time ten o'clock came last night and we hadn't heard from him, but really it's quite easy to see how it all happened. If it

72

had been anybody else but Bron I should have thought nothing about it – which, when one comes to think about it, is hardly fair to him.' He was determined to make himself believe that everything would come out well.

She agreed.

Evan picked up his Austin at Penfold's and Jenkins took him round to the workshop to see the Jaguar.

'This car will cost £60 to put in order,' Jenkins said. 'Am I to make out the bill to you, or to your brother?'

Evan studied the crumpled offside front wing and the deep scratches, as straight and as parallel as tramlines, running the length of the car.

'Then it's not insured?'

'Only in the case of a licensed driver,' Jenkins said. 'Otherwise the company accepts no responsibility.'

'But don't you take the trouble to ascertain whether or not a driver is in possession of a licence? Surely you should do that?'

'In this firm, sir, we always prefer to take a customer's word. Perhaps we shouldn't. We should find it embarrassing to ask a customer to show us his licence when he'd just assured us that he possessed one.'

'Are you suggesting that my brother told you a deliberate lie?'

'I'm not suggesting anything. I'm simply telling you that he informed me he possessed a driving licence and I took his word for it.'

Evan's interview with Inspector Fenn was also discouraging.

He had chosen a bad time. That morning the local paper had printed another leading article on the subject of unsolved crimes, and in doing so had provoked an acidulous phone call to the Inspector from the Divisional Superintendent. Overnight the words 'Fuck you' had appeared in vast letters in tar on the station's front wall; while the first post had brought an anonymous letter alleging that one of his men had been taking bribes. This was quite probable.

It was a moment when Fenn liked Wales and Welshmen less than ever before. 'Frankly,' he said to Evan, 'I can't see why you've come to see me at all.'

'Well, I thought it might be possible to straighten things out, or at least help to clarify the position.'

'Straighten things out? I don't follow you. In what way?'

Evan was nervous in these surroundings, found it difficult to collect his thoughts, to express himself. He was oppressed by the fortune-buffeted faces of three wanted men who stared back grimly at him from their portraits on the wall behind Fenn's desk.

'This is a small community with a kind of traditional interdependence. One wishes there was some way of restraining the zeal of a very young constable. Commendable as it may be —' Evan faltered.

'I'm still not quite sure what you're trying to say.'

Once again Fenn had the feeling that he was dealing with an oriental. There was a brown-skinned money changer in Aden Crater identical in speech, manner and accent with this man. The lost tribes? And why not? Bound to have lightened up a bit in colour in two or three thousand years. *Mr Fenn, the gold sovereigns of Queen Victoria are preferred for our market because of their richer colour. We shall be pleased to take any you can procure at the aforementioned price.* An oriental man. A Welshman of Aden with his feet in our camp and in theirs, who believed devoutly with upturned eyes and outspread palms in human corruptibility.

'A young and inexperienced constable,' Evan pleaded,

74

'hardly out of his teens, who sees a damaged and apparently abandoned car and jumps to conclusions.'

Some of these peasants wangled their way in and actually had the cheek to offer him, an inspector with seven years' service and nothing but commendation in the Metropolitan Police, slyly produced tributes designed to pervert the course of justice – such as fourteen pounds of bright yellow butter, a side of salt bacon, or even a laying pullet in a wicker basket. *A word from you in the right direction, Mr Fenn. Perhaps there's some way of softening the blow.'*

'Mr Owen, I'd like you to get this absolutely straight. I have no influence of any kind with the Swansea police, and if I had any, I certainly shouldn't dream of using it.'

'My brother is an excellent driver and a very careful one.'

'Nevertheless there was a collision in Swansea last evening shortly before the constable saw your brother in River Street, and a car that failed to stop corresponds to the description of the one your brother was driving, and which he was unlicensed to drive.'

'It couldn't have been Bron,' Evan said.

'Couldn't it? Why not?'

'Because he spent the whole of the afternoon in a cinema.'

'He told you that?' Fenn said.

'Yes.'

'And you believe him?'

'Of course I do, Inspector.'

Fenn was possessed by a huge irritation. This was a moment when he would gladly have reverted to sergeant if it offered the chance to be posted elsewhere. On one side the Chief Superintendent, with the Chief Constable breathing down his neck – 'I want results and I don't care how I get them.' On the other the Police Solicitor – 'Go ahead and use a bulldozer, if you feel you must, but I warn you, if nothing comes of it, he'll sue you and he'll win the day.'

The morning before they'd shown him a horrid mess wrapped up in a *News of the World* somebody had found in a waste bin in the park. 'You'll never make an infanticide charge stick. Not in these days,' the Station Sergeant warned him. 'Well get rid of it, for Christ's sake,' Fenn said.

Anger showed through a weak spot in Fenn's armour of professional discretion. 'Would you say your brother has a drop too much to drink once in a while?'

'Never. He hardly touches liquor.'

'And yet when the constable spoke to him in River Street last night, he couldn't articulate. He could hardly stand.'

'There must be a mistake,' Evan said. 'My brother may conceivably have been unwell, but you're suggesting he was drunk. That's out of the question.'

'When he was taken to the station he couldn't even give an account of himself.'

'He was sick,' Evan said. 'It sounds like an unusually severe bout. He suffers from these bouts from time to time.'

'Apart from the fact that it's an offence to drive a motor-car if your physical condition is such that you haven't control over it, the Police Surgeon formed a different opinion,' Fenn said. But here he was bluffing. The police's case against Bron was far from as foolproof as they would have liked. Witnesses had provided a description of the hit-and-run Jaguar, but nobody had been able to get its number, and it was unlikely that a charge of drunkenness while in charge of a car would be brought. The regular Police Surgeon had been off duty, ill, and by the time his locum had been found and had arrived at the station Bron's symptoms had miraculously subsided. This man had been described to Fenn as a hymn-singing Methodist who had shown himself not prepared to stretch a point in favour of the law. 'I make these tests because they're fashionable and I'm expected to,' he had said. 'But they impress me somewhat less than they obviously do you. This man may have been drunk an hour ago, but he certainly isn't now, and I don't care how much alcohol I find in his blood. I know a drunken man when I see one. A touch of common sense is a good thing to have in cases like this.'

'I've known instances myself when I would have been prepared to swear that a man was under the influence,' Evan said. 'But it turned out that he was suffering from a heart attack. In cases like this one should never be hasty in one's judgements of one's fellow men.'

Fenn managed somehow to get rid of him. As Evan was going through the door he remembered something.

'Your brother told our people at Swansea that he was just back from Australia. I suppose that's true?'

Evan stopped and turned round. 'No,' he said. 'It's not. I'm sorry if he told a lie, but I'm afraid it's understandable.'

Evan's solicitor handed him the agreement. 'I hope this is what you want. I thought it better to leave out all the frills. Not quite what we'd suggest in the case of an ordinary business partnership. Doesn't provide the safeguards. But this being a purely family affair, it's somewhat different. One assumes mutual trust. Perhaps you'd care to run through it.'

The agreement was very short. It took Evan two minutes to read it, and his first thought, resisted for only a fraction of a second, was, Can I really have intended this?

He was in a black mood – the victim of a violent swing of the pendulum from the optimism of the day before. Preoccupations seen under the huge curved glass of the sleepless night, the dread of far worse to come over the matter of the damaged Jaguar, and his chilly encounter with Inspector Fenn had left him with a feeling of hopelessness, while his defence of Bron seemed now to him to have exhausted his reserves of loyalty. Evan was quite prepared to believe that Bron had gone off on some wild, inexplicable escapade, involving a hit-and-run smash, injuries to others, possibly even deaths. In the background of his mind the arguments and counter-arguments of ten and fifteen years back raged again. Evan, passively, never certain in his conscience, had supported his father's campaign to put his brother into an institution, while his mother, supported by Dr Griffiths – still wearing the shreds of a threadbare liberalism – had resisted this solution and had won. 'These are things none of us fully understand,' Griffiths had said so often. 'For God's sake give the lad a chance to grow out of it.'

The argument of the nature of evil was always cropping up, with his father a dexterous champion both of the freedom of the will and original sin. 'Evil people,' Griffiths said, 'are defectives, or they suffer from brain damage in childbirth or the crimes perpetrated on them in childhood.'

'Possibly so, but they're still evil.'

Evan's father's voice spoke to him from the grave. *He's evil, or mad. Or both. Both if you like.*

'Any comments, Mr Owen?' the solicitor said.

'I don't think so. It all seems quite straightforward and to the point. I'll take it away if I may, and go over it with my brother, just in case we can think of anything else that ought to go in. Get in touch with you again in a day or two.'

Evan folded the agreement, put it into his pocket. They shook hands and he went out. He walked down the first flight of steps while his solicitor stood courteously at the not quite closed door of his office, then he began to run.

Evil or mad. Both if you like. He had left Cathy at the mercy of a madman.

Bron awoke in a cocoon of strangeness. He saw himself surrounded by the meaningless shapes of furniture against blank, white walls. He was placed in the centre of a vacant film set, and for a moment had the illusion, even, that he was watching a scene projected on a screen. Then a fly buzzed round his head; a thread of sound that was wound into a third dimension. A dark suit on a hanger was hooked over a peg with a sunbeam flickering on its sleeve. Where was its owner? Where was the man who had deserted it?

He could remember nothing of how he had come to be where he was, and he did not wish to remember. He had dreamed out a whole life full of the endless and pointless complications and plots of existence, and the dream had shivered into disconnected episodes, and then the episodes themselves had dissolved. Something had happened that was forgotten, and he had no wish to go back. The past had no existence, but in compensation the future was with him, linked to the present. This fusion was not complete, but time was unrolling like a carpet, and he was going with it, always seeing a few steps ahead.

This unfamiliar room was no longer unfamiliar. He'd been here before, and many times. And now his actions were mapped out, although their course only became clear from step to step as he passed through the stages of pre-vision. I will get out of bed, I will put on this abandoned suit, I will open the window startling away the pigeons on the sill, I will see a cat sitting on a low wall surrounding a pond which has green slime round its edges and is half covered by a willow tree.

The sun having gone into a cloud now presses up through it. A man on a plough carves initials on a mountainside with two entwined and arrow-pierced hearts. A bad smell comes through the window. This smell is the smell of death. It comes from the cat, and it will not go until the cat has gone.

I am me. My world is my world. Nothing exists outside me. I turn my head knowing I will see a red-faced postwoman on a bicycle coming up the lane. She exists only because I exist and for me. My world is a ploughman, a postwoman, circling pigeons, a sheep-dog snapping out of sight, the misted sun, the cat on its bed of dry fern on the wall top licking a paw. Only the cat I command not to be there.

In an instant Bron was beside the wall, stroking the cat, knowing that it would twist its head about like a child that likes to be tickled. I will grope and gather the loose skin in the nape of its neck, lift it gently so that it will not be frightened, and drop it into the slime. It will strike out with its forepaws like a swimmer, dragging itself forward a few inches, but the hindlegs will dig deeper and deeper into the slime, which will show as black where the green surface has been torn open. The moment has come for me to prise away a large stone from the wall and to drop it. It will fall a few inches in front of the cat's head, covering it with slime, and I will hear the faint whistle of the cat's breath as it struggles for air and draws mud into its lungs. Then it will cough once only, for the second stone will drop on its head pushing mouth and nostrils under.

At this moment I am free. I breathe in clean air again, and I smile and wave to the postwoman who turns her bicycle round and pedals off away down the lane. The ploughman on the mountainside has changed his entwined hearts into a tiger's head, and this I expected too.

And now I must go into the house. I open the door and find myself in a room with a polished table set for one, plate, cup, knife, fork, cruet, toast-rack, and four ticking clocks await me. The hands of all four clocks point to five minutes to ten, although seconds ago when I looked at my watch it was exactly twelve. I hear the sound of a tap being turned on over my head, and water running into a bath. I glance at my watch again, but now it agrees with the clocks and I see why. The clocks are speeding up. Their machinery whirrs inside their cases like sewing machines, and the minute hands are crawling round the dials. There is only one way to put a stop to this murder of time, and I collect the clocks, take them one by one to the door and throw them into the pond after the cat. Something shadows the side window and I see a boy's face peering in. I rush towards it and he turns and runs, his legs moving so fast that I can hardly see them as he floats out of sight under the mountain which the ploughman has now cleaned like a slate before going away.

Water running away overhead gurgles down a waste pipe. Something is waiting for me at the top of the stairs. Something that brought me here. I go up the stairs and turn into a passage that is dark and closed at the end by a low door with a brass handle. After three steps I know that I will find whatever I have come for beyond that door, after three more that what I have come for is a woman, and placing my hand on the door handle to turn it, I know that this woman will be naked.

I turn the handle and go in, and the clocks which I can still hear ticking in the pond slow down and stop. I see a woman's body, back to me, absolutely white and clear in the window-light of the small room in which everything else is dim and murky. This is a scene complete in every detail that I have stood staring at in a picture gallery. The woman has let a bath robe fall to the ground, and is in the act of bending to pick up a vest from a chair. She is motionless; painted on the dark background, a single breast visible under the outstretched arm groping with pointed fingers. I, too, do not move.

Then the clocks start clicking and we both move and she swings round to face me as I go towards her. She backs to the wall, crouching, casting the hollows of her body into shadow, covering her stomach with the vest clenched in her hands. We are both of us playing our parts exactly, like well-rehearsed actors, and not a gesture or movement is misplaced. Neither of us speak but we breathe in unison. I put out my hand and touch the vest and her fingers loosen on it, and I take it from her. The next move is to pick her up and put her on the bed. I know she will be submissive but this submissiveness, which has surprised me in the past, surprises me again. A conspiracy grows up between us. For a moment she is able to join me to see an inch into the future and understand that what will happen has happened. Sounds come from her but they are not protests, and when I separate her thighs she makes no attempt to close them. In every movement of her body she follows the blueprint of the inevitable.

And then I hear the shouting and the running feet and she snatches her body away from me. She is closed and void and gone, leaving me, as it had to be, with voices shrieking and doors banging in my ears. Everything is going with her and then gone, and I am coming back, full of disbelief. My mouth is dry, and my ears are ringing and I am lying on a bed in twilight. This is my brother's house, but I am separated by a silence from my brother and his wife. It is evening. What has happened?

Evan coming down the stairs was a man involved in a physical catastrophe that has crushed nerve-ends, torn away ligaments, cracked bones and sliced through veins and arteries. An instant of oblivion has been followed by a brief general paralysis, in the hub of which he helplessly watches the parts of his body that have slipped beyond his control, knowing only that he is alive. And then, as the machinery of the body moves again, he awaits, listening to the soft internal drip of blood, the onset of the pain that must come.

Everything else had been blotted from his memory by Cathy's eyes, staring up at him from the bed in the second before she had escaped through the further door and locked herself in the bathroom. This, like a scene from a film, had suddenly cut to a tract lying on the table top in the living-room: 'Cast thy burden upon the Lord and he shall sustain thee.' Clipped to the tract was a letter from the printers. *Dear Mrs Owen, we much regret that, as foreseen, time proved too short to have your order set in Westphalian Gothic, which you will recall was not in stock. To avoid disappointment we therefore took the liberty of substituting Modified Cunabulum, this being the nearest available to your choice, and trust that this meets with your approval.* Like a fantastic and meaningless episode from a dream, Evan remembered how the possibility that the printer might be forced into this substitution had taken up twenty-four hours of the life that was past and gone. He tore both tract and letter into hundreds of pieces and let them fall to the floor.

Now the active nerves were beginning to charge themselves with their load of suffering as the ice-age of his bereavement approached. A long fragment of paper at his feet with decipherable words took his eye – 'shall sustain . . .' He ground it with his foot into the rug until no more than a dirty shred remained. Not only did he no longer believe these crudely coloured lies, but never had. Polite pretences apart, men of Evan's kind were realists where the burdens referred to in the text were concerned. They bore their burdens themselves, or they were broken by them. The farmers of these Celtic wastelands recognized two Gods, neither of which had much to do with Christianity. The first was the God of the Chapel, seen as a kind of primitive group therapist, a club secretary, almost a Butlin's redcoat, who provided the excuse for lonely isolated people to come together, and kept them out of mischief at whist drives and day outings, and choir practices. This God was on the way out, and had virtually ceased to exist in the big towns. The second God was truly eternal: the Lord of nature, of pestilence and death, who had been feared in all men's hearts from the beginning of time. This God was known by his acts: the lightning that struck at the sheltering flocks and set fire to ricks, southwesterly gales at high spring tide, snow in April, frost in midsummer. He was the potato weevil, fruit blight, foot-rot, fowl-pest, glanders, foot-and-mouth, scab, a variety of parasitic worms, abortions and monstrous births.

The second God, aloof, detached and inaccessible at the back of the bland and grinning *maître de cérémonies* the rural Welsh pretended to worship, could not be cajoled or deflected from his purpose in any way, but Evan and his kind had learned to turn the tables on him in a most ingenious way by acquiring a perverse taste for his chastisements. They had learned truly to love ugliness, to love sorrow, hardship, crushing labour, the battle against the lusts of the flesh. No farmer – however rich by local standards he might become – ever thought of settling down to enjoy himself in the way other people did, because his enjoyment had come to consist in this tricking and defeating of God. At the slightest suggestion of life becoming a little less hard through an unpredictable success of some undertaking, he would nervously hurry to invest whatever gains he might have made into some project that guaranteed more struggle and misery. In this God-baiting game, Evan had always won so far, playing his hand in such a way that he had nothing to lose, and asking virtually nothing of life. But in marrying Cathy he had thrown away all his defences, and left himself as vulnerable as the softest of hedonists. And now God's moment had come to settle accounts.

Evan stood up. The sensation of an electric current running through his body had set up a vibration felt not even in his limbs but in the throat, eyes, stomach and bowels. The palms of his hands were wet and glistening.

He went into the kitchen, took off his jacket and hung it up, untied his tie, unbuttoned the shirt, and began to wash his face and hands at the sink. There were traces under his fingernails of the black, peaty earth of New Mill and Evan scrubbed them again and again until the last grain of dirt had been removed. A towel hanging on the roller by the sink was soiled, so he went to the linen cupboard, found a clean one, and used it to dry himself.

Evan climbed the stairs to the front bedroom, opened his wardrobe and took out a complete change of clothing; underwear, a white shirt with starched collar and cuffs, his thick, dark chapel suit, a black tie. He changed his clothing, dressing slowly with care. Several particles of fluff sticking to the surface of his suit were picked off between finger and thumb. Finally came the moment to put on the black shoes he always wore with this suit. Evan's shoes were the most important part of his wardrobe. He had paid six and a half guineas for them at the best shoe-shop in Swansea and they were the only touch of luxury he had ever allowed himself. These carefully polished shoes, fed with cream between use, kept in shape by their shoe-trees, were worn only on occasions of special importance, and were to Evan what a silk hat would have been to his grandfather.

The shotgun was kept in the toolshed, and Evan, meticulous in all his actions, had smeared the metal parts over with vaseline before putting it away after the time he had been obliged to use it in the previous year. Cleaning rags had been left folded up on a shelf near the gun, but in removing the vaseline he managed to transfer a small bluish smear to his jacket-sleeve. This he stopped to clean off with methylated spirit, going over the spot until no trace of grease was left. Next he loaded the gun with two cartridges and went back into the living-room.

Four faces awaited him, looking down from framed photographs on the walls. First in order came his father. His eyes were bold and eager but below them there was nothing but derision and melancholy and the constant bedfellowship with defeat. His mother, still young, fierce-eyed, smooth of feature and straight-nosed, viewed him with a kind of severe satisfaction. The central position on the adjacent wall was occupied by an elder sister of his mother with a classless raceless 1910 face, as common to the Teutons of the Royal Family of the period as the daughters of depressed Celtic farmers. The fourth family member was a sister who had died a hushed-up death in his childhood, and had been posed for her portrait in a sailor suit at the foot of the painted marble staircase which symbolized ultimate grandeur for people who climbed a step-ladder into the darkness of the room in which they slept.

Looking from one to another of these familiar ikons, Evan felt himself move closer to his forbears, not only to those portrayed here, but all the other faces he had never known, behind these faces: the faces of a thousand ancestors whose blood ran in his veins and from whose clay all these faces had been moulded. It was a sensation that could never have been embalmed in the lifeless terms of a credo, but it was pure religious emotion experienced for the first time in his life. Evan felt that his ancestors' eyes were upon him, not with disapproval, but with understanding. He realized that his careful preparation for the moment that was to come had been partly due to the respect he owed them, and it was out of this respect that he went to each picture and turned its face to the wall.

Evan then drew an armchair into the middle of the room and sat down to face the staircase, the shotgun across his knees.

At one moment during the timeless wait Beynon's expressionless face appeared, jaw drooping, at the window, and indignation twitched like the reflexes of a dead frog in Evan's brain. Why isn't he working? Why should he slack off the moment I'm not there to watch him? And once again the momentum of habit not quite run down showed itself when a sharp pain stabbed beneath his ribs. I've forgotten my medicine as usual. An automatic impulse almost brought him to his feet.

He heard the bathroom door open, then a quick scuffle of feet along the passage to the front bedroom, and a key turning in a lock. Again silence and the passage of time marked suddenly in the failing of the light outside. A leg went to sleep and he shifted his position. Within him the indifferent and complacent rhythms of the body continued as before. His bladder began to fill. He felt a squirm of peristalsis in the intestines and was obliged to release a little gas from the stomach. A persistent itch started in the thigh, and he removed his hand from the stock of the gun to deal with it. His organs and his skin were oblivious of crisis.

The key in the bedroom door turned again, and Evan heard Cathy at the top of the stairs. Her legs came into sight on the staircase and he levelled the gun and took aim.

Cathy came into sight slowly, visible first to the knees, then to the waist, then to chest and shoulders, before she was fully in view. She saw the gun pointed at her and stopped. She was wearing a dress that reminded Evan of the one she had been wearing when he had first seen her standing in the back row of the Retail Trades Association of Brynaron's choir, her small, thin, sweet voice overwhelmed by the vigorous sopranos and coloraturas of the other choristers. The plain blue high-necked dresses bought in bulk at a fifteen per cent reduction from Messrs C. & A. had been the choir's uniform for a season, and as Evan, stricken with love for the first time in his life at that encounter had often told Cathy since, she had never subsequently bought a dress that he liked so much.

With his finger on the trigger, Evan waited for Cathy to move. If she had turned to run Evan would have fired with the detachment of a young airman bombing invisible villagers in some tropical jungle. As it was, the foresight of the gun, wavering slightly, was directed at the centre of Cathy's chest, and suddenly between Evan and Cathy appeared the image of the small horror produced by his last firing of the gun. A year before he had discharged both barrels at close range at a roebuck amazingly caught in a snare set by one of the caravanners, and the animal, eyes bulging and gulping up vermilion blood, had continued to tug and leap and twist until Evan had reloaded and fired again for the third time.

Compunction slipped in the thin edge of its wedge. The thought of Cathy, her breasts shattered, ribs laid bare, heart punctured in a hundred places under the remains of the neat blue dress, became intolerable. A hand seemed to have been placed on the barrel of the gun, pressing it down.

Cathy moved. She began to come down the stairs towards him. Evan put the gun down, leaning it against the arm of the chair, and it slid on its butt and clattered to the floor. Her face was small and plain and pointed, the small eyes hardly showing between the pink, puffy lids. He noticed that she had taken off her wedding ring.

She passed him and went to the door and opened it. It was raining and the water drove into the room like a wind-blown curtain. Lightning suddenly showed all the farm buildings in silhouette against a white-hot sky veined with coloured fire, and when the thunder exploded the mountain above them seemed to have fallen.

Cathy shrank back. She had stood calmly within a hair's breadth of death, but to Cathy the gun's threat had been less intimidating than this. She was terrified of lightning. She stood there, the door half open, sprayed with the rain, wincing as the lightning glared on her cheek again.

Evan spoke. 'What are you going to do?'

She shook her head. 'I don't know,' she said.

7

For Police Constable Jones the day had not been strenuous. He had had one irate telephone call from Inspector Fenn over Division's decision not to proceed with any but technical charges against Bron Owen. A sheep had been found with an eye shot out. The first of the spring's normal crop of indecent exposures had occurred. About a quarter of the caravans were now occupied, and a girl occupant was said to be taking money for her services. Professionalism of this kind was anathema to the numerous free-lances of Cross Hands, and was liable to cause trouble. This was not to say that the local girls were narrow-minded. In fact the one who reported the matter to Jones had a husband, a long-distance lorry-driver who was known to return from his trips in the middle of the night sometimes and climb into bed with her and her seventy-year-old lover. Apart from such routine affairs Jones spent most of the day working on a difficult passage in the epic poem he was translating from the early Welsh.

He was a lonely man who would have liked to marry but had never been able to persuade a lively and ambitious girl to share his life with him. Cross Hands girls were realists. 'Get some promotion and it's O.K. by me,' was the invariable reaction, however tactfully wrapped up. 'I don't mind having a crack at living on £18 a week in Swansea, or some place like that, but you know what you can do with this dump.'

In fact all Jones had to offer apart from a miserable income was a home in the shape of a cottage rented by the police from The Metal. Jones's quarters had been designed to offer the scientific minimum of comfort and accommodation to the miners who had been paid twenty-eight shillings a week in the 'thirties. The Metal's four walls held water like a sponge; its main bedroom was too small to hold a normal double bed; its electricity was reduced to hardly more than a glow-worm glimmer in the bulbs when the village switched on in the evening; its water gushed brown from the taps when they were first turned on in the mornings; its Elsan closet was at the end of the garden and was visited at the risk of bombardment from stones falling from the cliff that overhung the village.

Jones would have liked to settle down with his feet up in front of the television on a damp evening like this, but for the fact that Cross Hands' location under a mineral-stuffed mountain made reception virtually hopeless. As it was, the only current entertainment was offered by the Saturday-night Hebron Chapel social. Cross Hands possessed eight chapels and twelve public houses – all built by The Metal who liked to keep its workers soaked in piety and the thin, sour beer brewed by one of its subsidiaries. Hebron, a grim, greystone building like a bus garage with pointed windows, threatened the village with eternity from a natural platform above the mean, terraced houses over which it had been built.

The hall – an amalgam of prefabricated army huts – had been put up at the chapel's side and here members met on social evenings to talk shop about salvation over meat pies and cups of tea at 2s 9d per head. For Jones, there was nothing to equal these occasions, when it came to keeping his finger on the pulse of village life.

Jones found that the Hebron congregation was present in full strength, with the notable exception of Evan Owen and his wife. Proceedings had reached the refreshments pause between recitations and songs, and the constable, camouflaged in a parson-grey suit, passed, cup in hand, from pie-chewing group to group.

Hebron was the chapel of the upper crust of Cross Hands, an exclusive club as well as a religious body, formed of leading shopkeepers and the small handful of farmers who did more than make ends meet, and membership was the highest social award the community had to offer. Smaller shopkeepers, the clerks and machine-minders of The Metal, and the more-or-less ruined farmers, were shared out among the seven inferior chapels, finding their levels not on a basis of income alone, but on many other local ingredients of prestige. Evan Owen would never have been admitted to Hebron purely on property considerations, but a familiarity with the classic form of the language spoken in the North made him a valuable asset as a lay-reader. The drawback to Evan's whole-hearted acceptance had been Cathy, and what was known or suspected of a pretty woman's past. Cathy was the subject of constant vigilance by the chapel's secret police; a body of ageing ladies who made themselves responsible for the purity of members' private lives, and recommended purges as necessary. In a way it was like league football, and members who fell below the standards called for by Hebron might be accepted by Ebenezer, just as Ebenezer rejects usually went to Moriah. But sometimes people who fell under a cloud left the village altogether and went to live at Sowbridge, five miles away – where there was only one chapel and organized worship was on the verge of collapse, but where television reception was good.

The atmosphere on this evening pulsated with excitement, and Jones soon found out that it was Cathy Owen whose reputation was being destroyed. The male members of Hebron, stamped in most cases with the discretion of successful shopkeeping, hadn't much to say, but their un-married sisters, the shock-brigaders of chapel morality, poured out venomous tittle-tattle.

Jones picked up a few samples of their opinion.

'Stayed at the Dragon with a commercial traveller, signed the register as Mr and Mrs Thorn. There's a name for you.'

'Not that I'm in the habit of going into places like that, but they say you could see her there any night.'

'There was this coloured fellow in Swansea. According to her he was the son of a prince, but he turned out to be a waiter in an Indian restaurant.'

'Judge not that ye be not judged, I always say. But there's no smoke without fire.'

'Whether there was a child or not, I'm not prepared to express an opinion; all I *can* say is that that was the talk at the time.'

Ivor Pritchard, a deacon, owner of the Cross Hands Supermarket, the biggest man in the chapel with the softest and most deferential voice, summed the matter up. Pritchard had been charged twenty-five years previously at Cardigan Assizes with a serious offence against a minor, but time and prosperity had cleaned the slate.

'One hears of certain things in the background that we're not at all happy to have associated with the name of one of our members – some of it pure surmise, perhaps, conjecture – but still . . .' The gentle purr of his voice trailed to a whisper, and he smiled ruefully as if apologizing for the quality of a poor cut of meat. 'And now this new unpleasant-ness.'

This new unpleasantness had been an identical anonymous letter slipped that evening into the letterbox of each of the four deacons, accusing Cathy of carrying on with her brother-in-law. Jones examined the specimen Pritchard had received. It was composed of newsprint words cut out and pasted on a sheet of paper. Beynon again, Jones thought. He pocketed the letter. 'But this isn't evidence at all,' he said.

Pritchard had the most expressive and sensitive hands, the hands of a surgeon, although they had never manipulated any instrument calling for more dexterity than a bacon slicer. Now they took the fears and prejudices of the congregation of Hebron and moulded them into a delicate sculpture of doubt.

Jones knew that Evan and Cathy had already been tried and sentenced. They were to be banished on grounds that, although no more than whispered in Cross Hands, would automatically debar them from membership of any of the other chapels. Within a few days old friends would cross the road or slip down the nearest side street when they saw them coming.

What was worrying Pritchard was, Would they have to tell the Owens the reason for their exclusion, and if so could an action for slander conceivably be brought?

'Don't worry,' Jones said. 'Evan will never do that. He'll have some pride left.'

But will he, though? he wondered.

An hour of the Social was enough for Jones. He felt depressed, and in the hope of cheering himself up he got out his Morris Mini and drove over to Sowbridge for a chat with a colleague who was stationed there, Constable Edwards.

Sowbridge, although only ten minutes away by car, was a different world. Its special character had been formed through some combination of winds and atmospheric pressure. The clouds that blew up swollen with rain out of the Atlantic and ruptured themselves on the mountain top

94

unleashed most of their burden of water on the western slopes, over Cross Hands, while Sowbridge often remained bone dry. There was no beautiful, fickle river running through Sowbridge to attract barbarous caravanners in summer, and drown sheep and cattle in winter in its floods. Sowbridge possessed no coal, iron or bauxite, so there were no industries and no mines. This meant that no-one had ever been buried alive, burned to death, or blown to pieces in pit disasters as had happened at Cross Hands on a number of occasions when the mines had still been in operation. Houses, with or without their occupants, had never been swallowed up when some old working caved in, nor been buried in black slime by the shifting of an ancient tip. The bursting of a criminally jerry-built dam, seven miles up in the mountains, and equidistant from each village, had unleashed its terrible waters in the direction of Cross Hands, and not Sowbridge, and it was Cross Hands that had received the King's condolences on the death by drowning of seventy-two of its citizens (forty-eight of them children) and had had a flying visit from the Prince of Wales who had stood bareheaded at their graveside and had said, 'This is terrible.'

Jones and Edwards were drinking beer in Edwards's sitting-room, facing the enormous television set that was the mark of Sowbridge's higher civilization.

Edwards was a past master of concealed inaction in the matter of his police duties, devoting the time this saved to natural history studies and the collection of fossils and geological specimens. 'One thing, you can't complain nothing ever happens,' he said. 'How's the Roberts case?'

'Died a natural death by the look of it.'

'I ran into the nephew in the pub the other day. Pleasant sort of chap. Cut above the average.'

'He did a very neat job. Not a trace of blood anywhere.'

'Manual strangulation, perhaps. Or maybe he suffocated them with pillows. That can be very effective.'

'It's not so much that they're murderous, it's this instinct to hunt in packs I can't stand. To take the latest case – I suppose you know Evan Owen?'

'I used to know his wife when I was at Brynaron. Cathy Thomas she used to be. Nice girl with a generous disposition.'

'She stepped out of line with Evan's brother. Or so they say. So the chapel's going to excommunicate them.'

'What do you expect? I wonder they don't stone them while they're about it.'

'They probably will,' Jones said. 'They're capable of it. The thing I don't understand is this special animosity they seem to have against the man. Evan, I mean, not his brother. After all, he can't help it.'

'It's a Mediterranean inheritance,' Edwards said. 'Cuckolds are unlucky. Something to do with the crops. Or the animals, I forget which.'

'The old women natter about the wife, but you can see it's the man they've got their knife in.'

'Some sort of matriarchal survival, perhaps. Who knows? Don't ask me.'

'I've had ten years of this kind of thing,' Jones said. 'You'd think I'd have got used to it by now, but I haven't. They're going to throw this poor chap out of chapel on Sunday. I wouldn't like to be there. Funny thing they don't object to incest, though. One of our leading citizens was caught under a hedge with his grand-daughter and nobody thinks any the worse of him.'

'Incest is different.'

'I was born in a lovely slum in Neath,' Jones said. 'I long for the city lights. My girl friend's a secretary in Swansea and they tell me she's been seen out with her boss. If I'm going to do anything about it at all, I've got to do something now.'

'What's holding you back? Why don't you apply for a transfer?'

'I have done. They won't give me one.'

'Why won't they?'

'Fenn says I'm too useful where I am.'

'You should get up someone's nose. All you have to do is to arrange to be soused next time the Superintendent comes down. Let him smell your breath a bit. He'll decide you work best under supervision. You'll be down on that beat on the docks at Ferryport before you know where you are.'

'That's a thought,' Jones said. 'That certainly is a thought, Maurice. I believe you've got something there.'

8

Evan locked himself in the box-room for three days, slept on the floor, came out noiselessly in the middle of the night to visit the lavatory, chew a little bread, and drink water. All three occupants of the farmhouse were engaged separately in coming to terms with the new climate of silence and withdrawal and all three were bewildered in their different ways. Bron lived parallel existences of interlocking reality and fantasy. Beynon waited to milk the cows until the milk was dripping from their udders, and carried out sullen, savage, short-lived attacks on the bracken on the mountaintop. The river, overflowing again at high tide, slipped a noose of water round three of Evan's mountain sheep and carried them away. When Bron broke the silence to ask after Evan, Cathy said that he had had a heart attack, and the doctor had said he must not be disturbed.

By Saturday night the rhythms of a lifetime's habit had begun their faint insistence, and Evan remembered that the next day was Sunday.

In the morning he got up at dawn, went to the bathroom and shaved off three days' growth of beard, dressing himself for chapel as he had done every Sunday since childhood. The routine came almost as naturally as eating and breathing. Just before nine o'clock, when the sound of life and movement in other parts of the house had just begun, he let himself quietly out of the back door, passed stealthily behind the cowshed and reached a short cut across the fields that brought him out on the road to Cross Hands a mile from the farm.

Fifteen minutes later Evan was on the outskirts of the village. This was Cross Hands as it had been before the first coal had been mined there, an early Victorian refuge of gaunt houses set among decrepit apple orchards. Farther on, the village built by the mining companies appeared to have been crushed in the jaws of an anvil before being thrust out of the way of the pit heads under the steepest part of the mountain. The background to this scene was a ridge of pigmy volcanoes – the old tips – their weed-encrusted surfaces gashed here and there with lurid chemical colours, and mists curling from them like authentic volcanic smoke into a sky that was streaked like a dirty window pane.

Sombrely clad farmers and their families were moving cautiously down on the village like tribesmen on the alert for traps and ambuscades. They were walking slowly, treading carefully round the edges of the innumerable puddles, talking already in hushed voices in preparation for the solemn undertones of the chapel. Occasionally a small black saloon car passed at a self-imposed Sabbath twenty-five miles an hour on its way up to Hebron. Outside the rain-stained and slightly lopsided building that bore the title over its door, MORIAH 1887, Evan caught sight of a small group waiting to go in that included his neighbour Phillips, but at his approach they turned away. He slowed down, almost stopped, his tiny store of confidence gone. Hebron faced him at the top of the hill, an implacable fortress of self-righteousness, a row of polished black cars parked outside, the deacons standing by the door and the sound of Cross Hands' only electric organ booming within.

Evan turned into a side street, walked up and down for five minutes and came back. Now the deacons had gone in and the doors were closed to. As he opened the door and slipped through, the congregation had just risen to their feet for the opening hymn. He was tip-toeing to his pew in the second row, and was half-way along the aisle before he saw that it was occupied. And then a sidesman was barring his way and Pritchard who had crept up on him from behind was whispering in his ear. They were trying to persuade him to sit in the visitors' pews at the back of the chapel. There was no disguising from himself what this meant. He turned round, as every head in the building swivelled in his direction, and hurried out of the door.

It was a mile across the fields down to the river, and Evan went down the wet hillside in a body-jolting, slithering scramble, falling twice and ripping the palms of his hands with brambles. These surroundings were too ugly to attract any caravanners, but there were a few shacks made from odd planks and packing-cases that would be occupied in summer by transient labourers, a class of gipsies who offered their black-market labour for half the fixed agricultural rates of pay. Here, with the open sea out of sight beyond the low hills and the cropped chimneys of ruined factories, the tide came up strongly, a surging ochreous flood, obliterating until the ebb the narrow course of the river through the tidal mud flats.

He reached the edge of the bank. The nearest shanty was a hundred yards away and there was nobody in sight. Evan raised his head for a last look at the sky, but swirling mists had covered it. He was past any fear. He believed that pain had no separate existence from memory, and since death erased memory, the pangs of death were a fiction. If I forget I shall not have suffered. All that was necessary was resolution. He looked down and saw below him nothing but glistening mud. The promised water was not there. It was low tide and it had drained back to the river's permanent channel a hundred feet away.

Evan sat down on the ground and tried to ease his body down the steep bank, struggling for handholds and footholds in the mattocks of coarse grass sprouting on the slopes of a precipice of slime. He slipped and plunged into a basin of putty-coloured mud that broke wind at the impact of his feet with a stench of decaying roots. Floundering on hands and knees, his limbs were sucked away from his body into a squelching morass of endless depth. His face was covered with mud. He tasted it under his lips, and drew it bubbling in and out of his nostrils. Evan saw a root like a withered arm sticking out of the bank, freed an arm and grabbed at it. Instantly with this automatic gesture of self-preservation a treacherous desire to live took hold. He tugged and struggled, freeing the second arm and then a foot, leaving the shoe behind. For ten minutes he rested before he could muster enough strength to haul and claw himself to the top of the bank. Here he lay down and waited for the violent beating of his heart to subside. When he tried to move again he realized from the pain behind his knee that he had wrenched a muscle in his struggles to free himself. Shivering with cold and from shock, he managed to drag himself the hundred yards from the bank to the nearest shack, and with the last of his strength he burst open the door. There was a camp bed inside and on this Evan threw himself down and went to sleep.

He awoke two hours later, stiff with cold, wondering why he should be lying in this gloomy cell with the cobwebs drawn like grimy curtains across the small, cracked window. Then the memory of his calamity returned. His life was extinguished, and yet he knew he was condemned to live and that he would never find the strength to go down to the river again. But there was a difference between Evan now and

Evan before the river had shown him death and then rejected him. In his extremity his last subconscious defences had collapsed. Something mustering among other names as pride had gone. Things that Evan could never have admitted to himself before, he was now prepared to admit.

He thought of Bron, and a fantastic suspicion that had sometimes half-emerged from the depths of his mind only to be hastily pushed back out of sight and memory, was now accepted as a hideous reality. Bron, Evan decided at this moment, was not his father's son at all, but had been begotten by the odious Dr Griffiths. A hundred incidents instantly crowded through the abolished censorship of his memory testifying to this new truth: intimacies that Evan as a boy had either sensed or seen, the secret gestures passed between his mother and the doctor, his father's unaccountable fits of weeping, once even the gross shuffling adjustment by Dr Griffiths of his clothing when he had come out of his mother's room. It was at about this time that Bron would have been conceived.

The physical resemblances between Bron and Griffiths that he had forced himself not to see, now clamoured for attention. Bron was the youthful counterpart of the old doctor – the double of the Griffiths Evan had once seen in a photograph from the time the doctor had been a houseman at Bangor hospital. And not only was he unmistakably the doctor's son in face and figure, but he had even inherited his mannerisms: the rolling walk, the moments of vacancy in the stare delivered by his protruberant eyes, even the trick of rubbing the corner of his nose with his thumb when in thought – as though determined in every way to assert the truth of a paternity so long denied.

Evan's old hatred of Griffiths now became indivisible from his hatred for Bron. Bron was Griffiths reincarnated through his own mother's flesh to torment him. And this moment when he, Evan, cowered here, muddy, half-drowned and utterly defeated, Bron who was Griffiths was defiling his wife, just as Griffiths had defiled the mother he had so painfully loved. The womb that had rejected his seed would gorge itself with Bron's, would fructify and bring forth its horrid fruit, stamped with the image of Bron and Griffiths. Griffiths' revenge would be total. Evan felt a hatred that was so violent that it steadied his nerves like a powerful restorative draught.

9

That first night Cathy lay awake until dawn behind the bolted door of the back bedroom. A little later, after less than an hour's troubled sleep, she got up, dressed, and packed a suitcase with whatever she would require to return to the independent life of a working girl. Her native fatalism had come into its own. It was the armour that made it possible to feel no great regret for what she had lost. The five years she had spent at New Mill had been happy in a negative sort of way, but the years before when she had shared a single room with another girl over a baker's shop in a Brynaron back street, seemed no worse in retrospect, and she was resigned to returning to them again.

She caught the first bus to Brynaron and waited about for Modes de Paris, where she had last worked, to open at nine-thirty. After that there was a further wait until the Personnel Manageress, a thin, stiff lady with a tight face and blue-tinted hair, came on the scene at ten-fifteen.

Cathy unfolded the reference she had been given by the firm when she left to be married shortly after she had risen to the position of Senior Sales Assistant, and the lady took it with no attempt to conceal a small grimace of surprise. Since Cathy's day the business had been absorbed by one of the bigger multiples. Senior sales assistants no longer existed. They had been replaced by 'consultants' who required many qualifications besides mere salesmanship. Applicants for this position were chosen by a selection board at head office after a three weeks' course in the company's methods and only one applicant in seven was considered suitable to be enrolled for the course. The Personnel Manageress let Cathy understand that she did not believe her chances were high.

After that Cathy worked her way along Brynaron's Golden Mile and the result was always the same, summed up in the routine hopelessness of the assurance, 'We'll put your name on our waiting list, and you'll maybe be hearing from us'. Cathy had the feeling that she wasn't taken seriously. Although in her five years in Cross Hands she had mixed among the élite of Hebron on terms that were hardly better than sufferance, she had picked up a certain fragile dignity, a sense of her own consequence which was neither found nor encouraged among girls serving behind the counters in Brynaron's lower-grade shops.

Cathy found Brynaron depressingly changed since the old days. There was no gaiety left in the place. The pretty, lively, coquettish girls she had worked with had been replaced by glum-faced teenagers who walked as though they were dragging chains. The shops she had worked in had become smaller, quieter and dingier. Their poorly dressed windows needed polishing and there was dirt on the glass surfaces in the show cases. In the evening when the lights came on they were less bright. Young people no longer wandered up and down the main street in provocative groups when the day's work was over. By eight o'clock Brynaron was deserted.

She was no further advanced on the road to independence but still determined not to go back home to New Mill. Loneliness and nostalgia drove her to take a room at the Dragon Hotel. Here a new climate of impersonality, even sternness, was evident. In the old days the Dragon had done its best to keep its customers within bounds by the use of jocular poker-work notices. Now there were blunt warnings: 'No singing.' 'No cheques accepted.' 'Rooms must be vacated by 12, midday.' Prices had gone up. Where a double room for a night of adventure could be had for 30s, the price for a single room was now 25s. At this point Cathy's precarious economic situation made itself felt, because having paid for her room she was left with only 4s 6d to cover the expenses of the next day.

The only remedy was to bottle up her pride and take anything that was offered as a temporary measure to tide her over the emergency. Pearsons was the cut-price store where Cathy had started ten years before and its employees were on the lowest rung of the shop assistants' social ladder, branded with contempt for the poor quality of Pearsons' goods, for the low wages they were paid, and the lack of comfort in their working conditions. At Pearsons Cathy found that the changes were superficial.

A Mr Hammett had been Assistant Buyer ten years before and now he was Staff Manager. Cathy found him seated in his glass-partitioned cubby-hole under a banner lettered with Pearsons' slogan: 'Spend to Save.' In a corner was an altar decorated with artificial flowers bearing a group of toilet articles tied together with plastic ribbon and a showcard, 'This week's Special Offer – *Sell it*'.

'Mrs Owen!' Hammett said. 'Mrs Owen. How very nice to see you again.'

Hammett had been notorious for his abuse of his power with the junior female sales-staff, irrespective of time and almost of place. Like his surroundings he had shrunk a little. He now showed more of his teeth when he smiled than before. His thick black hair had receded to a dense, felt-like strip pointing down the centre of his scalp. Fat had padded the line of his jaw, and he breathed noisily.

'And to what do we owe this very great pleasure, Mrs Owen?'

She explained. 'The thing is, I seem to find myself with so

much time on my hands. I was thinking you might be able to fix me up with something. I wouldn't object to something temporary if necessary.'

'What a pity you didn't come in last month, Mrs Owen, when we were taking on temporary staff for the spring sales. As it is, I'm afraid it would be a question of waiting until the autumn —'

He surveyed her speculatively but with the boldness he found had nearly always paid, starting at the knees and working up.

'I might be able to create some sort of position for you, Mrs Owen, but it would take a little time, and I couldn't promise anything unless you'd consider the packing department. You could make a start there right away.'

'The packing department,' Cathy said. 'That's where I started ten years ago.' It was staffed, she remembered, by fifteen-year-old girls and tired middle-aged women.

'I know you did, Mrs Owen. But then you've lost a lot of seniority.' He changed to a more solemn voice to repeat the old formula. 'Pearsons prides itself on promotion from the ranks.'

She shifted her position to get up, and he hastened to set his trap of a little hope. 'You would probably be called up to the counter to help out at rush periods. And once you were on the staff again I might be able to do something to help. These things have to be organized very carefully to avoid jealousies.'

Hammett continued his study of her body. He had known it hurriedly in a dark corner of the empty-cartons storage room on one or two occasions but had completely forgotten its geography. The way she was sitting had produced a slight bulge in the front of her dress. He now suspected that she was pregnant, and the idea of this made her even more desirable.

'Believe me, Mrs Owen, I'd like to do something for you. I sincerely would.' He was afraid she was slipping through his fingers, and an anxious whine had entered his voice.

'You'll probably remember there's a good deal of office politics goes on in this firm. I'd have to tread very carefully, or I'd find myself in hot water. You can't work with a disgruntled staff. The best thing really would be for us to meet somewhere outside the building to talk over the ways and means. Why don't you and I have dinner together?'

Cathy got up and made her excuses to go. He showed her to the office door, standing there with her for a moment then letting a hand drop to caress her buttock.

'I've always had a soft spot for you, Cathy, you know that, don't you? You understand it would mean taking a bit of a chance but I'd be prepared to do anything I possibly could for you. By that I mean putting you on the counter straight away. Why don't you give me a ring or just come straight in and see me if you change your mind. I'm always here. You know where to find me.'

Cathy was sent by the employment exchange to a bicycle shop (position filled), a hairdresser's (no experience), and The Metal (union labour only employed) before she gave up and telephoned an old friend who had done well, and who she hoped might be able to put her up for a few days while she went on looking round.

Elsie Collar and Cathy had shared a room together in their late teens and had formed a working team to attack the problems of existence under Elsie's leadership. Elsie supplied the ideas and Cathy most of the cash, as her friend changed her jobs almost weekly and was always short of money for clothes. Cathy knew that she was the better looking of the two, but Elsie deployed her personality with such effect that most people failed to notice that she was far from beautiful. An assistant bank manager who had once taken her to a roadhouse had said she was *gamine*. Whereas Cathy was truthful out of lack of imagination, Elsie was a fantastic liar who had been able to convince most people that her father was a retired brigadier who permitted her to work for pin money. She was full of native wit and stratagems. Most of Cathy's friends patrolled the main Brynaron – Cross Hands road on Sunday nights after chapel on the lookout for adventure but Elsie would borrow a car and have it break down at a time and in a place when she could hope to be rescued by one of The Metal's executives passing in his Bentley. Through this device she had succeeded in marrying an up-and-coming young tool-room superintendent.

A woman's voice answered the phone – giving the number with the cool, tinkling detachment of the speaking clock.

'Hello Elsie. That *is* Elsie, isn't it?'

'This is Eve Marshall speaking.'

Cathy remembered now that Elsie had switched to Eve in the last days of their partnership.

'Eve, this is Cathy. Cathy Owen. You remember me, don't you?'

'Cathy – what a wonderful surprise. How are you, Cathy? What are you doing with yourself these days?'

'Oh, nothing very exciting. Life goes on much the same as ever. I was in town for a day, and suddenly I thought it would be nice to give you a ring.'

'I'm so glad you did, Cathy. It's simply ages since I heard from you. I was beginning to wonder whatever had become of you.'

Elsie's own voice was quite unrecognizable in the straitjacket of a new English accent.

'Actually I've tried ringing you several times before, but the number's always been engaged or something.'

'I know, isn't it sickening? People are always telling me they can't get through. What with Henry's business calls and Nanny's boy friends and one thing and another. They seem to do most of their courting on the phone these days.'

'You've got a family then, Eve? I didn't know that. How lovely.'

'Two little monsters. One four and one two. Boy and girl. And you?'

'Nothing in that direction so far. Keeping my fingers crossed.'

'Lucky you. I feel terribly old sometimes.'

'It doesn't take a family to make you feel like that, Eve – time simply flies. Doesn't it seem ages since we had that room in Lammas Street over the baker's?'

'Absolute centuries. A lot of water has flowed under the bridge since then.'

'They were good times, Eve, weren't they? I often think of them.'

'Marvellous times.'

'Pity one can't stay young for ever.'

'I always say we ought to be born old, and get a bit younger every year.'

'Wouldn't that be wonderful?'

'Mind you, getting older has something to be said for it, Cathy. Responsibilities can be fun.'

'Remember that time when we went to Mary and Steve's party with all the queers, Eve, and Mary got drunk and we put her in the bath? And then Dickie Dark insisted on taking us to Aberystwyth in his Chrysler with that coloured boy?'

'I couldn't have been a member of that particular party. At least I've no recollection of it.'

'But you remember Dickie Dark, don't you? Surely you remember Dickie Dark?'

'Vaguely, no more than vaguely. The name rings a bell, but no more than that.'

'I always thought he was a bit of a favourite of yours, Eve. In the old days.'

'One sees so many faces, Cathy. They come and go.'

'That's true. That's certainly true. Then I suppose you don't remember—?'

'I'm a bit hazy about things these days. Sorry my memory isn't better than it is. A lot of water under the bridge. And what with this family, and social work and one thing and another, I seem to have hardly the time left to think.'

'Well Eve, I'd love to see you again. I really would. It would be wonderful after all these years.'

'It would be wonderful to see you again, Cathy. . . . I tell you what, why don't we meet up somewhere sometime for a drink?'

'I'd love that, Eve.'

'I'm afraid this week's not much good. We've got a whole series of boring parties to go to, but almost any day next week would be all right. . . . I tell you what – Henry will be away on Thursday and I'll be alone. Why don't we meet for lunch and take in a film somewhere in the afternoon? How would that be?'

'That would be marvellous.'

'Wait a minute – what am I talking about? I've got to sell hats at a charity bazaar on the Thursday. Could we make it the Thursday after that?'

'I'm free any time. The Thursday after that will be lovely.'

'Wonderful.'

'Lovely.'

'Absolutely marvellous. And now I really must dash,

Cathy. Henry's car is in for servicing, and I just remembered I promised to pick him up at his office in mine.'

'Bye-bye till Thursday week, then, Eve.'

'Bye-bye, Cathy. Be lovely to see you.'

She went straight from this scattering of the ashes of the past to the Dragon and asked to see Victor who was now Manager, and rarely seen by visitors. It seemed only yesterday that Victor had come on the scene fresh from a commercial college to be Assistant Receptionist, and success had put a mask of caution and scepticism over the schoolboy's face with its impudent schoolboy's smirk.

'Victor,' Cathy said, 'I'm going to be absolutely frank with you and put my cards down on the table. I've had a row with my husband and walked out. It looks as though I may be short of money for a few days until I find something to do. I have to have somewhere to stay.'

She waited for him to say something, tried to guess what was going on in his head behind that tranquil face, but Victor listened a great deal these days, and spoke no more than he needed to. He showed her out of his office then led the way to the reception desk where he reached down her key. 'All packed up?' he asked. She nodded.

Victor took her up in the lift to the fourth floor, they went along a corridor, up a narrow flight of stairs at its end, and stopped outside a low door under a steeply slanting roof. He opened the door, nodded to her to go in, and ducked his head to follow her.

Cathy found herself in a windowless cell smelling of linoleum and worm-riddled furniture.

'One of the chambermaids sleeps here,' Victor said. 'Her mother's ill and she's gone off for two or three days. You can have it till she comes back. O.K.?'

'You'll never know how grateful I am,' Cathy said.

She waited for him to go.

'I expect you'd feel happier if you were doing something for your keep,' he said, 'so I suggest you might care to give a hand in the kitchen.'

'Of course I will,' she said. 'I don't know that I'm much of a cook – but so long as it's nothing too complicated.'

'There won't be any cooking to be done,' he said. 'Just a bit of washing up. After the midday and evening meals. Say about four hours, that's all.'

'I see,' she said.

He glanced at his watch. 'Eight o'clock already. You may as well start now.'

10

From the trough of the wave Bron was carried on to the next crest, the prey now of a furious, bubbling euphoria.

He made a quick tour of the farm as far as he could decide its boundaries, and returned undiscouraged by the bogs, the soggy fields, the bracken, the gorse and the bare, eroded higher slopes. One of the innumerable books he had read at Hayhurst had been on scientific farming and Bron had read it twice, not for any conceivable practical use, but just as he tackled a textbook on higher mathematics for the sheer pleasure of involving himself in problems. Under its influence he saw the bald dome of Pen Gof planted – with the co-operation of the Forestry Commission – with young pines, and its flanks fertilized and contour-ploughed. Proper drainage was the next priority and with the elimination of stagnant surface water and marshes Bron's imagination painted over the sour greens of the landscape with the lively colours of grain crops. Logically from this followed whatever measures were necessary to place the river under strict confinement, after which the scrawny mountain sheep – the only breed that could tolerate local conditions – could be replaced by tenderer and fatter strains which would flourish in the new surroundings. In a second instalment of this vision the other farmers were inspired by the Owens' example to do likewise, and with the spreading of the new prosperity there would be money to clear the whole valley of Cross Hands of its old industrial wastelands, thus ushering in the new golden age of local farming.

Back at the farmhouse, Bron accepted the change in the rhythm of the household. The life of the farm seemed in some way to have slipped out of gear, but he was not surprised. He was accustomed not to grope after the cause of apparently irrational effects. In Bron the mechanism of forgetting differed from the normal. The archives of the normal brain are preserved imperishably in the subconscious. In Bron's case certain experiences were never filed either for conscious or subconscious reference. It was like the sightlessness of the blind man compared with the man who shuts his eyes and still sees darkness. Bron saw no darkness – he saw nothing. And this total excision of parts of his experience was normal to him. He was like a dreamer unable to question the haphazard and disjointed episodes of a dream. When questioned by Dallas as to whether other people's conduct did not from his viewpoint often seem irrational, Bron readily agreed that it did. The friend of today became for no clear reason the enemy of tomorrow. The world was more or less mad. He made allowances for it. At the moment he suspected an irrationality in Cathy's unexplained absence from the house, with Evan mysteriously ill, left in bed with no-one to care for him. And why was Evan now in the box-room? That, too, was inexplicable. Bron went to knock on the box-room door three times on that first morning, and there was no reply. He gave up.

About midday a police car pulled up in the yard, and the sergeant from Swansea got out. He wanted to ask Bron a few more questions about the damaged Jaguar, refused the offer of a cup of tea and came straight to the point.

'You stated at Swansea that you spent the whole of that particular afternoon and part of the evening in the Ritz cinema. I suppose you remember the titles of the films?'

'Sorry, I can't.'

'There was a main film, a supporting item, and the news,' the sergeant said. 'You must have seen one or two of the films twice.'

'I suppose I must have done.'

'Who was acting in them then? You must remember one or two of the actors.'

'I'm afraid I don't.'

'Did you see a comedy, a cowboy film, or what? Was it British or American? Where was the setting? If you spend five hours in a cinema you surely remember something you saw?'

'The point is I only went to the cinema because it was raining and there was nowhere else to go,' Bron said. 'I suppose I must have settled down straight away and gone to sleep. Films bore me.'

'You get in quite a bit of sleep, don't you?' the sergeant said aggressively. 'It sounds an unlikely story to me.'

'Does it? I'm sorry, but that's what happened.'

The sergeant seemed unwilling to go. He turned over the leaves of his notebook.

'Is your brother, Mr Evan Owen, about?'

'He's in bed, unwell.'

'Mrs Owen?'

'She's out.'

'Any idea when she might be back?'

'Afraid not.'

'Is this likely to be your fixed address from now on?'

'Yes, I told you that.'

'And what is your present occupation?'

'Farmer,' Bron said cheerfully. 'I'm going into partnership with my brother on this farm.'

The sergeant put his book away without a word; he went to the door and let himself out. Bron heard him drive away. By this time Bron was beginning to feel hungry. There seemed to be no food in the house, so he decided to walk down to the Salutation for a sandwich and a glass of beer.

Oakes was behind the bar, a little hunched like a boxer on the defensive, and black-browed when he saw Bron. There was no sign of Wendy. He mumbled a surly something in reply to Bron's 'good morning', served him with averted eyes and stumped away. Wendy was due back from a shopping excursion in about half an hour and Oakes hoped that Bron would have gone by then. Bron's name had come up in a violent row he had had with Wendy on the previous night. 'If he asks me to go out with him,' Wendy said, 'I bloody will. Why shouldn't I? You've got no rights over me.' Oakes went into his back room, slammed a few doors, rattled the drawers of his desk, tore a sheet off the calendar, crumpled it into a ball and threw it out of the window, hoicked and spat. He came back, picked up a glass, held it under Bron's nose and started to polish with angry concentration.

Bron took his beer and sandwiches to the other end of the bar, where the small farmer he had seen knocked over by the beatnik joined him, and Bron shared with him his vision for the future of New Mill. 'It's an attractive idea,' the farmer said. 'I imagine you'll have found all the money for it. Ten thousand for a kick off, I suppose?'

'That's the trouble,' Bron said. 'Funds. Evan tells me you can't expect anything from the banks these days.'

'Why not go to someone like the Borough Finance, then? They're operating a buy-and-lease-back scheme. Might give you a price for the farm and then let you have it back on a long lease. Gives you a chance to put whatever you get into more property and equipment. As it is the unit's too small. All the farms round here are too small. Have to be three times the size they are before they're a really paying proposition.'

Bron agreed with him. According to the textbook no unit under two hundred acres was much good anywhere.

'Anyway, there's nothing lost in giving them a ring. You'll find them in the book. Mention my name if you like. Billings. I'm hoping to do a deal with them myself if I can get them to see eye to eye with me on what my place is worth.'

'I'll do that,' Bron said. 'I'll give them a ring.'

The bus from Brynaron pulled up outside to deposit Wendy who slipped into the back entrance, hoping to avoid an encounter with Oakes before she had hidden her parcels away. But Oakes, hearing through the window the familiar squeal of brakes, the crunch of the heavy tyres, then the powerful sigh as the servo-operated doors closed to, dropped everything and dashed to intercept her.

'You're back then.'

'I'm back,' Wendy said. She had an armful of paper bags.

'You took your time. I expected you on the eleven-o'clock bus.'

'I had a lot to do.'

'See anybody you know?' Oakes couldn't stop himself asking the question.

She gave him a funny look, her lips compressed, and shook her head.

'What did you buy this time?'

'Among other things a dress.'

'That would be the third this month, wouldn't it?'

'The spring sales are on,' she said. 'You save money buying now. It's your pocket I'm thinking of.'

Oakes nodded in sarcastic agreement. 'I know.'

'Most women wait till they want a dress to buy it. I call that silly. I buy my dresses when the prices are down, knowing I'm going to want them sooner or later. Surely that's more sensible.'

'Much,' Oakes said.

Wendy went through to the room behind the bar, put down her purchases, flung her coat over the back of a chair, stood in front of the mirror to pat her hair in position, and began to touch up her lips. Oakes had placed himself between her and the door leading to the bar.

'I notice that none of the beds have been made,' Oakes said. He was determined to keep absolutely calm, but at the same time to leave no doubt in her mind about the way he felt about her neglect of her duties.

'That's Mrs Pugh's job.'

'It happens to be Mrs Pugh's day off. Our arrangement was that you would pitch in when Mrs Pugh had her day off.'

Wendy was darkening the eye-shadow on her lids. 'The beds won't be slept in till tonight.'

'It looks bad,' Oakes said. 'It makes the place look crummy. Clients have the right to expect their rooms to be made up by ten in the morning at the latest. They don't expect to have to sit about in a room that looks like a pigsty until three in the afternoon.'

'There's nothing to stop them going for a walk if they feel like it.'

'Do me a favour. Don't try to be funny. I hate going into a room myself at midday and finding the bed still unmade. It depresses me.'

'For God's sake give it a rest,' she said. She screwed on a pair of gaudy ear-rings. 'What do you think of them?' she said.

'Bloody terrible.'

'Sorry you don't like them. They're all the rage.'

'If you thought a little less about dolling yourself up, and a little more about doing your job . . . To tell you the truth I've just about had enough of all the mess around the place.'

'Why don't you do something about it, if you feel that way?'

'I intend to,' Oakes said. 'You can be sure about that.'

'Again? Not again? What's the new plan of action this time?' Oakes, she could see, was working himself up into a routine fury. She enjoyed these scenes as long as they didn't go too far. Instinctively she knew that they weakened him and increased her hold upon him.

'For a start I'll look after the bar myself this morning. Tonight and tomorrow, too, if necessary. That way you'll have no excuse not to get the house tidied up.'

'I wasn't employed to scrub floors.'

'And you don't.'

'Everything but, though,' she said.

Oakes puffed out his cheeks in an expression of ultimate determination. The moment for the final showdown had arrived. This was the confrontation at which would be decided whether Wendy was to remain an employee or would virtually become the boss.

'I must ask you,' Oakes said, 'to be so good as to do as I say. I told you to go upstairs and do the work you are paid to do. Now please go.'

She tried to pass him to go to the bar, but she was able no more than to glance through the glass-pannelled top half of the door before Oakes reached her. He pulled her back into the centre of the room where her parcels were, piled her arms with them, then thrust her through the farther door. 'And don't let me see you down here again until you've got the place straight,' he shouted after her.

Victory, he thought. Then he felt the need for a drink. He

slipped through into the bar and helped himself to a quick double whisky. Bron and Billings were talking finance over glasses that were half full at the other end of the bar. He went back into his room, and with the subsidence of his blood pressure his self-satisfaction began once more to ebb away.

Why hadn't Wendy put up the slightest resistance when he pushed her through the door? Why had she clattered away on her high heels down the passage and up the stairs, without the slightest protest or attempt to get back? The alarming thought occurred to him that he might have over-done his stand. Could it be that she had gone quietly upstairs to get her things together before leaving him – as she had so often threatened to do? Oakes knew that Wendy could walk out of the Salutation and walk into another job in Brynaron in five minutes. He felt an agonizing tug in the umbilical cord of emotional dependence that attached him to her, and which he knew he could never find the strength to cut. He had doubled her wages in the past three months, and spent a small fortune on her clothes. But it wasn't enough for her. She demanded a ring. He suspected that every time she went out of the place she pulled a fast one on him, and the way he tried to keep track of her movements had made him the laughing-stock of Cross Hands.

Oakes clenched his fists, saying to himself, To hell with her. If she wants to go, let her go. But in a moment he knew he would follow her up the stairs and try to make her see his point of view, before actually asking her forgiveness. 'Look here, Wendy, I don't expect to go down on my bloody knees every time I want you to do something for me. It's too bloody ridiculous for words.'

A door opened and closed on his crestfallen daydream. He turned round and Wendy was coming towards him in her new dress, treading lightly, smiling as if nothing had happened. She had decided against the ear-rings. His eyes watered with relief. For once she was going to forgive him without the usual prelude of humiliation. Wendy walked round him without a word and went through into the bar. Bron looked up as she came in, hardly recognizing her. She looked marvellous. A real beauty.

Wendy put her hand out to him across the counter, and Bron took the small, plump fingers in his palm.

'Hello stranger,' Wendy said.

When Bron came down on the Sunday morning he was relieved to find Cathy back, but chilled at the strangeness of her reception of him. He went back upstairs for the carnations he had bought her in Brynaron. 'A few flowers to cheer the place up a bit.'

He was disappointed when she showed no signs of pleasure or appreciation. She took the flowers, mumbled something and put them down on the sideboard.

Mechanically – because the very fact that she had returned to the house had plunged her into household routines – she got his breakfast. From this point on a set pattern of action would carry her through the day and, although she could not yet understand this, would sooth her distraught nerves. She went into the kitchen, put on a pot to boil, wound up a clock, closed a window against the rain, and came back. There was something she had to say to him, but she did not know where to begin. She stood looking down at him, noticing again and resenting his good looks. He glanced up. 'No breakfast?'

She shook her head.

'Not hungry?'

'I don't feel like it.'

She sat down and turned her head away, looking out of

the window, and now the change in her, which Bron had first ascribed to some trick of lighting, was more apparent. Her features seemed swollen and her eyes smaller. A boniness had appeared at the angles of her clothing. He would have said that she had lost weight.

'Sure you're feeling all right? You don't look well. Anything the matter?'

'I'm perfectly well.' Her dislike of him sharpened into fury. How dare he adopt this pose?

He pushed his plate away. 'Where's Evan?'

'I imagine he went to chapel.'

'He's up and about again. Well, at least that's something. Is he quite O.K. now?'

'It seems so.'

'There's something we ought to get straightened out. This business about a heart attack, for instance. I'm beginning to wonder if he hasn't been trying to keep out of my way.'

He waited for her to deny the suggestion before going on.

'If, as I suspect, he's been trying to avoid me, the question is why? I've given a lot of thought to it, and all I can suppose is that it's this wretched business about the car. Could I be right?'

'He was upset about the car, I suppose.'

'And don't think I can't see his point of view. He had every right to be. I turn up like a bad penny, and straight away the trouble starts – visits from the police, court cases in the offing. People live in a goldfish bowl in this part of the world. I suppose I've set this place buzzing with all kinds of talk. It was the same back in Morfa. It's always been the same. God knows, I do my best to stay out of trouble.'

For a moment he was back in Morfa again, hounded by sudden inexplicable antagonisms, driven in silence home from school by a white-faced headmaster to face his mother's tears and reproaches.

'I'm a human magnet where trouble is concerned. Anyone else can drive a car for years without having to show their licence. The first time I drive without a licence someone bumps me and the police want to book me on half a dozen charges.'

Bron was quite certain now – his certainty confirmed by Cathy's silences – that he had upset Evan, but the more he thought about it the less likely did it seem that the trouble over the car could be at the bottom of it.

'No,' he said. 'On second thoughts it can't be the car. The car business isn't important enough. I can't believe it's that. No, of course, I know what it is.'

She waited in suspense for what was to come.

'I wonder I didn't think of it before. It's this partnership idea of his. He's got cold feet about it, and I don't blame him. Well, anyway, I'm the last person to try to hold him to it if he wants to change his mind. Frankly, Cathy, he's had second thoughts about the partnership – that's it, isn't it?'

'He hasn't said anything to me,' she said.

'He probably wouldn't. He'd bottle the thing up and say nothing to anyone. Having once made the offer he wouldn't be able to bring himself to go back on his word. Still, we'll soon find out. I'll tackle him as soon as he gets back. If he wants me to stay on I'm perfectly happy to help on the farm on a wage basis. Or I can go and find myself something else to do. What I'll do is say to him straight out, "Look, let's forget this partnership business. Don't think I'm not grateful for the gesture, but it simply isn't necessary." Don't you think that's the best idea?'

She had lost her moment, and couldn't find the courage to go back.

'I don't know,' she said. 'I really don't know.'

. . . . .

Even the anticipation of seeing Wendy had been over-shadowed by this prelude, and Bron, on his way to the Salutation, had a moment of homesickness for Hayhurst, for Hayhurst's emphatic half-solutions to his problems, the absolute definition of its frontiers of conduct, its companionship, above all its accessibility to Dallas, the father-figure and the comrade with whom he had ventured into the labyrinth of his unconscious.

Bron walked on and Dallas would have shaken his head in disappointment and foreboding at the way he appeared not to notice the deep puddles. Freed from Hayhurst Bron had the sensation that he had become socially accident-prone once again. In Hayhurst he had been a member of a community on which common misfortune had imposed its own democracy. As a free man he was a misfit. Even without the police's knowing he was an ex-convict – he imagined he had done nothing to justify their checking on his record – he seemed naturally to attract their attention.

To some extent Dallas had foreseen this, warning him against too great a liking for the institutional life, and insisting that Bron's insubordinations had been planned in the subconscious to ensure the loss or remission of his sentence. 'I know you're probably happy for the first time in your life,' Dallas said, 'but you don't want to stay here for ever.'

Owen appears as a very lonely man, he had written in his notes. *He craves the society of others, craves their approbation and is deeply hurt when this approbation is withheld. He is generally popular with the other prisoners as he goes out of his way to assist them with their problems, and as the result of his educational background he is able to do this with some effect. Associates for preference with prisoners whose psychotic condition is particularly marked. Capable of compassion. Perhaps the need to feel that others are worse off than he. Normal life will tend to deprive him of the therapeutic value of such associations.*

'Is marriage ever the answer in the case of these isolated persons?' a colleague had asked Dallas.

Dallas doubted it.

'Owen is the kind of man who might take up with a prostitute, and would be very kind to her if he did. People of his kind with a whole range of psychotic syndromes often do. It's quite amazing how they contrive to see their girl friends' personalities like a photographic negative image. Completely idealized. The defects actually become virtues. I had a patient once who was a schizophrenic painter with a prison record. Painted nothing but the prostitute he lived with – always as a Madonna.'

'Do the girl friends reciprocate?'

'In the matter of affection? Rarely, except where there's some mental illness in their case too. It's quite extraordinary how many criminals are given away to the police by their girls. Some fundamental dichotomy of attitudes. The man makes atonement and attempts to reconcile himself with society through the woman, who becomes a mother figure. He expresses his anti-social feelings in other directions, from which she is excluded. The girl wishes to revenge herself on society, and she does this not only through him, but sometimes by bringing about his downfall. By punishing him for his love she settles another score with society.'

She's like a splendid animal in a trap, Bron thought. A captive – the butt of the crude jokes of these sour-faced, god-fearing farmers and a slave to Oakes's pathological jealousy. From the very first glance Bron had felt a current of understanding and affinity flow between them. He had had the sensation, too, that as their eyes met she had

126

appealed to him to rescue her from her predicament. But rescue her with what? For the first time he felt himself deprived of the powers of property and a future to be shared.

As it was Sunday the Salutation was theoretically closed, but the customers – attracted in greater numbers than on weekdays by the sin of lawbreaking – were going in by the back door, and Bron joined them. Wendy realized as though an electrical signal had passed between them that he had come in. She came round the bar to him and they stood in a corner of the room. He longed to put his arms round her. She smiled, and her eyes seemed moist. For a moment they did not speak.

'Has he gone?' Bron said.

'Until tomorrow afternoon. I'm all alone.'

'Where? Here?' he said.

'No, not here. I'll tell you why later. I'll meet you after we close up at half past ten. Wait for me by the water tower just down the road. You can take me for a drive.'

'A drive?' he said, feeling a nervous qualm.

'Yes,' she said. 'With luck it will be a full moon. If it isn't clouded over, I mean.'

11

Bron had kept out of Cathy's way since morning, and waited until he saw by the light in her bedroom window that she had gone to bed before he went quietly to the shed where the Austin was kept and unlocked it. He checked the petrol, glanced at the tyres, started up and quickly switched off. He was relieved now that Evan had not appeared. Bron could not imagine how he would have broached the subject of using the car again without a driving licence. As it was he proposed to drive the car with great care and the least possible distance, to pick Wendy up at the water tower, drive to the nearest place where they could conveniently park, and leave it at that. On further consideration he decided to clean himself up and get away without delay, and to drive over to the meeting place forthwith, even if it meant an hour or so's wait.

He bathed and had begun to shave when the lights went out. This happened often enough at New Mill, but this time it was a half-hour before they came on again and he could find clean underclothes and a shirt and finish dressing. Through the window the moon flickered through scudding clouds as if wired up to The Metal's undependable private lighting circuit. For once it looked like being a fine night. He was sorry now that he had not found some way of getting out of taking the car. He was beginning to feel a superstitious fear of attracting bad luck to himself.

The small noises downstairs seemed to have been going on for some time before his other preoccupations allowed him to consider them. Water rattled in the pipes as somebody turned on a tap. Faint sounds were coming from the direction of the kitchen. This could only mean that Evan was back. Bron looked at his watch and found that he was due at the water tower in just over twenty minutes. He had to make up his mind quickly about what was to be done. He would go down and test the atmosphere, and if – as he feared – Evan appeared unreceptive, set out immediately on foot to keep his appointment.

Bron did up his jacket, ran a comb through his hair, and went downstairs. The light in the living-room was on, and the door to the yard was open. The noises had stopped and Bron waited and listened. A minute passed and a sound started behind the kitchen door of someone scrubbing with a hard brush. Bron turned the handle of the kitchen door and pushed it open gently. Evan was there in his underclothing, his back to him, bent over the kitchen table, on which was stretched out a pair of trousers. As Bron came in he was on the point of dipping a scrubbing brush in a bowl of water.

'Evan,' Bron said. He went towards him smiling, and then stopped as Evan turned round, his hands behind him. Bron was startled. His first thought was, He's mad. Evan's face was bloodless, with the waxen polish of the face of a corpse. His nose was a small, sharp beak, and his mouth a lipless gash with ridged puckerings in the wax at the corners. The low-power naked lamp bulb hanging behind his head had completely drowned his eyes in the shadows of skull-like sockets. His feet were bare and mud-smeared.

'Evan! What's the trouble? Where have you been hiding yourself?'

A moment before there had been a large electric torch standing on the table beside the bowl, and then it was gone. Bron, flabbergasted, took another doubtful step forward and as he did Evan's hand came from behind his back. Something

129

flashed over Bron's left eye and crunched like an egg, and for an instant he was inhaling water gurgling through the nose. Teeth had appeared in the gash of Evan's mouth. Bron saw the torch come down again, turned his head away, and felt it thump on his shoulder. Until this moment he had been paralysed by a hypnotic surprise, but now as Evan raised his arm again, spittle boiling over the ledge of his lower jaw, small fishy eyes surfacing to goggle in the black sockets, Bron caught at the arm, twisted it and bent it violently back. Evan's ramshackle weightless body span and all his joints folded. Somehow a corner of the table had come between them, and as Evan went down Bron heard the soft gristly concussion of his face on the table's edge.

Like a jointless puppet Evan lay on the floor in his muddy underpants, his long, thin legs flexed like a frog's, head screwed round at an impossible angle to the trunk, a graze on the bridge of his nose that was filling with blood, and more blood trickling down from one nostril over the yellow wax of the top lip into the corner of the mouth and out again. He was breathing in noisy asthmatic rasps.

Bron's angry impulse died. He was sorry for the old man. Alarmed too. No one with a heart condition dare risk this kind of thing. He went to the sink, filled a cup with water and sprinkled a little on Evan's face. The reaction was instant. Evan began to scramble with his arms and legs as if trying to get a grip on an icy surface. He rolled over on to his knees. Bron put an arm round his shoulders to help him to his feet, but Evan threw it off.

'Evan, old boy, sit down and rest a bit. You're not well.'

Evan waved him away. He was reeling about in a most alarming manner, Bron stalking him, waiting to rush forward and catch him if he overbalanced. And then before Bron could reach him Evan made a dash for the back door, flung it open and disappeared into the darkness.

Bron stood outside the door for a moment, peering into the shifting patterns of moonlight in the yard. He could see or hear nothing of Evan. He went back into the kitchen, stood, head bowed in thought, for a moment. Two small over-lapping crimson circles appeared on the linoleum with tiny spear-shaped splashes at the edges. He raised his hand to his eyebrow, then looked at his blood-smeared fingers. The mirror showed him an inch-long cut, sagging open and fill-ing with blood again a second after he had tried to staunch it with his handkerchief. Take a bit of stopping, he thought. In five minutes he would be meeting Wendy.

It was at this moment – and for the second or third time since he had been at New Mill – that Bron had the sudden sensation that he was being watched. Out of the corner of his eye, through the opening of the living-room door, he caught a flash of movement. Pressing the handkerchief to his eye, Bron went to the door and opened it wider, but there was nobody there. What began as the crunch of footsteps became the wind plucking and tearing at the loose felt of an outhouse roof. My imagination, he thought – I'm upset.

Now he wished he could have put off the meeting with Wendy. There was blood on his shirt-front and no time to change it. No time to do anything but wipe his face with a wet towel, get out the car and set off.

Next morning Cathy came down to find Bron at the break-fast table with an empty cup and saucer in front of him. He was absorbed in balancing a teaspoon on the edge of the cup. She instantly noticed three things: the patch of sticking plaster over the eyebrow; the fact that his shirt-front was dirty; and that he was unshaved. She concluded that he'd been out all night and had only just come in. There was something disturbing about the atmosphere that she hadn't

131

got used to. And then she realized it was the silence. She hadn't got used to the absence of clocks.

Bron half got up. She found his smile strained.

'Where's Evan?' she said. 'He came home last night, didn't he?'

'He's gone to Aberystwyth. On the first bus. Left an hour ago.'

'Aberystwyth? What on earth for?'

'As I understand, to see a Mr Digby. Something about raising funds for more chapel building.'

'I've never heard of Mr Digby,' Cathy said. 'And it's the first I've heard about the chapel raising more funds.'

'I can only tell you what he told me,' Bron said.

She watched him, a little frightened. He had closed his eyes. He looked exhausted. 'What's the matter with your head?'

'That,' Bron said, 'is where Evan hit me. With a torch. I should have had a stitch in it, but I've probably left it too late now!'

'God,' she said.

'Last night I had the most extraordinary experience I've ever had in my life. I went down to the kitchen and Evan was there in his underclothes cleaning up his suit. I went up to him to say something friendly and before I knew where I was he was hitting me on the head with a torch.'

'I heard a noise but I was too frightened to come down.'

'The incredible part is still to come. He hit me a couple of times as hard as ever he could, then I managed to get him to drop the torch and he ran out of the back door – just as he was in his vest and pants – and that was the last I saw of him. All I could suppose was that he'd gone mad. Well naturally enough, the way things were one way or another, it was clear enough I wasn't going to be able to stay on here, so I decided to move out today. However, this morning when he comes on the scene it's just as if nothing has ever happened. He didn't even mention last night. I told him I thought we'd better drop the partnership idea and he wouldn't hear of it. He went and got the signed agreement and handed it over to me there and then.'

It was all wrong, Cathy thought. She didn't understand what had happened, but nothing made sense. 'When's he coming back?'

'He's not certain. Either tomorrow, or the day after, depending how long the business takes.'

'This talk about raising funds for the chapel,' she said. 'What did you say this man's name was?'

'Digby,' he said.

'He's never mentioned a Mr Digby to me. He tells me everything he does. I should have thought I'd have heard of him.'

'He was catching the ten-ten train to Aberystwyth to see his old friend Mr Digby. I particularly remember the old friend part. He was something to do with a Council of Free Churches, I remember.'

'But why should the chapel want to raise funds for more building when attendance is going down?'

'Search me.'

'Did he seem strange in any way?'

'A bit quiet, but all right otherwise. He told me to look after you while he was away. His actual words were, "I know Cathy will be in good hands."'

'And he was just quiet?'

'Quiet,' Bron said. 'Subdued, I'd say. I suppose it was to be understood considering the way he'd coshed me for no reason at all only a few hours before.'

'Was anything said about money?' she said. 'There's not a penny in the house. Nothing to pay the bills or for the housekeeping. We owe Beynon a week and a half's wages.'

133

'The only thing he said about money was that a representative of some h.p. firm would call for payment today and that either you or I – whoever saw him – was to put him off for a couple of weeks. Say he's away on holiday.'

She shook her head. 'That's incredible.'

'Why?'

'Because it's the same as telling a lie and I don't believe he's ever told a lie in his life.'

'It's surprising what you have to do sometimes when the money-lenders get their fingers round your neck.'

'He still wouldn't lie. I'm beginning to wonder if he hasn't taken leave of his senses. What was he wearing this morning?'

'The things he always wears.'

'You mean his ordinary working clothes?'

'I mean what I've always seen him in.'

'He'd never do it. He'd never dream of going to Aberystwyth or anywhere else in his working clothes. It's the last thing on earth he'd do.' Despite the gulf that had opened between Evan and herself Cathy shared with him some of the ignominy of the suggestion.

Bron nodded. 'It sounds out of character, I admit.'

'By the way,' she asked suddenly, and with a flattening of the voice, 'you went out in the car last night, didn't you?'

'I had to see someone. Why?'

'Oh nothing.'

'Mind you,' Bron said, 'although I told Evan I'd carry on with the partnership, I've decided against it on further thought. Whichever way you look at it and however repentant Evan may be at the moment for what he probably considers his un-Christian conduct last night, there must be some underlying antagonism. I'll stay on and do all I can to help to keep things going until he gets back, and then we'll have to see what's the best thing to be done.'

12

The phone rang at five past eight, and Jones who had been up since before dawn, working on his translation, picked up the receiver immediately.

Fenn was on the line. 'Nice to find you on the ball at this hour, Emrys.' Fenn's normally abrupt telephone manner had been injected with cheer by the news, received in the first post, that he had won £33 on the Pools.

'Just trying to catch up on some of the paper work,' Jones said.

'We just had a call here from someone who said there was a murder at New Mill Farm last night,' Fenn said genially.

'Not New Mill again.'

'The caller, as per usual, refused to give his name and hung up. Price, who took the message, thought he was trying to disguise his voice. The call was traced to a box at the junction of New Mill Lane and the main road outside Cross Hands. I don't set any importance to it. We've had two false alarms in the past seven days alone. All the same you'd better get over there.' There was a pause. 'Don't trouble to come back unless you've anything to say.'

Jones thought, He's smartening up. That means no report. I have to spend a morning on a wild goose chase and nothing to show for it. It's time spent whether it's wasted or not.

'That's a funny set-up all the same,' Fenn said. 'You got a copy of the C.R.O. report on Bron Owen?'

'I certainly did.'

'I suppose he's bound to give us big trouble sooner or later. That was a good start he made at Swansea the other day.'

'Don't worry, I'm keeping an eye on him,' Jones said.

Fenn's call was followed immediately by one from Evan Owen's neighbour on the east side of Pen Gof, Hughie Phillips. Phillips was one of a number of ruined farmers who had abandoned the ungrateful soil to live entirely off the rents received from caravan sites on their property. Phillips's site, on the highest point of Pen Gof accessible to wheeled vehicles, was called Glas Mor in recognition of a distant view of an inverted triangle of sea occasionally visible on the rare clear days. It was regarded as the choicest site in the area, and although it only took six caravans, Phillips made enough from it to start him on the upwards social road from the humblest of the Cross Hands chapels, known as Threepence in the Plate, in the direction of Hebron at the top.

'Emrys, I don't know if this is any good to you, but there's a good bit of poaching going on at Glas Mor.'

'What sort of poaching, Hughie?'

'There's a fellow up there setting gin traps in the open for pheasants. Decimating them.'

'A visitor?'

'One of the regulars unfortunately. Man called Stevens. English fellow. Big noise in The Metal. Although he's a customer of mine, I can't stick him. Fond of animals I am. You'll find the traps on the other side of the hedge between the site and the wood.'

This piece of information made Jones angry. He knew the type of man who kept a caravan at Glas Mor – a rich shopkeeper from Wolverhampton, or the overbearing owner of some small factory. Jones, proposing to call at New Mill Farm on his way back, got his bicycle out and set off straight away.

Although he detested caravan sites on principle he couldn't help feeling a grudging admiration for the way Phillips had gone to work there. Useless as Phillips had been as a farmer, Jones had to admit that he showed flair in his new enterprise. The place was well kept. Phillips had filled in the ruts in the approach lane and grown hedges all round the site to protect his rich clients from the depressing view of the low-class holiday-makers and their caravans that cluttered every flat space on the west side of Pen Gof, all the way down to the bed of the valley.

Beyond the site was an ancient tangled oakwood which had been too awkward for the original deforesters of Pen Gof to get at to be considered worth clearing. This miraculously supported a number of pheasants, game birds with a touch of the eagle about them, which had escaped there and survived by developing a resistance to the terrible climate. They avoided the foxes and domestic cats gone wild by spending most of their lives in the treetops.

Jones leant his bicycle against a gate and admired the site and its arrangements for a few minutes before starting his investigation. The six caravans spaciously dispersed about the field, were the largest and most expensive-looking he had ever seen. Only one appeared to be occupied and a vintage Rolls was parked close by. An area of the field surrounding the caravan had been transformed into a lawn, and a crazy-paving path flanked by lights festooned from poles led past an electric barbecue to a lavatory with separate entrances for males and females and the appropriate symbols on each.

The constable's reflections were interrupted by a faint and distant whimpering sound coming from the direction of the wood. He crossed the site, found a gap in the hedge and clambered through it. Here he was in a narrow field, with the wood all along the farther side beyond a low drystone wall. Almost the first thing Jones saw was a cock pheasant squatting with head erect in the middle of the field. He walked over to it and the pheasant waited for him but when he bent down to touch it it suddenly whirred away with a high-pitched pheasant's chatter, and Jones had time to see that one foot was missing.

After that he went back to the hedge and walked along it in the direction of the whimpering sound and stopped after he had gone a few yards. He soon found a dead pheasant in a trap, and round it in the grass a few grains of wheat. There were two more traps still set, and a third which had caught a wood pigeon, which appeared to have been killed and partially eaten by a cat. In the fourth trap Jones found the cat itself, which had ceased to whimper and moan and awaited him in spitting fear, tugging at its trapped fore-paw, with the bone showing pink and white under the shredding muscle.

Jones looked round for something to kill it with, but could find nothing but a half-rotten oak branch. He went back to the caravan and pressed the bell and a man in a dressing-gown opened the door. The man stood at the top of the low flight of steps and looked down at Jones. He closed the caravan door behind him and Jones had only the briefest glimpse of an interior of silk drapings and polished woodwork. 'Yes?' he said.

Jones said, 'I'm sorry to trouble you, sir, but there's a cat in a trap over there. I wonder if you have anything about I could use to put it out of its misery?'

He was a very tall man with a huge face, blue-veined cheeks and a short, sandy moustache, and he was looking at something over Jones's head in the remote distance. 'Wait a minute,' he said.

The tall man went back into the caravan and closed the door behind him. A window in the caravan slid up an inch and a little music squeezed out mixed up with the odour of frying bacon. A lark bounced up out of the grass near-by, trailing a slapdash melody. Two sheep passed with their lambs moving like quicksilver behind them through the clumps of heather. As Jones looked at his watch for the second time, the caravan door opened and the man came out again. He was now wearing an army officer's greatcoat thrown over his dressing-gown, and a pair of suède boots.

'This way,' he said.

Jones followed him to the Rolls. The man took out a key and unlocked the boot. 'Under that flap,' he said. 'The tool-kit. A hammer in it. Help yourself.'

Jones found the tool-kit, unstrapped it and took out the hammer and the man shut the boot, looking away.

'When you're finished with the hammer leave it by the rear wheel of the car.'

'Thank you very much, sir. Sorry to have bothered you in this way.'

'And clean it.'

He looked up at the sky, sniffed, pushed both hands into the pockets of his greatcoat and stalked back to the caravan, leaving behind him the faintest whiff of shaving lotion on the absolutely still air.

The cat, huge, agile and desperate, fought hard for its life, and Jones, feeling very sick, hideously bungled the job of killing it. Afterwards he took the body out of the trap and threw it under the hedge. Then he went down the hedgerow uprooting the rest of the traps. Peering into the brambles for any trap that might have gone unnoticed among the debris of dead bracken and leaves, he saw something glinting and picked up a silver cigarette lighter. He went back, threw the traps down by his bicycle and rang the doorbell of the caravan.

The tall man came out again. He looked over Jones's head and then down at him with a frown. This time he was in his pyjama trousers, with a bare torso tufted with greying sandy hair, and a towel round his neck.

'Well?'

'Does this happen to be yours, sir?' Jones handed up the cigarette lighter.

The man took it, held it between finger and thumb, looked at one side, then turned it over to look at the other. His left hand went down to scratch the base of his stomach under his pyjamas.

'Why should it be?'

'I found it over there by the hedge. There seem to be some initials on it.'

'As it happens, it is. Thanks. I didn't expect to see it again. Left the door of the caravan open when we were away the other day and somebody got in.' The strong, buccaneering face was suddenly weakened by a crafty smile.

'I wonder you didn't report the matter to us, sir.'

The weakness went out of the man's face as the frown came back. 'From previous experience I regard it as a waste of time.'

Jones said, 'We rather depend on the public's co-operation in this sort of thing. If crimes aren't reported to us there isn't much we can do. It's like trying to fight the criminal with our hands tied.'

'Please don't lecture me, Constable.'

Jones waited for the humiliation to subside before replying. He detested this man – this natural leader of men who scratched his pubes and looked at the sky while putting him so effortlessly in his place. This was the archetype of all

140

Englishmen who controlled the orchestra of their world with the slightest movement of head or hand, who shoved you aside with their voices, who could wear even creased pyjamas with absent distinction while men of Jones's calibre contrived to look fools in white tie and tails, who oozed so much power that village policemen who detested them seemed to lose control of their muscles and were forced to raise their hands in salute whether they liked it or not when one drew up in his car to ask a direction.

'May I ask if anything else was taken, sir?'

'A few trifles belonging to my wife.'

'Would you care to enumerate them, sir?'

'No, I would not. If I'm not bothered I don't see why you should be.'

'You're Mr Stevens, aren't you?' Jones said.

'Major Stevens. I also happen to be a county councillor, for what the information may be worth to you.'

'It's been suggested that you might be willing to help us in the matter of a complaint we've received of poaching with illegal gin traps.'

'And who made this suggestion?'

'I'm afraid I'm not at liberty to say.'

'Aren't you? Well, whoever they are, they're wrong.'

'Have you seen or heard anything of a suspicious nature going on in this neighbourhood since you've been here, sir?'

'No, I haven't, Constable. Do be a good fellow and go away.'

'My information is that these offences were being committed by some person living in a caravan on this site.'

The major looked skywards again, his frown deepening. 'Is this supposed to be some sort of interrogation?'

'It's a matter of routine inquiries,' Jones said. 'This happens to be the only occupied caravan, so far as I can see.'

'And what is that supposed to imply?'

'I leave that to you, sir.'

'I must ask you to go, and to go immediately.'

Jones had noticed a metal rubbish bin standing close to an incinerator a few yards away from the caravan, and now he walked across to it and took the lid off. There was a collection of feathers among the empty bottles and tin cans in the bin.

'I see you'll be having pheasant for dinner, sir,' Jones said.

'You're trespassing, Constable,' the major said.

'I'm carrying out inquiries in the normal discharge of my duties, sir.'

'But you happen to be on my property, and I've asked you to go. I've rented a space thirty yards square in which this caravan stands. If I ask you to leave and you refuse to do so you're trespassing, whether you're a policeman or not.'

'If you feel that way, sir, there's nothing more to be said for the moment. I'll go back and make my report.'

Jones was walking to his bicycle when the major called him back.

'You're from Cross Hands, aren't you?'

'That's correct, sir. Police Constable Jones.'

'Good. I'm playing golf with the Chief Constable tomorrow. I'll have a word with him about you.'

'I can't stop you doing so, sir.'

Jones's father had been a low-grade Spiritualist medium, a man whose inexplicable powers had been overshadowed for his son by his vision of a hereafter so trivial, so much resembling the present life in the most stagnant Welsh village, that for many years the boy had had a morbid fear of death. With this grew up an aversion for certain ill-defined faculties Jones was afraid he might have inherited. Under protest Jones saw further than he cared beneath the surface of things, and was the prey of atmospheres and intuitions. This was a disadvantage in a policeman.

At the moment, wheeling his bicycle down a rough, rain-eroded track on the southern slope of Pen Gof to come into sight of New Mill Farm, he felt the influence of Jones Senior's unwelcome bequest. A distillation of human un-happiness seemed to leak into its surroundings from the squat, drab, malproportioned house. They're all the same, Jones tried to assure himself. There were a dozen such farms living off the poorhouse fare Pen Gof had to offer. In every one of them five, six, a dozen generations had been expended in conditions in which real virtue was a luxury that couldn't be afforded and minor vices like miserliness and insensitivity had to be promoted to the position of pseudo-virtues under the titles of thrift and fortitude. To the psychic-*malgré-soi* Jones, affliction hung in the air over these places of doomed human endeavour like a cess-pit odour. Coming closer to New Mill he tried not to notice the ill-omened flight of a magpie, the presence of a crow on the rooftop, a posy of flowering blackthorn placed like an offering to the gods of misfortune in one of the downstairs windows.

As the ruts deepened he got off his bicycle again to pass the pond. Something in the slime under the new yellow buds of trailing willow branches stopped his eye. The gas-inflated corpse of a cat had popped up like a bubble out of the mud, and across and through the pond-smell Jones sniffed decay.

He wheeled his bicycle through the gate, gave a single knock at the door, rattled the letter-box, and while his hand was still on the flap, and without any interior sound of approaching footsteps, the door opened and Cathy was there.

'Mrs Owen, isn't it?'

'That's right. Won't you come in?'

The muscles in her face had tugged it into some sort of smile from which the small, red-lidded eyes remained aloof. She wore a cheap, stiff dressing-gown. Her hair, for the first time since childhood on long-leave from the discipline of curlers and hairdressers, looked like a pale, fluffy wig. It seemed to Jones only yesterday since he had seen her behind the counter at Marks and Spencer's and, as he remembered, had bought a pair of wool-and-nylon socks from her. The difference was depressing. Already she was part of the recognizable human furniture of Pen Gof. In the pre-war days, before the valley's export to England second only in importance to coal had dried up, she would have gone to London to be a slavey or a prostitute. Jones wondered if she was any better off as she was.

Jones said, 'I'm sorry to trouble you in this way, Mrs Owen, but someone made a call from a telephone box to Brynaron Police Station this morning saying that there was some sort of trouble at New Mill Farm. We don't treat this kind of thing very seriously, but we still have to check up that things are O.K.'

'There's no trouble of any kind here, Mr Jones. It *is* Mr Jones, isn't it? But thanks all the same for coming.'

Bron came in from the kitchen. 'This is Mr Jones,' Cathy said. 'Mr Bron Owen, my brother-in-law.'

'We've already met,' Jones said.

'Can I offer you a cup of tea?' Bron said.

'Not just now,' Jones said. 'It's very kind of you. I've got rather a lot on this morning.'

Jones studied Bron with what circumspection he could manage and with new interest. At the time of their last meeting he had been a petty offender. Now he was revealed as a violent criminal. A quiet-looking chap. Shy, almost. It was hard to imagine him with a gun or knife in his hand. Jones saw him as a younger, more vigorous version of

144

himself; a young man whose scholar's face would begin to emerge as soon as his hair began to recede. In the meanwhile Owen's introspective good looks had been thrown out of balance and given a certain raffishness by two and half inches of sticking plaster over the left eyebrow. He would be attractive to most women, and the moment he had come through the kitchen door everything about Cathy and the atmosphere of the room had changed. Jones assumed that they were sleeping together.

'While I think of it,' Jones asked, 'does that young fellow Beynon still work for you?'

'Still here, Mr Jones. He's probably down with the cows just now. Did you want to see him?'

'No, I don't think so, Mrs Owen, thank you very much. I just wondered if he was about the place, that's all. You've seen him recently, anyway?'

'He was in the yard half an hour ago.'

'Rather a queer kind of kid,' Jones said. 'Bit of a misfit. How do you get on with him?'

'Well, I really can't say we've got any cause for complaint,' Cathy said. 'He works very hard. That's the main thing. Evan says we couldn't find anyone to replace him.'

'And he's probably right there. They're all for the bright lights these days. Ten-pin alleys and café-bars. That's all that seems to interest them. Evan at home, by the way?'

'I'm afraid not, Mr Jones. He went out early.'

'Pity. I should have liked to say hello to an old friend. Must be months since the last time we had a chance to get together for a chat. Any idea when he's likely to be back?'

'He'll be here tomorrow, or the next day at the latest. He'll be sorry to have missed you. Any message?'

'Oh, I don't think so, Mrs Owen. Just say I called in and asked after him. I suppose he's gone up North to his old part of the country.'

'Aberystwyth actually, this time, Mr Jones. On business in connection with the chapel,' Cathy said. Her voice livened with the slightest possible injection of pride.

'Whether he decides to go on from Aberystwyth to Morfa while he's about it is another matter,' Bron said. 'Once you're in Aberystwyth it's no distance.'

'I expect that's what he'll do,' Jones said.

He made ready to go. He was trying to explain away the sadness that was as pervasive in the room as the smell of old curtains and chair covers in most of these Victorian farmhouses. Perhaps the Owens had not created this melancholy at all but had inherited it along with the ominous and prophetic birds, the floods, the bloodshot sunrises, and the scowl of Pen Gof into all the windows facing north. Cathy's tear-inflamed eyes and the sticking plaster on Bron's forehead, he did his best to believe, had no connection with it.

They saw him to the gate, where he got on his bicycle again.

'Thank you, Mrs Owen. Good-bye, Mr Owen.'

Nothing to say to Fenn, he assured himself. 'Don't bother to come back to me unless –' Fenn had said. Everything was in order. Everything explained. Only one anonymous telephone call in ten produced business, and this was not one of those occasions.

Jones made up his mind to go back to Glas Mor, where there was real work to be done. He would measure up the car-park and its surroundings, go back to his office and settle down to the production of a beautifully drawn scale-plan using the finest drawing paper, inks of two colours, calipers, a set-square and a steel rule engraved in centimetres. This plan would be clipped to a four or five-page typed report to be delivered to Inspector Fenn at the Brynaron station next day.

To be able to clear the field in readiness for this operation,

Jones felt it necessary to settle one very small doubt, and a short while after leaving the Owen farm he approached Agnes, the romantic conductress of the local bus, who was having a five-minute break for her elevenses at the Transport Café, Cross Hands, on the third run of the day into Brynaron.

'Agnes, good morning, my dear. Did Mr Owen travel up with you on the seven-ten this morning?'

'No, Mr Jones.'

'I thought not. Must have gone by car.'

The setback forced him on logically to Thomas Lloyd, ticket-collector at Brynaron Station.

'You know Evan Owen, don't you, Thomas?'

'Three of them,' Thomas said.

'Of New Mill.'

'Intimately.'

'In confidence, Thomas, lad – when did you see him last?'

'At the festival last September.'

'He didn't travel to Aberystwyth this morning, did he?'

'He did not.'

'Sure?'

'Couldn't be surer, seeing that nobody went to Aberystwyth.'

There was little point in going to discuss the fable of chapel business with Ivor Pritchard, that soft-voiced and timeless sexual deviant who as a Sunday-school teacher of old had spoiled Jones's taste for religion. Evan had not gone to Aberystwyth. He had not gone anywhere. Jones's guess was that he was hiding in one of his own barns, licking his wounds after whatever had happened to him at Hebron on the Sunday morning.

13

Two and three days passed, and nothing was heard of Evan.

The man from the agricultural machinery firm called as expected on the Monday and seemed only mildly surprised not to receive his cheque. He waved Bron's apologies aside. 'Please don't think I've called for the money. The purpose of these monthly visits is to help with any servicing problems that may arise. Your brother usually finds it convenient to give me the instalment cheque, but it will be quite in order if he posts it in to the company when he's ready. Tell him I'll look in as usual next month.'

Later that day a brisk young Mr Emmett with a ferrety, financial face called in answer to a telephone call Bron had made at the end of the week under the spur of an enthusiasm which had ebbed away. Bron had even forgotten the telephone call. Emmett explained the new sell-and-lease-back plan which he believed would be the salvation of such obviously under-capitalized farms as New Mill. He insisted in making a survey of the buildings and land, assuring Bron that he was involving him in no obligation of any kind. Bron told him to go ahead, and Emmett spent the afternoon on this task. At about tea-time he appeared again his face and hands violet from the scourging given him by the winds on Pen Gof. He took off his Wellington boots, washed the mud off them, and got down to figures. Bron listened politely but without interest to Emmett's vision of the lush paradise that Evan's share of the mountainside and the swampy valley beneath could be turned into, producing in abundance every type of crop grown in a temperate climate, for the sum the financial company were prepared to lay out. Between six and seven thousand, Emmett thought. A few hundred pounds one way or the other. Bron, who had concentrated with difficulty on what he had to say, thought he owed him the encouragement of asking how long it would take for the deal to go through if it were decided to go ahead. 'Oh, I should imagine we could let you have a cheque within the week.'

A mounting financial crisis began to draw Cathy and Bron closer together, and they were forced into an alliance – reluctant so far as Cathy was concerned, but still an alliance – to face the state of economic siege.

The bills began to pile up. Cathy was embarrassed to have to put off the baker when he asked for his money. This, she knew could bring about a general undermining of confidence in the tradesmen who supplied them, and soon lead to a stoppage of credit. A delivery of chemical spray sent C.O.D. could not be accepted. Cathy's greatest embarrassment had been Beynon's reaction to the news that he would have to wait a little longer for his money. 'I don't mind working for you for nothing, Cathy,' he had said, using her Christian name for the first time.

'I get the impression that that fellow can't stand the sight of me,' Bron said.

'It's not that. He's frightened of people.'

'And another thing – I don't much like the way he looks at you. Personally I'd like to see the back of him.'

'We'd be in a fine mess if he went. I can tell you that.'

They lived on their own produce. Bron's last few shillings trickled away. He could no longer go down openly to the Salutation for a drink. A week went by.

'Isn't there anything about the house we could realize money on?' he asked her.

Cathy unlocked a cupboard in the front bedroom where Bron still slept, and showed him a small collection of silver, blackened with years of disuse. Bron examined these articles with vague memories of burnished Georgian pieces decorating his mother's table on special occasions when Dr Griffiths had been invited to Sunday lunch. There was an ugly, old-fashioned gold watch with a heavy chain.

'I don't see why you shouldn't take that too, while you're about it,' Cathy said. 'Evan would never think of wearing it. He told me I could give it to the chapel sale last year but I didn't like to because it wasn't working. Tanners in Market Street might give you something.'

Cathy cleaned the silver and parcelled it up with the expertness she had acquired in her eighteen months as a packer and Bron wound the watch, shook it, held it to his ear, then dropped it into his pocket.

Tanners of Market Street, it turned out, were not only jewellers and silversmiths, but pawnbrokers.

'Whatever you do, don't let them know they're from us,' Cathy said. 'It would be bound to get round. It's the one thing that Evan would really hate.'

Tanners' main shop with its glittering jeweller's window-display was wedged among the multiple stores on the Golden Mile, but pawners or sellers were directed to a room at the back of the building, reached by an entrance in Blue Street.

Blue Street was Brynaron behind the scenes; a narrow twisting lane chiefly used as a short cut by people in a hurry, or at night as the best place to commit a nuisance in comfort. Its only shop sold trusses and jock-straps. The

Urban District Council had its public assistance office and its labour exchange here, and kept its waste-collection lorries in an old warehouse. Blue Street, joined to Market Street above it and Lammas Street below by numerous alleyways, was a perfect place to slip into and out of unobserved carrying household goods for disposal in the direction of Tanners' obscure entrance under the three brass balls.

Bron, dressed in his new Burton's suit, was seen by Tanners' Mr Storrs, a man of delicate movements and a gentle out-patients' department manner, in a room decorated with official notices and containing a single empty counter.

Storrs unpacked the silver with precise, surgical fingers, placing each article in a row at exactly equal intervals along the counter, the spout of the teapot pointing away from him at ninety degrees from the axis of the display. Before the last piece of wrapping paper was off he had fixed his maximum and starting prices, totted them up in his mind and rechecked the final figure, but there was a certain rigmarole to be gone through. While Bron looked on respectfully Storrs pretended to search for hallmarks. Next he took out an eyeglass and held the sauce-boat up to stare at its bottom with a sightless eye. He seemed interested in the watch, flicking its backplate off and probing in its interior with a pointed fingernail. At the end of this fictitious examination he waited, eyes raised inquiringly, and with a drooping, sympathetic smile for Bron to justify his presence with one of the routine excuses offered by all Storrs's customers.

'Seemed rather pointless,' Bron said, 'to keep all this junk hanging about the place when nobody bothers to use it any more.'

Storrs awaited the second part of the explanation. Bron should now have continued, 'and you can't even find the staff to keep it clean,' but he didn't.

'Quite so, quite so,' Storrs said. Forty years of life at Tanners had not been wasted. On a narrow front it had made a philosopher of him, convinced him empirically of certain human truths. All men were brothers under the skin. He loved his work in purchasing and pawnbroking, the most fundamental part of a business in Brynaron's most fundamental street. The art of buying, Storrs believed, was more refined than that of selling.

'And what do you feel you should get for the articles, sir?'

'I'd prefer you to make me an offer.'

In preparation for the small deception Cathy had forced on him, Bron noticed, to his amusement, that he was using a con-man's nondescript overseas accent that could have been mistaken for city-Australian, or even American.

'And you say you haven't any price in mind?'

'Well I suppose I have, but you must know what you pay for this kind of thing.'

The limit Storrs had set himself was £100. 'We might go to £75,' he said.

'And you can't do better than that?'

Bron's voice announced that he was going to take Storrs's offer. Storrs shook his head. 'I wish I could.'

The quick nod of agreement made him a little wary. Excessive trust in such negotiations was found in people out of touch with the real world, such as professional soldiers, lighthouse keepers and criminals, and Storrs found himself unable to put Bron in either of the first two classes. Had Bron been offering him jewellery or an expensive camera, Storrs, dropping his voice to an undertaker's whisper, would have asked him for proof of ownership, but with silver plate and an old watch – even one that had some antiquarian value – he was on fairly safe ground.

'Will a cheque be in order, sir?'

'I'd very much prefer cash. I'd like to do some shopping while I'm in town.'

'Well actually, sir, it's a matter of regulations. I'm not sure whether I can persuade Mr Tanner to stretch a point in this case. I'll go and see.'

'I'd be most obliged if you would,' Bron said.

Storrs went into his office and got down the purchase book. He opened his cupboard, poured himself a small mid-morning sherry, bit a digestive in half, chewed and swallowed, took out a clean linen handkerchief and wiped his lips carefully. The chances of illegal possession in goods of this type were less than one in a hundred, and it had been more than a year since a thief had crashed the barriers of Storrs's intuition and sold Tanners a haul of stolen property.

He went back to Bron, his smile congratulatory. 'I've had a word with Mr Tanner and he's agreeable to making an exception in the circumstances. Would you be so kind as to write your name and address in our book?'

Bron wrote, 'Herbert Lawrence, Rosemount, Haverford-west,' while Storrs went away to get the money.

A week passed without news of Evan.

'We ought to get in touch with the police,' she said.

'Give it another day or two.'

'Do you think he could have gone to Morfa?'

'There's nothing to stop him phoning or writing if he had. In any case, I can't see he had anything to go for. He told me that he'd made a clean break with all the people there when he and Mother decided to move down here.'

'I can't help wondering if he had a heart attack and landed up in hospital somewhere.'

'Even if he had the hospital would have been in touch with us long ago.'

153

'The great mystery,' she said, 'is why he should go off like that in his working things. It doesn't make sense.'

'Well actually, it... it's a matter of explanations. I'm not sure where I can persuade Mr Father to stretch a point. Is...'

Bron began to feel the need for occupation. He rang the employment exchange, told them of his book-keeping experience, and they found him the names of several firms who had vacancies. But when it came to the point Cathy brought herself to ask him to put off leaving. 'I could never stay in this place by myself,' she said. 'There's something about it. I don't know what to say. It gives me the creeps.'

Gradually the belief was growing that Evan would not come back, and this thought begat a hope that she was too ashamed to admit to herself. Life had changed. Even Pen Gof's usurpation of half the sky couldn't keep the spring out entirely. Every year at this season something in her stirred a little, tried to raise itself up and was smothered. This year it moved again cautiously, and then more strongly. A little fresh, happy human vulnerability had survived after all. Soon she was a girl again who had shed five years of resignation, and was entitled to hope, and who found herself thrown into the company of a cheerful, engaging and considerate young man.

Bron felt the change in Cathy's spirit, but of its cause he guessed nothing. He longed to find some way of using his time and in the end made overtures to the hostile Beynon who, cornered in the cowshed and unable to solve the problem by turning round and running away, was obliged to speak at last. He refused the cigarette that Bron offered him.

'What about that bracken-clearing job of yours?'

'It's finished now. The seed's in.'

Bron was amazed at the boy's deep bass voice.

'What have you got on today?'

'The cows.'

'I know. What else?'

'I've always got plenty to do.'

'All right, I'll give you a hand.'

Bron followed Beynon and cut him off again when he'd taken the cows down to the field.

'Where do we start?'

Beynon went to the toolshed and got out a shovel and a pickaxe.

'If you're not used to the work, it's a waste of time.'

'Well, we'll see about that.'

In between rain-squalls Beynon was digging a ditch to drain the water from a small, flat, marshy area on the mountainside where Evan believed that something could be cajoled into growing. Bron helped himself to a pick and shovel, put on an old army surplus gas-cape and followed Beynon up the mountain.

They started work. 'We'll only get in each other's way,' Beynon said.

'I'll make a start lower down the slope,' Bron said, 'and we can join up. How deep do you want it?'

'The deeper the better.'

Bron struck down with his shovel, put his foot and the weight of his body on it, then lifted out fifteen pounds of squelching turf, and threw it aside. Beynon looked on with one side of his big mouth hooked up in a grimace of contempt.

He shook his head. 'It's not strength, it's knack. It's knowing how to handle the shovel.'

'I was watching you the other day,' Bron said. 'May have picked up a tip or two.' He pushed the shovel in again, lifted the turf and peat and threw it after the first shovelful. He enjoyed any excuse for physical work.

F

Beynon started work higher up, and an hour later with the thin rain washing the sweat from his face and panting with fatigue, he put his shovel down to compare his output with Bron's. Bron's ditch was almost double the length of his, the turfs neatly banked along each side. He showed Bron his blue, empty gums in a cat's snarl. 'Made sure there weren't any rocks down there, didn't you?'

'You have to be smart in this life,' Bron said.

Later, when they had to join forces with pickaxes to remove some boulders, there was a near accident. Beynon's pickaxe flew off its handle and missed Bron's head by inches. Bron couldn't be absolutely sure whether or not there was something more than carelessness and chance in this incident, but thereafter he watched Beynon carefully, kept farther away from him and made sure that Beynon never got behind him.

The same post brought a summons to attend Brynaron Magistrate's Court on a charge of driving a car without being in possession of a valid driving licence, and an account for damage to Penfold Motors' Jaguar of £55.10.0.

There were other heavy bills which had to be met without delay. The selective weed-killer spray sent C.O.D. had to be paid for, at a cost of £27, and there was £36 to pay for grass seed. Neither of these things could be done without, and both were urgently needed. Spring was the time when outgoings were at their heaviest after the long economic breather of winter.

'I don't quite see what we're going to do,' Bron said, 'if the place is to be kept going.' The money raised on the old silver was either spent or earmarked for spending. The bank would not even discuss the possibility of releasing funds from Evan's account without Evan's sanction.

'We'll have to sell a few sheep,' Cathy said. 'There's nothing else for it.'

'I can't imagine Evan would much care for the idea of that.'

'It's either that or the farm comes to a standstill as far as I can see. Evan's ordered 500 week-old chicks for delivery next week. How are we going to pay for them? And there's still the h.p. instalment on the equipment to be found. After all, Evan's made you a partner whether you want to be one or not, so I suppose you've a right to use your own discretion.'

Bron rang up the auctioneers at the market.

'It's up to you, of course. You certainly won't find any difficulty in getting your price. The very reverse. Unusual time to sell, but you know best. We shall want some written authority, of course.'

Next morning a dozen sheep were rounded up and carried off to market in the auctioneer's lorry.

Bron's second meeting with Wendy was brief and shrouded in security precautions. It took place shortly after dark in a terraced house in the same row under the mountain as the house occupied by Constable Jones – which was also the police station. The location was described in a note slipped to Bron by his friend Billings and, persecuted by yapping dogs, Bron went to the fifth garden from the end of the row and sat on a boulder that had crashed into it from the slope of Pen Gof, until a back door was opened and a light switched on.

Wendy awaited him in a dwarf's bedroom and they crouched, fumbled and clung to one another in what space was left by unnecessary furniture and a steeply sloping roof. Total privacy was unknown in a Cross Hands company house and Bron and Wendy's tender murmurings were interrupted by family conversations which reached them without loss of clarity through the floor, and the groans and the snufflings of an invalid in the next room. This was an old lady whom Wendy was officially visiting.

There was little time for embracing. 'I've only got half an hour,' Wendy said. 'Never know when Oakes will decide to come round and check up on me. He's got one of his fits on.'

Bron was surprised. Little had been said about Oakes at their first meeting. Little had been said at all.

'I can't tell you half of it, darling. I've had a hell of a time. A hell of a time. Can you imagine a man who goes to the trouble of bugging anyone's room. He even has some gadget fixed to the telephone to spy on me. It used to cost him twenty-five guineas a week to have me followed.'

'Don't talk about it now,' Bron said. 'Forget about it.'

'For example, if I go shopping he'll want to know all the shops I went to and how much time I spent in each. "All right," he'll say, "that leaves an hour unaccounted for. What about that?" Supposing I say, "I went to have my hair done," he'll ask me which hairdresser and then get them on the phone to check up.'

'Why do you stand for it?'

'It's one of life's mysteries. It's something I can't explain myself. Something I've got myself into and I've got to get myself out of, I suppose. We have the most terrible rows. I've had to keep out of sight for days on end with the black eyes he's given me.'

'One thing's sure – I'll never understand women.'

'You see – oh, I don't know how to explain it – he wasn't so bad in the first place. Things got this way gradually. He's still kind enough in his way when he hasn't got one of his fits on.'

158

'You certainly can't go on like this.'

She wriggled away from him on the bed to reach her watch on the bedside table. 'God. We've only got another ten minutes. . . . Last time I told him I was going,' she said, 'he cut one of his wrists. His doctor got round me to stay otherwise that would have been that. I'd made up my mind.'

With only a few minutes of her, Bron didn't want to waste time discussing Oakes, but he couldn't get Wendy away from the subject. She was less gay than she had been the first time and there were moments when she seemed depressed.

'Anyway, things are bound to come to a head one way or another, because his divorce comes through on Friday and he's going to expect me to marry him.'

'Don't talk about it,' he said. 'We've only got five minutes left.'

He tried to take her in his arms again, but she pushed him away. 'Oh darling, I've been kicked around. I've had a hell of a life. Oakes is one of nature's gentlemen compared to some of the others. I don't know why all these things should happen to me. Do you know why?'

'Because you're generous,' he said. 'You don't know how to defend yourself. It's always the same – the soft ones go under.'

'Have you ever been to a remand home? Have you ever been to an approved school?'

'Not quite that, but something like it,' Bron said. He had given up his attempts.

'If some rich man's wife goes into a shop and helps herself to a pair of stockings she doesn't want she gets bound over. If it happens to be me it's Holloway at eighteen years of age without the option. I've been through the mill, Bron. I can tell you that.'

What he liked about her was that she didn't try to cover

159

anything up. Anyone else would have told him only half the story. To Bron it had been a display of her credentials. Any homeless girl who finished up at eighteen in Holloway Gaol could be excused anything thereafter in Bron's eyes.

'When I'm with you,' she said, 'I relax. I can tell the truth.'

'Why don't you stay with me?'

'Let's face it,' she said. 'I'm a weak person. A very weak person. I couldn't get by on my own. Hence Oakes with all his faults, I suppose. I've been in trouble most of my life, and I have to have someone to look after me. Can't stand on my own feet, that's the story. If you were in a position to ask me to go away with you, I don't know what I'd say. I'd probably say yes.'

It was Oakes that Bron worried about too. He was sorry for the man. But if Wendy decided to get rid of him on her own account, that would be different. 'If it comes to a show-down, you know I'll be there waiting,' he said.

Oakes grabbed her as soon as she came through the door. She knew that if she gave him half the chance the inquisition would start. He'd want to examine her dress, her under-clothes.

'Where have you been?'

'You know where I've been.'

'Who've you been with?'

She pulled herself away from him. If it came to a fight she knew she could hold her own. Her arms under the womanly fat were more muscular than his.

'That is my business.'

'I'm going to kill you,' Oakes said.

She laughed. 'It's now or never for you, Harry boy. You know what I mean. So make up your mind quick, because it's your last chance.'

14

The reporter from the Brynaron *Observer* found Cathy alone. He was an ambitious young man on his way to Fleet Street who knew how to handle people and in particular women, and to apply the slightest possible twist to the opinions they voiced to make these opinions more generally readable.

'How long exactly has Mr Owen been missing?'

'Missing?' she said. 'Well, we haven't really thought of him as missing at all.'

'Well, absent from home, then?'

'It's nine days now.'

'Are you worried, Mrs Owen?'

'Of course I am.'

'Was Mr Owen ill? Has he ever suffered from loss of memory, or anything like that?'

'His heart isn't too strong, but he's all right if he remembers to take his medicine.'

'Have you done anything about it so far? I mean, have you made any efforts to trace him?'

'I don't see that there's very much we can do.'

'What about the police? Have you contacted the police?'

'Not so far.'

'Why? Don't you think you should?'

'I don't really know. I suppose I didn't want to bother them. Not at this stage.'

'You didn't think they'd want to be bothered? Is that it?' He shook his head with knowing sympathy. This reporter proposed to use the deficiencies of the police as a stepping stone to higher things.

'I don't know what to say. People bother them all the time with such silly things.'

'Shouldn't have imagined they'd have thought a missing husband a silly thing to bother them about. I may be wrong.' The reporter wrote something in his book.

'I'm afraid they haven't been too energetic in the past in cases like this. Too busy chasing motorists for parking offences, I suppose. In the end people begin to lose confidence. As you say, it's a waste of time going to them. I mean, what's the point?' He smiled with huge persuasion, shrugging his shoulders.

'What's the point?' she felt obliged to echo, and he wrote in his book again.

Next day a news item appeared in the *Observer* under the heading 'Missing From Home', and readers were referred in small bold type under the paragraph to 'editorial comment on another page'.

IS IT NORMAL TO DISAPPEAR?

The news that yet another local man is missing from his home is disquieting, and acts as a timely reminder that over the past two years alone no less than seven other persons have been reported missing in this area, and that no single case has so far been satisfactorily cleared up.

Yesterday a member of our staff spoke to the local police authorities and was somewhat surprised to learn that they were completely unaware of Mr Owen's disappearance. The police spokesman took it upon himself to assure our representative that 80 per cent of such disappearances are eventually found to have a normal explanation.

Unfortunately we cannot share the complacency of the police's approach to this problem. Even if we accept the very unlikely figure given, we feel obliged to ask ourselves what happens to the unfortunate 20 per cent for whose disappearance there is no normal explanation? At what point, too, is it decided that such a disappearance is abnormal? Surely it is abnormal to be missing from one's home for many months, or even years?

When our reporter called on Mrs Owen at her farm he found a distraught woman who had not reported her husband's disappearance because she thought it 'a waste of time'.

We urge the police to take every possible measure to restore what is rapidly becoming an understandable collapse of the public confidence.

Detective Sergeant Broadbent came out of the explosion – the tempest of urgent memoranda, the angry long-distance calls between Division, Brynaron and London, the personal interview of Brynaron's Member of Parliament with the Chief Constable, the hints of transfers and demotions. He was a recent graduate of the Police College, and arrived in his own sports car laden with photographic and X-ray equipment, textbooks, and an as yet unused laboratory kit in a black leather case.

Bron was away in Brynaron when he called at New Mill Farm.

'So you thought it was a waste of time going to the police, Mrs Owen,' Broadbent said.

'I don't remember saying that at all,' Cathy said. 'I know they put it in the paper.' He was a nice informal young man, unlike any policeman she had ever seen before in his sports jacket with the flap at the back, and his flannel trousers. She could see he wasn't offended.

'You probably didn't,' he said, smiling to put her at her ease.

'I looked at what they put, and I thought, surely I didn't say that?'

'They seize on something and distort it beyond recognition,' Broadbent said. 'Anyway, not to worry. . . . Do you mind if I smoke?'

'Of course not,' she said.

Broadbent took out a pipe and began to fill the bowl. 'Eleven days now, isn't it?' he said. 'I wonder if you would show me where Mr Owen keeps his private papers?'

She opened a drawer in the desk standing in a corner of the living-room. Insurance policies, but no personal insurance, car logbook, copies of hire-purchase contracts, a batch of old receipts, a few letters to be examined at leisure, a bankbook showing Evan's account to have a credit balance of £112, and the possibly significant fact that £55 had been drawn out three days before the disappearance. There was a writing pad with an unfinished letter bearing the date of the fateful Sunday. *Dear Mary, Thank you for replying so promptly. I know I can always rely on you. The situation here seems to be worsening rapidly –*

'Is this your husband's handwriting?'

'Yes,' she said.

'Who's Mary?'

'I believe she's some cousin he keeps in touch with. I've never met her.'

'Can I borrow these letters for a day or two?'

'Certainly.'

Broadbent tore the sheet off the pad, and put it with the rest of the letters in a cardboard folder he carried in his briefcase.

'I wonder what your husband meant when he said that the situation seemed to be worsening rapidly? Any idea?'

'None at all, I'm afraid,' she said. 'We haven't been very flush for money lately. He may have meant that.'

164

'Mr Owen left home early on the Monday morning. Is there anything that strikes you as particularly surprising – I mean apart from the fact that he should leave home at all – in the circumstances under which he left?'

Cathy thought about it. 'Yes,' she said. 'He was wearing his working clothes. I can't understand him doing a thing like that.'

'How do you know he was wearing his working clothes?'

'Because Bron saw him before he left.'

'Oh yes, of course. Bron was the last person to see him.'

Wearing his old clothes, Broadbent thought. Interesting how this was following the blueprint of similar mysteries he'd read up for the occasion. 'Let's go over the events of that Sunday again, Mrs Owen, if you don't mind. Now when exactly did you last see him?'

'I *heard* him go out in the morning to go to chapel.'

'Yes, but when did you last actually *see* him?'

'Well,' she started, 'it was a day or two before that. I hadn't been home. I'd been staying in Brynaron.'

He looked surprised. 'A holiday?'

'I'd been looking for a job.'

'Ah-ha.' He seemed to expect some explanation.

'I felt there wasn't enough to do here to occupy my time, so I decided to look round for a job.'

'Of course. And you came back —?'

'On the Saturday.'

'And you didn't see your husband on the Saturday night? You didn't occupy the same bedroom?'

There was no point now in not telling him the whole truth.

'We'd had a bit of a row before I left. I slept in the back bedroom.'

'And your husband?'

'Evan slept in the box-room.'

'Mrs Owen, are you absolutely certain, beyond the

slightest possibility of doubt, that it was your husband you heard go out on the Sunday morning?'

'Oh, absolutely.'

'Why are you?'

'Because of his cough,' she said. 'His cough always gives him away. He's got one of those dry coughs. It's unmistakable. I heard him coughing as he went down the stairs.'

'And when did he come home again?'

'Not till the Sunday night.'

'Was that unusual? Would you have expected him to stay away all day?'

'No,' she said. 'I expected him home for lunch. I kept his lunch hot for him until half past two, but he didn't turn up.'

'Any idea why?'

'I suppose he hadn't got over the row,' Cathy said.

'And nothing like that had ever happened before?'

'No, never. My husband was a man of very regular habits.'

Broadbent noticed that she'd referred to him in the past. It was most revelatory. Quite clear she doesn't expect to see him again.

'What makes you so sure that Mr Owen actually did come home on the Sunday night.'

'Well, apart from the fact that Bron saw him, I heard him coughing again. I was in bed and I heard someone come in the front door and then I heard him cough. He coughed two or three times and then I heard him go into the kitchen.'

'At about what time would you say this was?'

'Soon after ten. I'd gone to bed early because I had a bad headache, and I'd been in bed about an hour when he came in.'

'And then a little later Bron came in?'

'About half an hour later it probably was.'

'What did he do?'

'I heard him go into the kitchen too.'

166

'Did you hear them talking?'

'I don't remember. I don't think so.'

'Would you have been able to hear if they had been talking.'

'Indistinctly,' she said. 'I think so.'

'Wouldn't you have expected them to have something to say to each other?'

'I don't know. I never thought about it.'

The answers were beginning to slow down. 'Did you hear anything at all – any sounds from the kitchen?'

She was thinking twice now before she spoke, trying to anticipate the next question each answer would provoke.

'Sounds of any kind?' he asked with a kind of hypnotic gentleness.

She realized that her hesitation had committed her.

'I think I heard a noise. It could have been anything. It wasn't very loud.'

'Any idea at all what it could have been?'

'It might have been a box falling off the shelf, or something like that.'

'A heavy box?'

'Something like the box we keep the grass seed in. A wooden box.'

'A wooden box,' he said. 'A bit of a crash, in fact.'

'The kind of noise a box makes when you knock it over.'

'And after that – any other noises?' he said.

'I don't think so.'

'Try to remember. I'm sorry to bother you like this, but it's rather important.'

'I'm trying to think.'

'Didn't someone come out of the kitchen eventually?'

'They must have done. Yes, of course they did. Someone went out of the back door. That must have been my husband, because I heard Bron go out at the front.'

167

'How would you have known that it was Bron who went out at the front?'

'He told me in the morning. I heard whoever it was go to the shed and start up the car, and he told me he'd taken the car out next morning.'

'So he went out in the car?'

'Yes,' she said, thinking, What a fool I am. There'll be more driving-licence trouble now.

'Was he away long?'

'Quite a while.'

'An hour – two hours?'

'I don't know,' she said. 'I dropped off to sleep and then I heard him come in again. Maybe two hours, maybe more. I really couldn't say.'

'Mrs Owen, forgive me for asking a rather direct question. Were your husband and your brother-in-law on good terms?'

He saw the stubborn look come into her face. Now he had a hostile witness to deal with. Well at least we know where we are. The moment had come to set the trap.

'Why shouldn't they have been?'

'Wasn't there some trouble over a car? I'm sorry, I'm obliged to ask these questions.'

'I don't know of any trouble,' Cathy said.

'I may have got my facts wrong, but I understand your brother-in-law borrowed a car and damaged it, and that your husband was upset.'

'No, I don't think so,' she said. 'There was some question of changing our present car and I think Bron was attending to it for my husband. There was nothing for my husband to be upset about.'

The last thing this woman wanted, Broadbent thought, was to see her husband back again. He wasn't sure yet whether she knew that he was dead, or just wanted him dead.

Now the trap was ready. 'Mrs Owen, I believe your husband suffered from a heart condition. Do you think that it could have had any bearing at all on this mysterious business?' Broadbent had spoken to Evan's doctor less than an hour before his visit to the farm. 'It turned out to be indigestion,' the doctor said. 'Wind round the heart, if you like. We did an electrocardiogram to be on the safe side and found he had some slight alteration in the T-waves. Not significant.'

'I'm sorry, I don't follow.'

'He had a bad heart. Could he conceivably have dropped dead?'

Broadbent waited for the snap of the spring.

'He could have done,' she said. 'He'd been worried that something like that could happen if he didn't take it quietly.'

'So he might easily have gone for a walk in some isolated place and have had an attack. It's not inconceivable that he could have fallen into a river.'

'He had these fits of dizziness,' she said. 'When he went up the mountain to work sometimes, I used to wonder if I should have let him go. He used to be grey in the face.'

Broadbent nodded with sympathy. 'A sick man, in fact.' From this moment on he believed that the chances of Evan's being still alive were slight.

He got up, put his pipe away, then as a matter of afterthought asked her, 'Would you mind if I had a look round now I'm here? Just a matter of routine.'

'Why should I mind? Help yourself.'

'Is that the kitchen?' He opened the door for her and then followed. It was the first piece of virgin investigation in the field that had fallen to him. In all the other cases he'd interested himself in local C.I.D. men had descended like amateur archaeologists on some ancient site uncovered by the plough and enthusiastically obliterated all the evidence that might have been assembled for expert study. Fore-warned had been forearmed, as repainted interiors and re-placed furniture sometimes proclaimed.

In these remote farms they fought a rearguard action against the fickleness and disorder of nature with the rigid discipline of their own surroundings. In this kitchen where the Owens would spend four-fifths of their waking lives they had ranged the basic equipment of living round them with barrack-room precision. Plates were severely paraded in order of size along the dresser, cups suspended in rows, jugs dressed by the left. Each object occupied its own inviolable territory, placed at its own fixed point at the bisection of invisible lines and the apexes of triangles in the geometry of the room. Exactly in the centre stood the table, its legs in slight, permanent depressions in the linoleum, and four straight-backed chairs faced each other solemnly across the scrubbed wooden surface. Outside a magician's cloth of mist might be lowered at any moment while the landscape's components were snatched away and rearranged by storms. Inside, everything was in its place, to be found instantly, even with the eyes shut. Order was a form of solace.

The walls were impeccably distempered in cream, and the woodwork painted a dark chapel-brown that knew its place. The floor was linoleum-covered with a large rug by the electric fire. A faint smell of home-cured salt bacon hung on the air – a smell that no amount of washing and polishing could eradicate once it had taken hold. Cathy was hovering at his back, absently shifting the position of articles that had been misplaced by a fraction of an inch.

'When you came down on the Monday morning, Mrs Owen, did you notice anything unusual about this room?'

'Nothing that I can remember.'

'Whatever it was that fell over must have been picked up then?'

'It must have.'

'Everything was just as it is now?'

'Absolutely,' she said.

Broadbent moistened a finger with spittle, bent down and rubbed at the linoleum with a circular motion by one of the table legs, and then again in a corner of the room.

'Do you happen to remember when the floor was scrubbed last time, Mrs Owen?'

'I went over it with the mop yesterday,' she said. 'The last time it got a proper scrub-out was before I went away.'

There were a number of minute cracks in the centre of the linoleum where the wear had been greatest. If things went well the linoleum would have to come up and the central area, which had had a thorough cleaning at some time recently, cut out and sent to the lab. So far there was nothing to justify this.

A large scullery came next with an old-fashioned open gate, which was normally the most promising focus of interest in such a case.

'Has this been cleaned out recently?'

'One day last week,' she said.

'Since you came back from Brynaron?'

She nodded.

'What was in it?'

'Just ashes.'

'Where did you put them – in the rubbish bin?'

'Yes, but it's been emptied since then. We've got a place where we tip rubbish.'

'It doesn't matter,' he said. 'When did you last have a fire in this grate, by the way?'

'Back in the winter. It helps to keep the house warm, but it doesn't draw well.'

Broadbent opened a cupboard. 'What do you keep in here?'

'Dirty linen,' Cathy said.

At the bottom of the bundled-up sheets and a tweed costume of Cathy's waiting to go to the cleaners he found a neat brown-paper parcel.

'Happen to know what this might be?'

'It's probably something belonging to Evan.'

'Mind if we open it?' he asked. He untied the careful knots, unfolded the paper and took out a dark suit.

'It's Evan's,' she said. 'It's his best suit.' There was no mistaking her surprise.

Broadbent took the trousers and held them up to the light of the window. He scraped at the cloth's surface with a fingernail.

'Looks as though somebody's been having a go at cleaning it up, doesn't it?'

He folded the suit again and made a poor version with the string and brown paper of the original parcel.

'I'd better take this with me,' he said. 'And now I'd like to have a look at the car.'

Mary Lloyd taught French and English in a girls' school at Builth Wells, a cultivated woman, shapeless in cardigans, who lived alone in a small flat among pot-plants and books.

'I haven't seen him since he got married. No, I have never met the wife. My cousin Bron? Well, why beat about the bush? He was no good from the start.'

Broadbent said, 'I've been obliged to go over Mr Owen's personal papers, and I gather that you kept in close contact.'

'We used to see quite a bit of each other until the marriage took place. We still correspond regularly. I believe he feels rather isolated where he is and I've plenty of time for letter-writing.' She plucked nervously at a row of seed pearls and gave him a smile that carried undertones of grievance.

Broadbent showed her the unfinished letter he had found in Evan's desk.

'He rang me up in the end,' she said, 'so I suppose there wasn't much point in sending it. I'd gone to bed. There isn't really a great deal to do here in the evenings, so that's what I usually do after I've marked off the books.'

'This would have been the Sunday night, would it?'

'The Sunday night. I can't tell you the time, but I think it must have been quite early. I'd just dropped off to sleep.'

'Can you recall what was said?'

'Well, he was agitated. Things with Bron had turned out badly – as of course they were bound to. He'd been betrayed by those closest to him. Everybody hated him. He felt his life was endangered, etc., etc. He just went on like that. I suppose he had to have someone to talk to.'

'And did you take this seriously?'

'I knew that he was quite certain to fall out with Bron. As for the rest – well, he was capable of hysteria.'

'And you didn't consider you were justified in informing the police.'

'Good heavens, no. I telephoned him next day and his wife said he'd gone to Aberystwyth. For various reasons I was not particularly anxious to discuss his problems with her.'

'Mrs Owen didn't seem concerned in any way about this trip of his?'

'Far from it. I should be most surprised to hear that she felt any concern even now. I suppose I shouldn't have said that. You see, I was the repository for all his troubles.'

Broadbent compressed six interviews and the travelling they entailed into the next few days.

The fruitful visit to Tanners the pawnbrokers was the result of an old hand's tip from Inspector Fenn. 'It never does any harm to go round to pawnshops and see if anything's been flogged. Whatever the motive these villains can't resist the chance of flogging anything they happen to get their hands on. It's given them away over and over again.'

Broadbent was severe with Mr Storrs, who well remembered Bron from Broadbent's description.

'Are you in the habit of buying articles without verifying the identity of the person that offers them for sale?'

'We usually do that,' Storrs said.

'But you didn't in this case.'

'It's rather a matter of using one's judgement. We try to avoid offending the customer. Of course, the purchase is entered into a book and signed for.'

'I shall want that to get a photostat made of the signature.'

'With all due respect,' Storrs said, 'I believe you'll find from your own records that we've made very few mistakes indeed in the fifty-odd years we've been in business.'

'Have you any idea why this man should have given a fictitious name and address? Surely if the articles were his to dispose of there wouldn't be any point in his doing this?'

'I'm afraid that isn't necessarily so. Pride sometimes enters into it.'

Broadbent was running through the stock book. His forefinger stopped at an entry.

'We've sold the plate,' Storrs said reluctantly.

'I see that. And at a very nice profit too. A hundred per cent, eh?'

'We often have things on our shelves for years on end. By the time you deduct the overheads there's surprisingly little in it.'

'What happened to the watch?'

174

'The watch is in our workshop. It requires adjustment.'
'I'll take it with me,' Broadbent said. 'Write you a receipt.'

He started to flog the brother's possessions as soon as he was out of the way, Broadbent thought. Incredible. Why couldn't he have lain low for a month or two? Still, it was these blind spots of the imagination, this impatience, this lack of forethought that made the criminal.

The motive of financial urgency was underlined by his conversation with the auctioneer.

'It's certainly unusual to sell stock at this time of the year, although not unheard of. If people are going to displenish they usually do so in the autumn, by which time the animals have got some fat on them. The problem in this part of the world is carrying stock over the winter. After that it's plain sailing. I gather that the money was somewhat tight in this case.'

Mr Emmett of Borough Finance, too, agreed that Mr Owen had seemed hard pushed for cash. 'Let's face it,' he said. 'People who come to us usually are. We run what we call a buy-and-lease-back scheme. The idea is to provide a sort of financial blood transfusion for under-capitalized properties like this. Mr Owen rang us up and I went to see him myself. His main concern seemed to be how soon we could make payment if the deal went through.'

'And having sold the farm to you, was there anything to prevent him simply putting the money into his pocket and clearing off with it?'

'Nothing at all, except that he would in effect be selling us the farm at a price that would be somewhat below its market value.'

'However, he'd be getting the money a lot more quickly than if he put the farm up for sale in the ordinary way?'

'Oh, indeed yes. In a matter of a few days as compared with a number of weeks or months. Buyers for this kind of property are few and far between.'

There was the matter of Bron's conflicting stories as to where Evan had actually gone after he had left the house on that Monday morning, and the first to be demolished was the legend that he had been called away to Aberystwyth on chapel business.

Mr Pritchard, interviewed in an office at the back of his store, shook his head, and the fat on his pendulous cheeks quivered with the violence of his denial.

'I am afraid, Sergeant, there was no question of Mr Owen going on chapel business to Aberystwyth or anywhere else. No. No.'

'You're very emphatic.'

'Well, I am very surprised indeed that such a suggestion should have been made. As it happens, Mr Owen had been suspended from membership of Hebron.'

'Can you tell me why?'

'There were rumours. Talk,' Pritchard said. He had pursed his lips and appeared by his gestures to be weighing something in a finely poised balance.

'About the wife and the brother, I gather,' Broadbent said.

'It would be un-Christian to say more, Sergeant.'

'I could have told you he didn't go to Aberystwyth,' Constable Jones said.

'I wonder you didn't,' Broadbent said.

'Mr Fenn can be very discouraging. He wasn't in the slightest interested until the newspapers started giving trouble again. I've been told to keep my nose out of what doesn't concern me before now.'

'What about this second story Owen told the hire-purchase people about his brother going off on a fortnight's holiday?'

'It was very inconsistent of him,' Jones said. 'I found it hard to explain why an intelligent young fellow like that shouldn't at least remember to stick to the same story.'

Broadbent saw the company's representative.

'Can you suggest any reason at all why Mr Evan Owen should have wanted you to come back in two weeks' time?'

'Frankly, I can't.'

'Has Mr Owen ever been behind with his payments?'

'A day or two sometimes. Not more.'

'Isn't it unusual to collect hire-purchase instalments in this way?'

'The purpose of these regular visits is not to collect hire-purchase instalments, it's to keep an eye on the equipment and to service it when necessary. Mr Owen chose to hand me his instalment payments when I called, but that was entirely up to him.'

'Were you surprised when you were put off in this way?'

'Exceedingly.'

'It's never happened before, I suppose.'

'Never.'

Two experts from Scotland Yard accompanied Fenn's amateurs for the descent on New Mill Farm. They searched the house, went over the walls, tapping them with hammers, took up a number of floorboards, removed nine square feet of linoleum from the centre of the kitchen floor, poked about under tons of old equipment and stores in the out-houses and drained the pond. The pond yielded excitement in the form of a short iron bar, and the surprise of four undamaged and expensive-looking clocks.

They interviewed twenty-three persons whose business might have brought them into the neighbourhood of the farm at any time on the fateful Sunday, but only one had anything to report. This was the post-woman. 'I saw him drowning a cat. The face of a fiend he had. I told him I was going to report him to the R.S.P.C.A., and he only laughed at me.'

A letter which should have been delivered on this day to Bron by the morning post was held up until the afternoon delivery, and a few minutes after it had come into Broadbent's hands he phoned the office of the Australian High Commissioner at Australia House. The information he was given sent him hurrying back to New Mill where Bron was courteously doing what he could to assist the investigation.

'I didn't know you were thinking of emigrating, Mr Owen.'

Bron didn't seem in the least concerned by this new line of inquiry. 'I'm not really.'

'But I understand you wrote to Australia House asking for details of assisted passages?'

'That's true enough. It struck me as a possible alternative to staying on here if Evan decided against going on with this expansion project we'd been talking about.'

'Where do you keep your wife?'

'I'm not married.'

'But in your letter you specifically asked for details of passages for married persons.'

'I might decide to get married. If I emigrated I probably would.'

'Anyone particular in mind?'

'Not at the moment.'

'Mr Owen, may I ask you something? How did you get on with your brother?'

'Very well indeed. Everyone got on well with him.

He was a man who always put everybody else before himself.'

'So they tell me. That's a nasty place you've got over the eye.'

'I should have had a stitch in it. Walked into a piece of guttering hanging down from the roof after that gale the other night.'

'Very dangerous. You could have lost the sight of an eye.'

This encounter was discussed with Constable Jones and Edwards. 'Interesting,' Broadbent said, 'the true criminal type.' He had recently read two Victorian authorities, Lombroso and Lauvergne, on criminal physiology, and was still under their influence.

'In what way?' Jones asked.

'He's very hairy, for one thing. Eyebrows practically meet in the middle. Hair on the backs of the fingers too. That pallid complexion is characteristic.'

'The man's been in clink for five years, Sergeant,' Edwards said. 'You wouldn't expect him to have a Riviera suntan.'

'This is different. This is a different kind of pallor. Did you notice his eyes, too? That stare. Lombroso found a fixed stare present in the case of 15 per cent of the criminals in the prison at Milan.'

They were in the Swan at Llansarn, a village three miles from Cross Hands to which they had been sent by a report of a recently dug grave not far from the roadside. This was found to contain the corpse of a large dog that had clearly been run over by a car.

'That chap at the end of the bar,' Jones said. 'Fellow with the suède shoes who's just come in. What would you say about him?'

Broadbent applied the standards of Lombroso and drew a blank.

'I don't know. What is he? A commercial traveller?'

'Could he be a criminal?'

'He could be. In a small way. Most of us could. False pretences, or absconding bailee, or something like that.'

'That's the famous Roberts,' Jones said. 'Knocked his uncle and auntie off. Wouldn't stop at anything.'

'I shouldn't have thought it. What was the motive?'

'Money. They had a bit of property. He wants to buy that mountain you can see from the station at Cross Hands. It's a kind of craze with him.'

'He's not a criminal type all the same,' Broadbent said. 'A bit screwed up at the most. Anyway, there's an exception to every rule. Very much doubt if he'll murder anyone else, all the same.'

'He won't,' Jones said. 'Not unless they try and keep him from getting that mountain. I wouldn't like to be in the shoes of anyone that did, though.'

Broadbent reported progress to Fenn.

'The lab report's just come through. Positive. Two blood groups on the linoleum, AB and AO. There was a fight. A fair amount of AO blood on the suit, and traces in the boot of the car.'

'I was fearing this,' Fenn said.

'Fearing it, sir?' Broadbent was startled into formality.

'Yes, fearing it, Sergeant. It's going to be a severe pain in the crutch for all concerned.'

'I don't know about that, sir. I'd say we'd got the case pretty well sewn up.'

'Would you?'

'Within a matter of days of his brother's disappearance Bron Owen was flogging his bits and pieces. He sold some of the stock and was in touch with a firm about selling up the farm itself. We know he told different stories to different people to account for his brother's absence, and I've just found out he was making plans to clear off to Australia. With a woman.'

'Who?'

'I don't know. Probably the sister-in-law. It's common knowledge they're having an affair.'

'Common knowledge,' Fenn said. 'How often I've seen people trying to pass that off as evidence.'

'You don't sound enthusiastic, sir.'

'I've learned not to be – the hard way. Any weapon?'

'They found an iron bar in the pond. Doing tests on it now. They're not too hopeful, though. Oh yes – Owen rang up a cousin the night he disappeared and told her his life was in danger.'

'So we've got a murder on our hands?'

'I would say so.'

'But no body.'

'That's all we've got to do. Find the body.'

'Well, I hope it's soon found for all our sakes,' Fenn said. 'I can't tell you how sincerely I mean that.'

An unsigned correspondent reported having been on a cliff-top with a girl ten miles from Cross Hands on the Tuesday after Evan's disappearance and seeing someone dump a heavy object into the sea from a boat. From the description the man in the boat could have been Bron. The location of this happening was given in such a way as to enable Broadbent virtually to pinpoint the spot where the water had closed over the long, sack-like shape, and after a visit to the clifftop,

Broadbent went on to Milford Haven, hired a diver and went out with him in a boat.

The diver looked up at the cliffs and down at the water.

'This some sort of a joke? I've been here before.'

'What do you mean by here? In this cove?'

'No, here. Just where we are now. A lobster fisherman was supposed to have knocked his partner off and dumped the body last year.'

'Coincidences can happen,' Broadbent said.

'Not this kind of coincidence. The sea's a big place. What do you want me to do?'

'Just tell me what's down there.'

'I can tell you now. Ninety feet of water like a London fog at midnight. Rocks as high as houses and holes you could drop a bus into. You really want me to go down?'

'Now we've come as far as this.'

'It's the Government's money,' the diver said. He got into his rubber suit and Broadbent helped him on with his aqualung and he went over the side.

Broadbent waited, swallowing his saliva, fighting down the nausea, while the black dolphins of water raced past and the wind scooped the tops off the waves and smashed the spray into his face. The boatman struggled with the oars to hold the boat in position.

The diver surfaced and Broadbent pulled him over the side of the boat. He took off his mask, spat out a little blood and shuddered.

'How was it?'

'I already told you.'

'No signs of anything at all?'

The diver pointed to the cliffs towering above them that appeared to be made of shattered iron, with huge sections in the act of breaking away and about to fall into the water. 'It's like that underneath. You don't even have to go down there and look. You know by experience. Boulders thirty feet high piled on top of each other. You know they're there because you can feel them. Can't see anything at all.'

'Like looking for a needle in a haystack in fact.'

'Under water,' the diver said.

The next expedition was to the top of Pen Gof and Edwards, taken by surprise while making a Pueblo rug, was compelled to act as guide.

'At least we've got a nice day for it,' Broadbent said.

Edwards looked at the sky which was blue to the horizon in all directions. A small cloud the colour and shape of a pearl balanced on the summit of the mountain like a ball on the snout of a performing seal. 'Yes, we've got a nice day for it,' he said.

It took an hour and a half to reach the summit and find the small cavern indicated by the informant. By this time visibility was down to fifty yards and the fine particles of drifting rain had soaked through both men's uniforms.

'Used to be an old hermit fellow up here when I was a kid,' Edwards said.

'Lucky for us,' Broadbent said. There was a packing-case once used as a table, and the remains of a chair, and they managed to make a fire with these.

'What are we supposed to be looking for?' Edwards asked.

'There was some talk of bones.'

'Sheep's skeleton over here. Bird's too. Might be a chough's. If so, quite a find.'

Broadbent was standing at the mouth of the cave staring out at the shapes forming and dissolving in the mist. 'It's clearing a bit, we may as well get going.'

.   .   .   .   .

There were other wild goose chases in which reinforcements from other districts collaborated with a degree of hope or cynicism often corresponding with their length of service. Under the spur of a widening interest by the Press which had now reached the London Sunday newspapers, more and more policemen arrived in Brynaron. All the wells in an area of twenty-five square miles were pumped dry and examined – some for the second or third time. Two small lakes were dragged. The charred contents of a barn that had mysteriously burned down were sifted and analysed. Digging in several likely spots unearthed several ribs and a femur which turned out to belong to a girl, about eighteen years of age, buried in early Celtic times. A collection of putrescent flesh hidden away under a bridge was identified as slaughterhouse offal. Even Fenn found himself involved, being persuaded to visit a Spiritualist medium who wrote to say that she had been able to contact Evan's spirit in the other world. A vague but impressive message delivered through this woman caused Fenn to lose three days, secretly and ashamedly poking about in the debris of a number of ruined cottages.

After a week of muddle, rumour and frustration another visit made by Broadbent to New Mill Farm produced a breakthrough.

'I seem to remember seeing a large-scale ordnance map last time I was here. Can you put your hand on it?'

Bron went straight to a drawer and got out the map. He was helpful but enigmatic. In cases like this Broadbent expected to be met with injured innocence or heavy sarcasm. A criminal type as presented by Lombroso, but in no more than the physical details.

'What are these pencilled crosses?' Broadbent asked.

'Old mine workings they don't show on the map. My

brother tells me he's lost a few sheep down them at one time or another.'

Dotted lines showed an old road leading to one of the workings, and Broadbent went back, collected his cases of equipment and drove to the spot.

Disused for half a century, the road had disappeared under a dense blackthorn thicket, but a heath fire had cleared the undergrowth the previous summer and tyre-tracks showed of a car that had recently used it. He parked the car out of sight and walked up the road. The tyre-tracks stopped just short of an iron gate jammed half-open. The tread-pattern was still clear in the mud, and Broadbent congratulated himself that although it had rained every day for the past week, there had been no obliterating downpours. He got out his Leica, fitted a close-focussing attachment between the body of the camera and the lens, and took a series of photographs of nine-inch sections of the tyre-pattern in the mud. Then he got out a tape-measure, measured several footprints and also photographed them.

Inside the gate an old administrative building was falling to pieces, shedding its bricks all round, and beyond this the blackthorn closed in, a twenty-foot high palisade of interwoven thorns, a jungle that had swallowed up all traces of the mine's existence apart from a ruined chimney-stack. Broadbent struggled painfully round the perimeter of the thorn-choked ruins. In several places he found natural entrances into the thicket, offering a choice of paths all of which soon ended in barriers of spiny branches. There had been old earth-subsidences producing earthquake effects among the undergrowth, and once he climbed across ruptured terrain to stare down into a chasm into which the remains of a building had been stuffed. It's down there all right, Broadbent thought. Somewhere down there. But we're never going to find it.

15

Height about 5 feet 8 inches, probably stocky build, wearing poor-quality mass-produced shoes, tendency to swivel on balls of feet suggests rolling gait. Abnormally short steps and dug-in heels suggest this man was carrying a heavy weight. Tyre imprint shows make, size and tread-wear characteristics identical with tyres fitted to Austin car inspected.

Against the experts' reports and the cautious commendations of Divisional Headquarters, Fenn, returning from a visit to the Police Solicitor, maintained a stubborn lack of optimism.

He called a conference to discuss the latest moves.

'We still haven't got a body. Don't let's deceive ourselves, the evidence we've got here is far from conclusive. Bloodstains sound dramatic but they don't always add up to much. People cut their fingers. One of the local cleaners used to send us a suit once a month without fail. Never a month went by without the arrival of some bloodstained garment till we managed to talk them out of it. Minute bloodstains on a kitchen floor don't amount to anything taken by themselves. That's where people work and that's where they cut themselves. If it had been splashed all over the walls and ceiling it would be a different thing.'

Fenn turned over a page of his notes. 'This business of the

car being driven to an old mine-working and our friend carrying something heavy out of it. Well, really, it doesn't have to be a body, does it? We all realize that Sergeant Broadbent's done a good job here, and I certainly don't want to pour cold water on his enthusiasm, but as the Police Solicitor points out, what we're not told is *when* the car was driven there. Once again, a minute trace of blood was found in the boot of the car. It may have been Evan's. It probably was. It was from the same blood group. We can check that much because he'd been a blood donor. It also corresponds to the blood found on the suit and one type of blood on the linoleum. Very significant, you might think, but the Police Solicitor didn't get excited about it. Nor did he think it important from our point of view that Bron should have said his brother told him he was going to Aberystwyth and then given the hire-purchase fellow a completely different story. Perhaps his brother *did* want to put the hire-purchase people off for a fortnight, as he says.'

The moment had come for the public reprimand of Constable Jones, who had recently fallen into deeper disfavour.

'We have to thank Constable Jones for his prompt discovery that in actual fact Evan Owen never did go to Aberystwyth, a piece of information he only recently thought fit to pass on to me. I have said before and I say it again: investigations of this kind are to be recorded in a written report on the same day as they are undertaken.'

Jones's attention was recalled by the mention of his name. He had been at his old trick of classifying the citizens of Brynaron as they passed the station window by their height. He accepted the reproach calmly. He was only the last link in a chain of injustice.

'The weakest spot in our case is the woman's statement that Bron went out in the car at about 11.00 p.m., and returned several hours later. Could she be certain that it *was* Bron she heard go out? The answer is no, she couldn't, and any defence counsel worthy of his salt would pounce on this kind of vagueness and use it to tear the case to pieces. Always remember that Mrs Owen is going to be a hostile witness. Whatever she may have said already that she felt might incriminate our friend, she'd take back when we put her in the witness box. Remember, if this goes for trial it's going to attract one of the most clued-up defence counsels in the country. As things stand now he'd make mincemeat of us.'

Broadbent wanted to ask a question.

'Isn't it a fair assumption that by the time Bron started to flog his brother's effects he knew he was never coming back?'

'It's an assumption – just that and no more. On the other hand he went to a local pawnshop. Surely if anything that's a point in his favour. I should have thought a clever criminal with the high I.Q. this man is known to have would have been smart enough to go farther afield if he'd committed a murder. The same with that suit of Evan's. Surely the first thing he'd have done was to get rid of it if he'd murdered him?'

'Why do you suppose he gave a false name at the pawnbroker's, sir?'

'He may be a compulsive liar. That doesn't make him a murderer. Any other questions?'

'Did the Police Solicitor think the partnership agreement was all above board, sir?'

'He said that he couldn't understand any man in his right mind agreeing to it and signing it. Evan's lawyer told him it was drawn up in accordance with his client's instructions and there was no more to it than that. As it is there's nothing to stop Bron Owen selling up the farm tomorrow, pocketing

188

the money and clearing out. The agreement's been sent to the handwriting expert for an opinion on the signature but it's hardly more than a formality.'

Jones had lost interest in the proceedings. It was a case that was condemned to a still birth, so – as all the local men agreed – why worry? In over a hundred years only two cases had been brought successfully where no body had ever been discovered. Jones would not even be there to observe the successive stages of defeat. On the previous day he had been called to the office of the Chief Constable who had listened to Jones's version of the encounter with Major Stevens. He had impressed Jones as a friendly and democratic man. 'You seem to have been rather tactless, that's all. However, there are such things as politics – more's the pity. You'd better concoct a letter of apology. Make it quite short. You needn't grovel; just say you had no intention of appearing discourteous. Send the letter to me and I'll forward it with a covering note.'

'I'm not sure I could do that, sir,' Jones said.

The Chief Constable appeared not to hear.

'And see that I get it within three days.'

Now that the moment of change was upon him Jones found the prospect of it less enticing than when it had seemed remote. Life in Cross Hands was cramped but lived against a dramatic background, and he had developed a real affection for Brynaron. For him its unique atmosphere was compounded of its misted oriental landscape, under a town hall softened to a pagoda shape; the mysterious smell that lay over it permanently of shellac on fused electric wires: collisions passed from truck to truck as the goods trains jogged endlessly backwards and forwards in its shunting yard. A very special town. After the conference he would go off alone to wander in its streets, enjoying these delicate pleasures perhaps for the last time. At this moment he wondered whether the girl was worth it. Shouldn't she have been ready to share his life wherever he happened to be?

Fenn's nasal London voice came back into focus, charged with renewed scepticism. 'Does the fact that this man may be thinking of clearing out of the country mean a thing? I take leave to doubt it. I'm told by the office of the Australian High Commissioner that they get any number of apparently idle inquiries. Our friend told Broadbent that he wanted a second string to his bow if nothing came of all these schemes for turning the farm into a paying proposition. It could be true. He may also be thinking of getting married or taking up with some woman on a permanent basis, and despite all the rumours the woman doesn't have to be his sister-in-law.'

It seemed to Jones that the faintly perfumed letters he received weekly from Neath had grown shorter and happier, which was a bad sign. One day in the near future he expected to receive an ecstatic one of a single paragraph, and after that they would cease altogether.

'My great objection to pressing ahead with this thing,' Fenn said, 'is the absence of motive. Anonymous letters don't mean a thing. I could paper the walls of this office with the collection I've got – but we haven't much evidence, apart from a phone call made to a good lady in Builth Wells, to suggest that those men weren't on brotherly and even affectionate terms. As for the good lady in Builth Wells – I have my doubts. The police up there say she's a bit of a neurotic – one of these old dears living alone who sometimes imagine things. A minute quantity of blood on the linoleum belonging to two blood groups. Well, Bron Owen says he hit his head on a bit of guttering, and his brother may have cut his finger. Bron didn't have to kill his brother for his property because he was going to get that anyway.

And now in conclusion, I'd like to remind you that Owen is a clever man with a good nerve and a pleasing personality. He'd make an excellent impression on a jury. Any final questions?'

Jones raised his hand. 'Do you believe Owen murdered his brother, Mr Fenn?'

'Of course I do,' Fenn said. 'But we happen to know the kind of man we're dealing with, and the jury won't.'

A few minutes later the meeting broke up and Fenn signalled to Jones to stay behind.

'Well, Emrys, what about that letter?'

'I'm afraid I can't write it, Mr Fenn. I'm sorry.'

'I expected you'd say that,' Fenn said. 'You know what it means, I suppose.'

'I do indeed,' Jones said.

'Well, I'll be sorry to see you go. I'd never have believed it, but I will. It's been an education to work with you people. Quite an experience. Do you want another day to think it over?'

'I've made up my mind, Mr Fenn. It's back to the beat for me.'

Fenn clapped him on the shoulder. 'Don't quote me, but in this case I think you're doing the right thing.'

Leaving the station, Jones made for the better end of the town. Soon the Salvation Army's headquarters, the second-hand furniture shops, the working cobblers and the fish-and-chip bars were behind him. He passed Penfold Motors where the damaged Jaguar had been renovated and replaced in its position at the front of the showroom. The open door of the Municipal Baths puffed its chlorinated breath over him, and then immediately the Golden Mile of Market Street started with a Lyons self-service. Jones went in, lined up for a cup of weak, milky tea, took a packet of digestive biscuits, and carried his tray to a table.

He sat there for ten minutes while his tea got cold, dabbing occasionally with a spoon at the creamy scum on its surface and thinking unconstructively about the future, as the customers stopped their nibbling and sipping, glanced at their watches, got to their feet and started for the door.

Alone at his table, and almost alone in the café, Jones soon had the feeling of being under observation. A youth was sitting four tables away and every time Jones looked up their eyes met. After a time it occurred to him that the youth appeared to be signalling to him in something like deaf and dumb language, and he finally realized that this apparently half-witted boy was Beynon, but a Beynon seen for the first time wearing jacket and tie and with the hair that had previously hung over his ears cut short. The beetle-browed, shaggy Beynon of old, who had reminded Jones of the imaginative reconstruction of the skull of some kind of proto-man in a work of popular science, was no more. In his place was a rodent-faced young man who, as Jones studied him again to make quite sure he was not mistaken, raised his right hand and wagged his forefinger at him.

Jones got up, took his packet of biscuits, and went to sit down at Beynon's table.

'Weren't you supposed to come and see me more than a week ago, Beynon?'

'I did, Mr Jones. I called at the station twice and you were out both times.'

'Bit of a liar, aren't you? Lucky for you I've been busy, or I'd have come to see you. What's all the sign language about, anyway?'

Beynon showed his empty gums in a nervous smile, and once again his face was the face of pre-history. 'I've been following you – waiting for the right moment. I saw you come in here and I knew that was my chance. I knew everybody would clear off at two o'clock.'

'Gone off your head, Beynon, have you?'

'I wanted to speak to you in a quiet place like this where we wouldn't be noticed. If you go to the police station everybody knows about it.'

Lives in a world of his imagination, Jones thought.

'The police are supposed to have their regular contacts, aren't they?' Beynon said. 'They meet them in café-bars and places like that. That's how they work.'

'On the telly they do anyway.'

'Mr Jones, I know more than most people do about what goes on around Cross Hands.'

'I suppose you can't spend half your time looking into other people's bedroom windows without picking up a few facts.'

'I've done with that kind of thing,' Beynon said. 'It's other kinds of information I mean. More important things. Would they pay me for it?'

'No, they wouldn't.'

'It doesn't matter anyway. It's not the money that counts. I'd be prepared to work with the police for nothing.'

'You'll be lucky not to see more of the police than you want to if you don't change your ideas. You still read those sex magazines?'

'I've given them up, Mr Jones. Gone over to crime now. I've got subscriptions to *True Detective* and *Amateur Sleuth*. I hope to be a detective one day.'

'It's an improvement on being a peeping Tom.'

Beynon, on the brink of revelation, waited while a customer passed with a tray and sat down five tables away.

'I've got a very important piece of information for you, Mr Jones.'

'In that case you'd better come to the station.'

'Can't we talk about it here first?'

'What's it all about, Beynon?'

'I'm told they're looking for Mr Owen.'

'You *know* they are. Everybody in Cross Hands knows they are. Hasn't Mr Broadbent taken a statement from you yet?'

'Not so far. I stayed up the mountain for three days when I heard he was talking to people. I wanted time to think things over.'

Jones was beginning to wonder if there mightn't be something at the back of this. It was a case where disbelief might prove the best midwife for the truth.

'The trouble is, Beynon, you're a born liar. You live in a world of dreams.'

'I don't think they're going to find Mr Owen. Not alive anyway.' Beynon stroked the corner of a nostril in a sly gesture.

'Why not?'

'I'm not prepared to say any more at this stage.'

'You will if I take you to the station.'

'I'd like to arrange a meeting with the detective sergeant who's on the job.'

'He won't listen to a word you say. I've already told you. You've got a better chance with me. At least I'm listening. Come on, let's have it. Why don't you think they'll find Mr Owen?'

'I'm a key witness,' Beynon said. 'You'll get nowhere without me.'

'All right, we'll get nowhere without you, Beynon boy. Let's forget it.' Jones looked at his watch and pushed his chair back as if to get up.

'Wait a minute, Mr Jones. If I tell you all I know, will you put in a good word for me?'

'A good word? Why? What about?'

'If somebody put in a good word I might get an official commendation, and that would help.'

'An official commendation? For telling the truth?'

'Mr Jones, you don't get anywhere in this world without someone to pull strings for you. This is about the only chance I'm ever going to have. I'm on my own.'

'I know you're on your own, Beynon, and if I could see you were doing anything to make a man of yourself I'd help you in any way I could. What do you want to tell me?'

'I saw Bron Owen hit Mr Owen,' Beynon said.

'Where and when?' Jones asked.

'In the farm kitchen, on the night he disappeared.'

'What exactly happened, and where were you?'

'I was there in the house. I happened to be going past and the front door was open, and I could hear that something funny was going on so I went in. The light was on in the kitchen and it sounded as if there was a fight going on. I pushed the kitchen door open and I saw Bron Owen hit Mr Owen and knock him down.'

'Did he hit him with some kind of instrument?'

'He had a big torch in his hand.'

'And after that?'

'Well, Mr Owen was lying on the floor with his eyes shut, and Bron Owen was standing over him. Evan had a lot of blood on his face.'

'What else? Did you see any more?'

'No, because Bron Owen turned round and I was scared because I thought he'd kill me too if he caught me. So I ran out of the house and went and hid in case he came to look for me.'

Jones got up. 'I think you and I had better take a walk down to the station together.'

16

It rained all day and all night. The weather was the worst at that time of the year in living memory. Rain changed to sleet and back to rain. The high fields were covered with seagulls taking refuge from the sea, and the bottom of the valley was a lake of weak tea with the river curling on its surface and throwing up agitated wavelets, like the barely submerged body of some huge serpentine monster. For the first time the pond in the farmyard overflowed and floated the small, bluish, hairy balloon of the carcase of a drowned cat almost to the step of the front door. On the second morning the summit of the mountain was snow-covered and as the clouds lifted a huge eyeless face was to be seen sketched in bare rocks on the snow, and this, until the snow began to melt, smirked down vacantly over the sopping landscape of Cross Hands.

Bron forced himself up the mountainside but was down in the farmhouse again by mid-morning. The cold and the stiffness were no longer in the skin and in the muscles under the skin, but in the bones themselves, and the position of each joint in his body was marked by a small, deep-seated aching.

He gave Cathy a defeated smile. 'Beynon didn't show up,' he said.

Cathy was scrubbing the kitchen floor, temporarily patched up with linoleum from the box-room. She mopped and rubbed at the sweating surfaces of paint and woodwork all day long.

She got up, dried her hands and pushed back her hair.

'He's gone,' she said.

'Gone where?'

'Just gone. He left a letter saying he was going. That's all.'

'Puts us in a bit of a spot, doesn't it?' Bron said.

'It's not going to be funny until we find somebody to replace him.'

'We can't replace him,' Bron said. 'I've already made inquiries at the exchange. Out of the question. You can't get an experienced cow-hand to come out here even if you offer fifty per cent over the odds.'

'This weather can't go on for ever,' she said. 'In another two weeks we'll be into June. The damp's in everything. The hens have gone off laying, and they're off their food.'

'We've lost three more lambs,' Bron said. 'The ravens got a couple yesterday. They must have been sick. Wouldn't have gone for them otherwise. I found another one frozen stiff today. God knows how many sheep are going to go in these floods. We ought to get them up the mountain but there's no grass for them. It's like mid-winter. Be foot-rot next, I suppose.'

'It can't go on like this,' she said. 'It's practically June. If only the rain would stop it wouldn't be so bad. We can manage the cows together. We'll have to leave the sheep to get on with it as best they can and hope for the best. Hang on somehow until Evan gets back.'

'Until Evan gets back!' he said.

Bron curled back a piece of plaster over the palm of his right hand and peered under it.

'How is it?' she asked.

'Better,' he said. 'Practically right. But I'm not going to be able to do much with this hand for a day or two. Trouble is I've gone soft. A few hours' work and I come up in blisters. I thought I was going to show old Beynon how to dig ditches, but it wasn't long before he was showing me.'

'Take that plaster off,' she said, 'and I'll put on a clean one. I only hope you haven't got dirt into it.'

She took a clean plaster out of a tin, stripped the backing off and put it over the open sore at the base of his finger.

'What made him decide to take off, after all?' Bron asked. 'Got the letter handy?'

'I burned it,' she said. Bron thought he noticed a change in her voice and decided not to press the point.

'He was a nasty little piece of work,' she said. 'I'm not sorry to see him go. He said he wanted to go and live in a town.'

'I never told you,' Bron said, 'but I suspect he tried to do me in a few days ago. The head happened to come off a pick he was working with and missed me by inches. I don't think he's right in the head.'

There was a moment of silence while Cathy made the tea. Bron held his cup in both hands and felt the painful return of the circulation in his finger tips.

Cathy forced herself to broach the subject that had been uppermost in her mind for the past few days.

'What do you think made Phillips change his mind about selling the land?'

'I don't know,' he said. 'We're just out of luck, I suppose. It's just as well the way things have turned out.'

'But how are you going to be able to go ahead with your plans if we can't get the land?'

'I couldn't anyway. Not on my own. I don't know enough about this kind of thing. It has to be faced, I'm beaten before I start. This is a time when we need Evan.'

'You're depressed, that's all. So would anybody be in

your boots. If only this weather would break things would look quite different.'

'And anyway, even if I had the know-how – the big question is, have I got what it takes in other directions?'

'Of course you have.'

'I suppose you know I've been a not very well man . . . over a good many years?'

'Evan said something about it,' she said.

'Well,' Bron said, 'it may have taken its toll.'

'No, it hasn't. It hasn't done anything to you. You're no different from anybody else.'

'It's a thing you're not really supposed to talk about,' Bron said. 'One theory is that talking about it can make it worse.'

'Don't speak about it if it upsets you. I understand.'

'It's all right now,' he said. 'There's no trouble now. They finally put me right at Hayhurst. They used to think this kind of thing was incurable. The psychiatrist there was very good. They have drugs these days that will cure anything short of death.'

'They cured you!' she said.

'Yes,' he said. 'And it couldn't have been a closer thing. I was finally cured just before I got out. I even had the feeling that an attack was coming on just after they let me out, but Griffiths gave me something and it passed off. The time I had the trouble over the car – remember? If I'd have been going to have an attack, I'd have had it there and then. As it was I took the stuff that Griffiths gave me, and no more trouble.'

'What are these attacks like?' she asked.

'I can't tell you because I don't know anything about it. A funny sort of feeling comes on for a day or two when it's on the way. A feeling of excitement. Things seem to become unreal. You're real but nothing else is. After that it's all a blank. The next two or three days don't exist. That's when the trouble happens. I never remember a thing afterwards. They call it automatism.'

'How do you know you didn't have an attack this time?' Cathy asked.

'It's just one of those things you can't explain. I know I didn't, that's all. I felt very sleepy for a day or two, and then I was all right. Going to sleep in that cinema may have had something to do with it.'

He thought again, trying hard to remember. This was what Dallas had called the period of clouded consciousness, and very little of it remained in his memory – a few trivial events were sketched like some Impressionist drawing on a vaguely suggested background.

'A curious thing about all this,' he said, 'is that at these times other people seem to me to behave strangely. For example, both you and Evan seemed very strange to me for a day or two. That's another reason for feeling that I had a lucky escape. Why, for example, should you have appeared cold and distant about the time that Evan disappeared, and after that you were just as you were before – kindness and consideration itself? The answer obviously is that it wasn't you or Evan, it was me.'

'Has it always been like this? All your life?'

'It started when I was a kid at school. The worst thing of it was I didn't even behave like epileptics are supposed to behave. I never had a real fit – nothing like falling down and frothing at the mouth or biting my tongue. People always thought I was shamming mad. They didn't even know I was an epileptic until I was sent to a prison where they had one of the first electroencephalographs. Even when I was at Hayhurst the Senior M.O. told me I was putting on an act. I got the birch when I was nineteen for something I didn't know I'd done.'

'How terrible,' she said.

'It wasn't too bad,' he said. 'The birch wasn't too bad. They gave you a half-pint of stout if you lost much blood.'

'Aren't you bitter?'

'Why should I be? I wasn't any worse off than anyone else. None of the fellows in prison asked to be born psychopaths, or sex maniacs, or whatever they were. As it turned out, I was curable. If you're a psychopath you aren't, but you have to take your punishment all the same.'

'Yes,' she said. 'You were curable. How lucky for you. You're quite sure you're cured now?'

'I'm cured all right. A few months on some new wonder drug, and that was that. There was a chap in my cell in Hayhurst who couldn't sleep unless he stole something every day. We used to arrange for him to pinch odds and ends from us. He always gave them back. Something happened to his brain that made his life not worth living if he couldn't steal. In a few years' time they'll have invented a wonder drug for him too. We had an old man doing ten years' preventive detention for stealing a bicycle worth four pounds. The real trouble was he was born too soon. If he could only have put it off a few more years they'd have been able to give him a course of tablets instead of putting him away for the rest of his life.'

He remembered a joke shared with Dallas. 'The Guest Star we used to call him – the second me, that's been living in my body running up bills for me to pay. That was Dallas's name for him. Unlike me he had a short temper. If anyone trod on the Guest Star's corns he let him have it but it was quiet, peaceable me who was given Restricted Diet, No. 1, Solitary, and loss of remission of sentence. In the end he turned out too smart for once, because when he got me an extra two years for assaulting a prison officer I qualified for psychiatric treatment.'

Cathy had been trying not to ask him the question but an impulse took her by surprise. 'Bron,' she said, 'what do you really think happened to Evan?'

He didn't seem surprised. 'I don't know.'

'He's dead, isn't he?'

'I don't think so. As a matter of fact I've got a new theory. I think he's had some sort of an attack of the kind I used to have. It probably runs in the family. There was some mystery about my sister's death. We were never told why she died. It may have been the same thing. Evan used to say my brain was damaged when I was born. He said the doctor bungled the delivery. Nowadays, thinking about it all, I'm not so sure.'

'Evan's dead,' she said. 'Nothing will convince me he isn't dead. For three nights running now I've dreamed he was dead. I dreamed he was under the ground somewhere.'

'Dreams don't mean anything. The thing's preying on your mind.'

'He's dead,' she said. 'I'm as sure he's dead as I'm sure I'm alive. What are we going to do?'

Bron put an arm round her shoulder, trying to calm her.

'The police think he's been murdered,' she said. 'They talk about routine inquiries, but they think someone murdered him.'

'They're bound to. Especially after they found that suit of his.'

'And so does everybody else. When I go into Cross Hands people cross the street to avoid speaking to me. The girls in the Co-op wouldn't serve me. That's why Phillips said he wouldn't sell his land after all. They all hate us.'

'You're beginning to imagine things,' Bron said. 'It's all this constant strain on the nerves. Why should they hate us?'

'Don't you understand? Everybody thinks that we've put

Evan out of the way because there's something between us.'

He shook his head, truly astounded that she could have entertained such an outrageous thought, astounded that she could believe that anyone could exist capable of such mental slander. In the first moment of seeing Cathy he had seen her as pretty and desirable, then instantly this spontaneous admiration of a man for a woman had been thrust out of mind as disloyal to his brother. Cathy became the asexual female presence in the house – a sister towards whom he felt an increasingly brotherly affection. He was unable even to imagine the existence of physical relations between her and Evan, and had she ever become pregnant he would have been a little shocked. An incredible possibility suggested itself.

'Was that by any chance why Beynon cleared off?'

'Yes,' she said, 'that's why Beynon went.'

It was Beynon's letter that had put her in this frame of mind, he thought.

'If only we could leave this place and go somewhere else,' she said.

'That really would set the cat among the pigeons.'

'Somewhere where nobody knows us,' she pleaded.

'It's out of the question for a dozen reasons. First and foremost I can imagine what the police would think.' Somehow or other there was nothing wrong with being under the same roof with her alone, but to go and live somewhere else with her (and in any case, where?) was unthinkable. 'And incidentally it might take quite a bit of explaining away in another direction,' he added, but she didn't seem to hear.

She had reached the point when she could no longer hold back the question. 'Bron, where did you go on that Sunday night when you went out in the car? Can you remember?'

'Of course I can remember.' Then he saw what she meant and laughed. 'You're wondering if I could have had an attack. Don't worry, I remember the occasion in every detail.'

'You were out a long time, weren't you?'

'A fair time,' he said.

'Most of the night,' Cathy said. 'I woke up when you came in and looked at the clock.'

'I know it was late when I got back.'

'That detective asked me and I told him I heard you go out in the car. I'm very sorry I did.'

'You couldn't have done anything else if he asked you. You heard me go out. What else could you have said?'

'They're watching you. They're checking up on every movement you've made.'

'Routine inquiries,' he said. 'They're bound to. It doesn't mean a thing. They check up on everyone.'

'I'm going to take it back,' she said. 'I'm going to deny I said it.'

'But why?' he said. 'Why?'

She wouldn't answer directly. 'Why should they force me to say anything? I'll take it back.'

'Don't do that whatever you do. They'd only think you've got something to cover up. If you're innocent the only thing is to tell the truth.'

'In that case what made you tell an untruth about that cut you got over the eye? Didn't you say you told them you cut your eye on a piece of guttering?'

'Yes, but I realize I shouldn't have done it. I thought it was the best way to save a lot of questions, but it was a mistake. Lies always complicate things in the end.'

'Can't you tell me where you went?' She knew it was a question he wanted to evade, and it was this added to his other reticences that finally convinced her. But with this suspicion that had finally become certainty came the resolution that she would stop at nothing to protect him. She defended herself to her own conscience and the world by claiming this tragedy as a family affair. This is our business. Evan is gone and nothing can bring him back. Leave us alone to make the best of what's left of our lives.

At this moment Bron came to the conclusion that he might as well tell her. 'I was out with a friend. A girl friend,' he said.

'Oh,' she said. 'Oh. I hadn't any idea that you knew anybody like that.' Her voice was flat.

'I didn't say anything before,' he said, 'because there are complications. She's not free at the moment. We hope to get married eventually, but just when I can't say.'

She longed for it to be a lie – tried hard to believe that this was his way of trying to throw her off the scent. 'Do I know her?' she asked.

'I shouldn't think so,' he said. 'I don't believe she's accepted locally. She's a girl who's had a hard time of it. She's keen on emigrating, and that's what we might do, but it's early yet to say. It all depends how things work out.'

'I hope everything works out well for you,' she said. Please God don't let it be the truth, she prayed. In a sad little fantasy she saw herself in the police station being interrogated, lying for him and refusing whatever they did or said to budge from her story. They would have to release him because they could do nothing with him. After that he would turn to her in gratitude. She retained a childhood habit of believing that if you wanted anything enough it came true.

They heard the splash of water as a car was driven up through the deep puddles standing in the lane, then the sound of tyres gouging into the wet gravel as brakes went on hard outside the gate.

Bron went to the window. 'Our friends are here again,' he said.

17

In the nature of things, the Detective Chief Inspector
shared between two divisions was bound to appear upon the
scene, attracted like an art-dealer who has heard rumours of
an uncatalogued Franz Hals that has turned up in a provin-
cial saleroom. It was an interesting case, and one that might
quite easily make the legal textbooks. Hardly had Fenn and
Broadbent started their interrogation than there was a
phone call ordering them to await the Chief Inspector's
arrival before proceeding with the investigation, and now he
had arrived to take over.

He gave Fenn and Broadbent a talk on cases of murder
where no body had been found. 'The last case offered a number of interesting parallels,' he said. 'Farmers once again –
partners in an unprofitable concern. The accused man put
forward the ingenious plea that his partner had been kid-
napped and conveyed behind the Iron Curtain. Much of the
evidence was strikingly similar, and one found the same
curious carelessness on the accused man's part in all the
accessory details of the crime.'

Every few years the fashion in interrogation technique
changed, and the Chief Inspector's was almost a period
piece. It marked a swing of the pendulum from the school
of 1939, when it was believed that suspects could be startled
into telling the truth, and interrogators had been known to
dress themselves like Alpine guides in *Lederhosen*, or even
conduct investigations from the low branches of a tree. The
Chief Inspector's training belonged to the next phase when

the investigator cultivated a false sympathy and tried to see life through his victim's eyes. It was an approach that engendered the maximum of suspicious hostility in the suspect and was soon dropped, and only a few old-timers, protected by the system of seniority, persevered with it. 'The trouble is,' the Chief Inspector said to Bron, 'that you fell for this hoary old fallacy that a charge of murder can't be brought unless a body can be produced.' He was benignly understanding about this common mistake.

'It's natural and understandable in a way – almost a matter of common sense – but it happens not to be true. If there's sufficient evidence to make it quite obvious that a murder has been committed the law accepts this evidence and finds the accused man guilty of murder whether a body is available or not.'

They sat in the interview room in Brynaron station and Bron smoked the Chief Inspector's king-size cigarettes, feeling both surprise and curiosity. He proposed to let the Chief Inspector talk on as long as he liked, to save himself the waste of energy of disputing point by point the minor pieces of evidence the Inspector might produce, and then when the right moment came demolish the whole structure of his case by the production of his trump card. He found it surprising that he should be in the position in which he found himself and yet very little in his life had been predictable or even explicable in rational terms.

'Naturally,' the Chief Inspector said, 'we'd like to have a body but we can do without it, and I'll try to explain why.'

In the background Broadbent produced a faint chirp of exasperation, inaudible to the Chief Inspector, but audible to Fenn. Broadbent and Fenn had been allowed to take notes but not to intervene. 'In my experience,' the Chief Inspector had said, 'it's fatal to surround a suspect with a lot of shouting policemen. In nine cases out of ten he just buttons up. The thing is to draw him out.'

'If one entertains this particular fallacy,' the Chief Inspector said, 'only one thing is paramount – the disposal of the embarrassing end product. You look round for a satisfactory place of concealment, believing that once you've found it you can fold your arms and sit back. I was, by the way, most impressed by the way you tackled this problem – the painstaking reconnaissance of all the suitable sites. I gather you used the marked map the indefatigable Sergeant Broadbent found at the farm.'

Bron had nothing to say.

'Please interrupt whenever you feel like it. Don't just let me talk on if there's a query of any kind. This isn't meant to be a one-man show. The map was marked with pencilled crosses showing the location of all the mine shafts in the area. This led to the discovery of the tyre marks of the car you used – and, of course, your footprints. You did drive the car up that lane, didn't you?'

'I did – and if Sergeant Broadbent had asked me I'd have told him so.'

'Well, at least we're getting somewhere. All your subsequent actions bear out this theory of mine that you believed that all you had to do was to make this body you'd got on your hands disappear. What could be better for your purpose than an old mine shaft? And having found this perfect place for concealment – and given this misconception of yours – why take elaborate precautions to cover up your tracks? You struck your brother to the ground —'

'Excuse me, Inspector, he fell.'

'Why split hairs? He fell – but you struck him first. At least that was the sequence of events according to an eye-witness's statement we have.'

Bron was certain that the Chief Inspector was bluffing,

208

but decided against further interruptions. He took another cigarette from the proffered case, and the lines at the corners of the Chief Inspector's kindly eyes deepened in gleeful benevolence.

'What I'm pointing out is that you didn't make much effort to cover up your tracks. You killed your brother, cleaned up the kitchen floor in a perfunctory manner, undressed the body, put it in the boot of the car, drove to the mine shaft and threw it down. I should have thought that you would have burned your brother's bloodstained clothing, but you didn't bother to do so. From this point on this misplaced confidence of yours makes you positively careless. You give conflicting stories to explain your brother's whereabouts, and when you start selling articles of his property – understandably giving a false name to the purchaser – you go to the nearest pawnbroker's. I personally should have thought, too, that it would have been prudent to let weeks or months pass before starting negotiations for the sale of the farm and making your preparations for departure to Australia. But there it is, you thought it simply didn't matter. The clue to all your actions is to be found in this one basic fallacy of yours.'

Broadbent had drawn a design of concentric circles and triangles in his notebook. There were no notes to be taken. The purpose of an interrogation, he had been taught, was to encourage a suspect to talk. The more he talked and the less the interrogator had to say the better. One let a suspect know as little as one could of what one had up one's sleeve. By these standards the Inspector's performance was a catastrophe.

All the Chief Inspector's efforts were directed towards the production of a mood of confession, accompanied by the slow building up of a belief – however hopeless the prospects might look – that some sort of deal was possible. This inevitably involved him in a double problem, because being a religious man he was compelled to delude not only his victim but himself. He had to encourage a climate of mutually acceptable make-believe, and exorcize the spectre of fraud by a self-deceiving pretence of offering value for money. 'We can help each other,' the Chief Inspector was bound to say sooner or later in these discussions. 'You can help me, and I can help you.' He tried very hard to mean it. It was a moral trapeze-act, an illusionist's perform-ance carried out not only for benefit of an audience, but himself. Hopes and promises were produced from nothing, displayed, then whisked away with a flourish of a silk scarf. It was a performance polished by many years of practice.

'Occasions arise,' the Chief Inspector said, 'when the police can be of more help than any defence counsel, how-ever good. In this case we know there was quite a fight. Blood from two groups was found on the linoleum. Hence, too, your cut over the eye. You may have been provoked beyond endurance. Self-defence. I can't promise at this stage – but a word in the right direction . . . manslaughter ?' He seemed to be putting a question to himself which Bron was allowed only accidentally to overhear. To Bron he said, 'We don't want to be vindictive.'

The question was, Could the obvious premeditation be muffled up in some way? Even the Chief Inspector's acro-batic conscience doubted it. But let's see, let's see. He was like an early aeronaut trying to coax some rickety contrap-tion of spars and wires into the air. Nothing was clearer and more damning in this case than the premeditation. 'I suppose the most unfortunate thing from the premeditation aspect,' he said, 'is that forged signature on the partnership docu-ment. And yet surely it shouldn't be beyond the bounds of possibility to get over that. Given goodwill on both sides.

Your brother's solicitors confirm that he instructed them to draw up the agreement, so the inference is that he only dug his heels in when it came to the signing. The forgery *could* have been post-mortem.'

Bron laughed. 'Sorry, Inspector, you better check on your records. Forgery isn't in my line.'

'I gather that,' the Chief Inspector said, with a trace of disappointment. He had hoped for immediate collapse at this stage. 'Our handwriting expert said it was a typical first attempt. Nine out of ten non-professional forgeries are tracings. Our man didn't even bother to use his microscope. Apparently you can see the depressions in the paper's surface with the naked eye.' He brightened. 'Of course it might help if we're trying to get round the premeditation angle.' His voice changed as he posed himself another question: 'Couldn't the fight have been over the brother's last-minute refusal to sign?' Privately, he wondered whether this forgery couldn't even be left out of the evidence if Bron decided to co-operate. Ten to one the jury would still bring in a verdict of guilty, but it gave him a chance.

'Well, what do you say?' the Chief Inspector said. 'Any chance of our getting together over this?'

'I'm afraid not, Inspector,' Bron said.

'I'm sorry. Very sorry indeed. You're an intelligent man. I should have thought you'd realize which side your bread was buttered. May I ask why?'

'It's nice of you to suggest you might get the charge reduced to manslaughter, but it doesn't even interest me. If my brother's dead I had nothing to do with it.'

'Wouldn't you agree that the evidence that you did looks pretty complete?'

'I would,' Bron said. 'So complete that there might be a miscarriage of justice but for one fact.'

'And that?'

'I've got an alibi.'

'Have you? How interesting. Are you prepared to say what it is?'

'Yes,' Bron said, 'of course. I'm supposed to have killed my brother on the Sunday night. As it happens I can account for my whereabouts on that particular night.'

'And produce corroborating witnesses?' the Chief Inspector asked.

'A witness,' Bron said. 'I hope one will be enough.'

Central Records Office had supplied the salient facts of Wendy's past: soliciting, shoplifting, larceny, being concerned with another person in the presentation of indecent performances for money. Broadbent who had expected a garish, painted harlot was surprised to find a respectable-looking, pleasant woman, with what he still thought of as a touch of class. She was perfectly agreeable to going down to the station with him there and then. 'Can you wait a moment while I put on something different?' She dressed quickly and with care for the trip to Brynaron. Broadbent found it hard to imagine the quietly immaculate Wendy in a long night of rough and tumble lovemaking in the back of a small car, or the ruined buildings of Foxes' Mine. 'You carried your brother's body in and threw it down the shaft.'

'No,' Bron said. 'I took the girl there.'

'Then how do you explain the fact that there are only your footprints?'

'She asked me to carry her. She didn't want to get her shoes muddy.'

There was a small domestic interlude when Oakes had to be dissuaded from getting into the car.

'Do you mind if I come too?'

212

'You can come by all means, sir, if the lady wishes to be accompanied, but the interview will be in private.'

'And you can't give me any idea at all of what this is all about?'

'I'm afraid I can't, sir.'

'Be a good boy and don't make a fuss,' Wendy said. 'I shan't be long, will I, Sergeant?'

'I shouldn't imagine so, madam.'

The Chief Inspector, too, rather fell for Wendy. Wonderful what a girl like this can do if she ever decides to take herself in hand. Could go a long way. Be opening charity bazaars yet. If only they could get rid of the ponces. It was the ponces that drained the life and soul out of them. With this one the boot was on the other foot. Clever girl. He liked her.

'Do you know a Mr Bron Owen of New Mill Farm?'

'He's the short brother, isn't he? Yes, I know him. As a customer.'

'Is he a friend of yours?'

'No more than any other customer. In our business you're expected to be friendly with everybody. Do your best to remember everybody's name. They expect it of you. If they ask you to have a drink with them, you have a drink. You know how it is.'

The Chief Inspector nodded with sympathy. 'Of course.'

'They try to tell you their troubles. People are always on the lookout for a listener.'

'And in Owen's case it was no more than that? You held yourself aloof as you always do?'

'Definitely. I don't suppose he's been in the place more than half a dozen times.'

'Then you've quite certainly never been for a car ride with Mr Owen?'

'I've never been for a car ride with Mr Owen or with any other customer. It isn't done.'

The Inspector could see her in ten years' time, iron-clad in her virtue.

'Why – has anybody suggested that I have?' Her eyebrows were raised at the idea.

'I must be quite frank with you. Mr Owen has made a statement to us in which he says that he has been on intimate terms with you.'

'How fantastic,' she said. 'How absolutely fantastic.'

'You've never accompanied him in a car to a place known as Foxes' Mine?'

'I've just said I've never had anything to do with him whatever beyond serving him a drink, and passing the time of day. Quite apart from anything else, I happen to be getting married shortly.'

'I didn't know that,' the Chief Inspector said. 'Please accept my congratulations. Anyway, it can be assumed you'd be prepared to stand up in court and say you'd never been out with him?'

'I very definitely would.'

'It's most unlikely it'll be necessary,' the Chief Inspector said. 'I wonder incidentally if you can remember what you happened to be doing on the night of the 10th?'

'When was the 10th?' she asked. 'I'll have to think. What day of the week was it?'

'A Sunday,' the Chief Inspector said.

'The Sunday before last?'

'The one before.'

'There's no trouble about that,' she said. 'I went to the pictures with our housekeeper. After that we came home and made some supper. We probably put on a few gramophone records after supper – we usually do. We'd have been in bed by about midnight. That's the way it always goes.'

'And you didn't go out of the house again that night? I'm sorry to have to insist like this. We have to get everything very cut and dried.'

She pardoned him with a quiet smile. 'No, I went to bed, and I went to sleep. I've got an alarm clock that wakes me at a quarter to eight, and until that bell rings I don't so much as stir.'

'Thank you, Miss Frost. I think that's all. Thank you very much for coming, and the sergeant will drive you home.'

The Chief Inspector had an afterthought as she was going out. 'It's most unlikely that we shall want to see you again, but will you be about if we do?'

'For another two weeks,' she said. 'After that we'll be on our honeymoon.'

18

Bron, who had been held on remand for over a week and was flagging from interrogations, revived instantly at the sight of Dallas's cheerful face. Once again he was amazed by the youthfulness he had grown accustomed to at Hayhurst, the juvenility emphasized by the small defensive beard sprouting from the point of the chin. Dallas found Bron on the whole apathetic. As soon as the warder had gone, locking them together in the dingy interview room, Dallas had explained. 'This is quite unofficial. I'm not supposed to be here at all. Have to be very careful about infringing other people's territorial rights.'

Four weeks had passed since Bron had last seen Dallas, and now he realized that he had never been released from his dependence on this young man. In a matter of minutes the false self-sufficiency of the past month crumbled, and Bron understood that he needed Dallas as much as ever before.

'It's a bit too early to say we've fallen on our feet,' Dallas said, 'but I've had rather a stroke of luck with the doctor here.'

'Not a bad sort of chap, I thought,' Bron said. 'More human than one usually finds them.'

'The bedside manner conceals a heart of stone. Nothing he used to enjoy better than a hanging. Told me he once refused to certify a poor fellow suffering from general paralysis of the insane. They had to carry him in to be topped.'

'Where does the luck come in then?'

'I happen to have hit on the weak spot. When he was a student a man called Weber once patted him on the head and took him out to lunch at Simpson's. As a result Doctor Parkinson has a sort of proprietorial interest in the Sturge-Weber Syndrome his friend discovered. As it happens you exhibit the Sturge-Weber Syndrome.'

Bron laughed. 'What's going on here?'

'Didn't I ever show you your cranial radiographs?'

'No,' Bron said. 'You didn't.'

'Funny. I always meant to.' Dallas was beginning to worry now that Bron might refuse to co-operate. There was another problem too about spelling things out – Dallas didn't believe that the possibility of eavesdropping should be ruled out. The interview room tried to capture the atmosphere of a club, with a deeply dented settee, a couple of armchairs upholstered in scrofulous brown leather, and two darkly misted Victorian oil paintings. A ring-worm of light fom the invisible sun trembled on the dusty bathroom-glass of the window. Were these places ever fitted with listening devices?

'I may have decided that it wasn't a good thing,' Dallas said. 'However there doesn't seem to be any reason why you shouldn't know now. You have fairly extensive calcifications in the occipital area, which of course explains all the other symptoms, the delusions, the sensory hallucinations, the sub-cortical paroxysmal discharges shown in your EEG, and so forth.'

'This is all news to me.'

Bron's voice boomed dangerously in the sparsely furnished space. The room had shrunk and the walls had thinned. Dallas felt the presence of the warder alert under his pose of boredom behind the door, with its small speakeasy flap half-opened outwards. And could that greasy landscape in its chipped gilt frame conceal a microphone?

A shuffling squad of men marched up the corridor towards them and then away and Dallas threw urgent words at Bron through the clumping of their boots.

'Confusion . . . mutism . . . panosmia . . . trismus . . .'
He wanted to shout, For God's sake use your head, you fool.

Bron's sceptical and stubborn smile remained.

'Dr Parkinson,' Dallas said, 'was most interested in the radiograms. He pointed out a small calcification in the rear parietal area I'd actually overlooked. I explained to him that in the nature of things my experience in the field was bound to be limited.' Since Dallas kept the radiographical records nothing was easier than to manipulate them. With calmness and with resolution he had obtained typical Sturge-Weber Syndrome radiograms and substituted them for those in Bron's file, which were supremely unrevealing. He had gambled on the chances of Parkinson being energetic and suspicious enough to have his own radiograms done being negligible, and the arteriogram would be a fussy business to repeat.

And now this Welsh peasant seemed to be refusing to be saved. He had either given up or was on the point of giving up – of surrendering to his native fatalism.

This was to have been Dallas's last effort to justify himself to himself before leaving the prison service. A week before he had dined with the Governor at Hayhurst and mentioned the possibility of resigning. 'I've had a ringside seat for three years at the spectacle of men being punished for illness. What we're trying to do here is cure pneumonia by taking a man's clothes away from him and pushing him out into the snow.'

The Governor apologized for his own inefficacy. 'Write to your Member of Parliament. I just pull the levers on this machine. No real reason so far as I can see why they shouldn't pull themselves.'

218

A jog-trot of feet resounded in the corridor again. Dallas pulled his chair closer and screamed at the man, 'Please try to co-operate. I can't do anything without your co-operation.' What a psychiatrist I am! he thought. I try to compensate for my failure by this obsession with a single patient.

The warder opened the door, his jaw muscles recovering from a yawn and his left hand just withdrawn from scratching at his crutch.

'Did you call, sir?'

Before the door had closed behind him again, Bron said, 'I always understood I was virtually cured when I left Hayhurst.'

'There wasn't a hope of it,' Dallas said.

'That wasn't what you told me.'

'It wasn't advisable to tell you all the facts. You wouldn't have given trouble if you'd been kept under sedation. That was where we fell down in our arrangements. What I should have had was the power to commit you to a county asylum on release, but I hadn't. Even if you'd been a raving madman there was nothing I could do about it. As it is I'm sure you had a seizure a few days after you went out. Everything I can find out about your doings points to status epilepticus followed by automatism. Take this famous alibi of yours. Much as you believe it yourself, it's the most transparent piece of fantasy.'

'You've put your finger on a raw spot,' Bron said. 'The business about that girl is the one thing that really worries me. I'll never understand what made her do what she did.'

'She didn't do it,' Dallas said.

Bron could see it all as if it had happened to him only the night before, clear-cut in every detail. The memory of this betrayal made him want to weep. 'We went to a house,' he said. 'I could describe everything about it. The stairs creaked and the key in the bedroom lock turned the wrong way. There was a religious text about God's love on the wall.'

'But you don't know the address. Am I right?'

'No, I don't know the address. It was dark. There was a path running along the back of some gardens, and the arrangement was she'd leave the back door open and the light on.'

'I'll bet no one saw you,' Dallas said.

'And you'd win. They didn't. She was living with a man and she had to make sure he didn't get to hear about it. I could take you to the place.'

'I doubt it,' Dallas said. 'I think that after all the explorations of the human mind we've undertaken together you should be ready to admit that this could have been a kind of dream state. This form of dream can carry as much conviction and be as fully detailed as the waking consciousness. I don't say I'm particularly impressed by police methods but they're supposed to have checked and rechecked on this woman's story. They say they're convinced she's telling the truth.'

Bron said, 'I think perhaps it's time one thing was established. Do you think I killed Evan?'

'Put it this way, I think you're capable of it. Whether you did or not is of less importance to me.' It cost Dallas some effort to make this bold declaration and he gave Bron a cautious side-glance to see how he was taking it.

Bron was scrutinizing the texture of the past: the reality of Wendy's flesh, the interlocking logic of his motives and actions. At the most there had been occasional losses of sharp focus. Only Evan's rage remained inexplicable.

'There wouldn't have been any point in it,' he said. 'It would have been senseless. I had nothing against Evan.'

'Except possibly the subconscious realization that he had

something against you. You hadn't anything against that warder at Wandsworth either, according to my notes.'

'I suppose I have to believe you,' Bron said. 'I obviously can't trust my own reason or my memory any more.'

'I'm your friend. I want to help you to decide the best course to be taken. That's why I came here.'

Bron said without enthusiasm, 'I saw the man who's going to defend me yesterday. He's supposed to be pretty good.'

'I've heard all about him. He's out to carve his initials on the world.'

'He seems to think he may be able to get me off.'

'He might too. That's the trouble. Five years ago, you can say it's ten to one they would have hanged you. There's nothing they'd like better than to hang you now, but all these articles in the Sunday supplements about possible miscarriages of justice have made them a bit nervous.'

He thought it was a fifty-fifty chance.

'As high as that, eh?' Dallas made a face. 'Doesn't it worry you?'

'I can't work up any excitement about it one way or the other. I'm a disappointment to him so far.'

'This counsel of yours has got his name to make. We have to remember that. It could be a sensational trial, and a big lift for him if he managed to bring it off. You might be acquitted, but the whole point is you don't really want to be, do you? You can't tell me you enjoy freedom. From the chats we had at Hayhurst you made it clear enough you felt you'd had some of the best times of your life there.'

'I got used to the life pretty quickly.'

'But the thing is you've never been able to make the same adjustment to life on the outside. There weren't any problems in Hayhurst. It all made sense. That's why, whether you realized it or not, you were determined to stay on as long as you could.'

221

'You're probably right. You always have been so far. What should I do then? Tell this chap I want to plead guilty?'

'As it happens I think we can do better than that. I told you Parkinson's on our side. The next step if you agreed would be to get a second opinion from Northfields.'

'Northfields – that's for life, isn't it?'

'Her Majesty's Pleasure.'

'Same thing.'

'Not necessarily. It depends on all kinds of things. I can't say any more than that. You'll just have to rely on me. I'm doing everything I possibly can.'

'What's it like?'

'An improvement on Hayhurst. They make quite a fuss of people who aren't stark staring mad. You'd be in one of the élite blocks, rubbing shoulders with introspective chaps taking correspondence-course degrees. Probably put you on parole in a month or two and give you the run of the place. Relative sanity's at a high premium.'

'Northfields didn't have a very brilliant reputation in the prisons.'

'It's all part of the policy. They want to keep out the riff-raff. Obviously it doesn't do to let the idea get round it's a kind of Butlin's camp. You'd take to it like a duck takes to water. I remember your telling me you wouldn't have minded going into a monastery. Well, this has got most of the things a monastery has to offer, but I should imagine you might find it somewhat more varied in its appeal.'

Out of politeness he makes a pretence of being interested, Dallas thought, but in reality he's not. He doesn't want to go on. What I'm fighting is not the bright legal boy who wants to see his name in lights but the death-wish that's always ready to fill the vacuum when hope and desire are at an end. The man from Northfields would come down, and

222

Parkinson in his new role of angel of mercy would go into battle on their side. But could Bron ever be induced to do the minimum that was required of him? If only the death penalty hadn't been dropped Dallas knew that Bron would have been lost to the reckless self-interest of his counsel and his own urge for oblivion.

19

Overnight almost, the atmosphere at Cross Hands had changed and the cauldron of public excitement settled and cooled. On the threshold of summer, spring arrived at last, daubing the dour valleys with sunshine, and sweeping away the staleness and the claustrophobia of a winter that had lasted six months.

The gates in the grim Italianate entrance of Northfields opened and closed on Bron and he disappeared from sight and in most cases from memory. Losing interest in him, the Brynaron *Observer* also dropped its recent obsession with unsolved crime and cleared the decks of its columns for the silly season, which came earlier and stayed later in Brynaron than in most other parts of the country.

With the installation of a new transmitter, television reception was much improved in the area but religious attendance declined steeply. That summer the number of caravans increased by fifty per cent, spoiling what was left to be spoiled of the accessible valleys. A half-dozen more farmers gave up the struggle, turned their fields into caravan sites and joined a new class of idle poor. This year the summer visitors were more violent, destructive and immoral than ever before, and the newest sport was the slaughter with ·22 rifles of the salmon that risked the stretch of river passing through the caravan encampments.

After their strenuous late winter, the police rested on their laurels. Detective Sergeant Broadbent went back to London carrying a letter of congratulations from the Chief Constable. Inspector Fenn applied for and was given a transfer, burning a small mountain of anonymous letters before he left. Police Constable Jones received a disciplinary posting to Ferryport, a rapidly growing slum built round an oil refinery by the sea. Police Constable Edwards spent a tranquil summer working on a contribution to *British Ornithology*, entitled *Diet as a Contributory Factor in the Population Decline of the Chough*. For this he received four guineas.

On Midsummer Day five children of Cross Hands lost their lives when the ground subsided into an old mine working. This tragedy pushed the juvenile drug addiction and high-diving grandmothers off the front page of the Brynaron *Observer* for two weeks, and the paper pointed out with justification how repeatedly it had drawn attention to this danger in its columns. Rumours of a national inquiry proved to be premature.

Local ex police-suspects had a good year. Roberts, whom the police had lost all interest in, began to show discreet signs of prosperity. He bought most of the land on Pen Gof at give-away prices, equipped himself with the latest tractors and bulldozers, and it now began to seem as though the mountain was about to meet its master at last. People stopped calling him by his Christian name.

Morgan the lobster fisherman had never looked back since his partner's disappearance. This year for the first time the exporters had moved into the lobster market and were paying big prices. Morgan bought a calendar watch, a new outboard engine with a self-starter, and moved up two chapels.

Oakes married Wendy, and after their return from their Majorca honeymoon Wendy set about the transformation of the Salutation into a roadhouse with continental cuisine. Oakes retired into a shed in the back, became absorbed in the construction of model railways and was rarely seen again except at the controls of a miniature locomotive into which he could just squeeze. When beatniks from a caravan site invaded the Salutation Bar and Grill one summer's night a Cypriot waiter who had been a weightlifter threw one of them into the street with such violence that he broke four ribs. A case for assault heard at the Brynaron Sessions was dismissed.

Cathy sold New Mill Farm to a generous and sympathetic Roberts for a small sum – other potential buyers being excluded from the market by the farm's aura of mystery and death. She gave part of the money to a pair of needy sisters, banked the rest, leaving it untouched, and went to work again at Pearsons. After a week in the packing department Mr Hammett proved as good as his word, and she was promoted first to the counter and soon after to the position of Assistant Buyer. She was often lonely and the other girls at Pearsons regarded her as middle-aged. An attempt to renew her friendship with Eve Marshall failed after Eve's husband Henry – who turned out to be practically a dwarf – had made a pass at her at a cocktail party. One night she had a nightmare in which she was visited by the ghost of Evan who tried to describe to her his predicament in Hades. 'I'm enclosed in a crystal,' Evan said. 'A sort of cameo with two faces. Weekend passes are rarely given, but there it is.' She woke up weeping.

Constable Jones took an immediate liking to Ferryport, the natural greyness of which was relieved by a cosmopolitan population, many of them Easterners made to feel at home by the Welsh inability to dislike any foreigners but the English. Half the town smelt of crude oil and its derivatives, and the other half of curry, and kindly, promiscuous Welsh girls snuggled up with turban-wearing men among the pampas-grass and laurels of the local park, as soon as twilight came. It was a town where rest was pleasantly disturbed by the nostalgic moaning of ocean-going ships. Men quarrelled in ten languages in twenty-seven waterfront taverns. The harbour offered the spectacle of many fish floating belly-upwards in the vivid, multi-coloured sea. Seagulls that had fed on poisoned waste occasionally fell dead from the sky in the streets. Jones missed only the fogs of Brynaron, which could have no existence in a town swept endlessly by Atlantic winds.

His first lodgings were in a tenement block occupied largely by members of a tribe from Mysore. Here he shared a flat with two laughing bus-conductors who played an instrument with eighteen strings, kept incense-cubes burning on their mantelpiece, and presented him with red- and blue-dyed cakes on their feast days. Jones wrote to his girl friend Elizabeth to mention the subject of marriage again. She had just celebrated her thirtieth birthday and with this landmark in mind she took a secretarial job with the refinery at Ferryport and within weeks they were married.

Jones benefited in almost every way by his change in status, and the only drawback to the fact that Elizabeth earned fifty per cent more than he did was that he felt unable to complain when she was kept late at the office and came home smelling of cigar smoke. They soon took a semi-detached suburban house with what Jones found an exciting view of storage tanks, and cranes wavering behind them like the antennae of sensitive insects. The main problem to be faced by any policeman new to the Ferryport scene was the one of his personal safety. New men, usually arriving under a cloud, were treated like unsatisfactory soldiers in the Continental armies of old by being placed in positions exposed to the enemy's fire. In this case the firing line was the Ferryport waterfront. Jones soon learned all that was necessary to survive – summed up in the art of never being on the scene when trouble happened. There were safe and unsafe streets, and the patrol through the unsafe areas had to be covered at practically a run, and the maximum amount of time used up keeping out of sight in alleyways only used by the marijuana-maddened toughs from the waterfront to relieve themselves.

One night Jones had just slipped through the shadows along the hundred yards known as Tiger Drag, where a policeman had had his jaw broken in three places only a month before, and was just about to dodge into an old graveyard for a quiet smoke when a voice spoke at his back.

'Hullo, Mr Jones.'

Jones turned round to face whoever it was had been stalking him, backing nervously into the wall.

'Don't you recognize me, Mr Jones? I'm Beynon.'

A tall figure hunched up in black leather had come up out of the shadows. Brass studs twinkled faintly in the light of a distant lamp. A brow, nose and jaw jutted boldly under an unfastened helmet.

'Not you again, Beynon? You're beginning to haunt me. Don't say you followed me here all the way from Cross Hands.'

'I got a job at the refinery, Mr Jones. Saw you passing the other day, and I thought we ought to meet again for a chat.'

'What's happened to your face, Beynon? Your face is different. It's almost unrecognizable.'

'It's the teeth, Mr Jones. I got a new set of teeth. They've filled my face out. My girl friend insisted on it.'

'A girl friend, eh?'

'Her people are Italians. Own a café. Her dad's going to

228

take me into the business when we get married. I got a motorbike too.'

'You fell on your feet right enough. Bit of a change from the old days up at New Mill, eh?'

'You're dead right, Mr Jones. You get in a rut, that's the trouble. You get in a rut.'

'You're well out of that, Beynon. That was no sort of a life for a young lad like you. That solitary existence you used to lead. Very unhealthy.'

'I seen you pass the café, Mr Jones. More than once. I been wanting to speak to you, but I didn't like to. I kept putting it off.'

'I don't see why you should have done that – even if our relations were a little strained once or twice in the past.'

'There was something I wanted to say, but I didn't know how you'd take it. It's been worrying me. I can't sleep at night.'

'What have you been up to now, Beynon? Come on, let's have it.'

'It's not what I've done, Mr Jones. It's what I haven't done. It's about Evan Owen.'

'Somehow I had a feeling it would be. What about him?'

'I'm not so sure he's dead.'

'Considering that statement you made, I'm surprised to hear you say that.'

'He could be. I don't say he isn't. But on the other hand he may not be. There's a doubt in my mind. Sometimes I lie awake at night and think of Bron Owen in Northfields.'

'That sounds a bit like a bad conscience to me.'

'How long will they keep him inside, Mr Jones?'

'Thirty years maybe. Probably the rest of his lifetime.'

'I thought it was ten years for murder nowadays.'

'If you're sane. Owen's a criminal lunatic.'

'And he won't get out under thirty years?'

229

'I'd say it was very unlikely.'

'That's a long time. Thirty years, eh? You can't really imagine it, can you?'

Jones agreed with utter sincerity. 'No, you can't imagine it.'

'That's terrible. That's really terrible. Thirty years. You got to feel sorry for him.'

'Being sorry for him won't do him much good, Beynon. I suppose you *were* telling the truth when you said you saw Bron Owen attack his brother?'

'I swear to God I was, Mr Jones. What I didn't say was I saw him kill him. I didn't say that. I can't be sure he's dead. That's why I wanted to speak to you.'

'He's dead as far as the law's concerned. His widow's inherited his property and his brother's in Northfields for killing him. There's no more to be said.'

'Mr Jones, I think I saw him on the morning after that night when his brother's supposed to have killed him.'

A door had opened in the blank wall near-by discharging a little sickly light and an infant's wailings. 'I think we'd better take a walk together,' Jones said.

The end of the street closed to a narrow embrasure on the night sky of the port, which was always pink. In this flushed haze derricks whined and rattled eternally. In between the raising and lowering of cargoes, gusts of beer-inflamed laughter, music and silence.

'What makes you think you saw Evan Owen?'

'I don't see who else it could have been.'

'Where were you?'

'Up by the oak forest on Pen Gof. I decided after what happened I didn't want to stay on at New Mill, so I got a few things together and locked up my cabin, and I thought I'd walk over to Sowbridge by the short cut to see if Roberts would give me a job. When I was up by the oak forest I

230

thought I saw Mr Owen going along the path about a quarter of a mile ahead of me.'

'You either saw him or you didn't see him, Beynon.'

'It was either Mr Owen or his ghost, Mr Jones.'

'And I suppose you believe in ghosts.'

'Not in Ferryport, I don't, Mr Jones. But on Pen Gof I do.'

Jones was inclined to agree with this summing-up of the phenomena of the occult.

'The trouble was you couldn't see much for the mist but I still don't see how there could have been any mistake. He went into the wood ahead of me, and after that I didn't see him again.'

'By this time you were on Roberts's land, weren't you?'

'I believe so, Mr Jones. It's hard to say. There aren't any landmarks up there.'

'What surprises me,' Jones said, 'is that you didn't say anything about this before.'

'I tried to tell Sergeant Broadbent, but he didn't want to know about it.'

'And also you weren't exactly upset at the thought of Bron Owen being in bad trouble, were you?'

'I didn't like him all that much, Mr Jones. That's a different thing to wanting to see him put away for thirty years.'

'You were jealous of him. You hated him like you hated almost everybody else. A poisonous young fellow, weren't you, now you come to think of it?'

'I've changed since then, Mr Jones.'

'And not too soon.'

'I've talked about my problems with my girl friend's family. They've helped me to see things in a different way. If there's anything I've done wrong I'll do anything I can to put it right.'

'If there's anything you've done wrong it's too late to do

anything about it now. Besides which I'm personally of the opinion that that imagination of yours has always been far too vivid. You lived on your own too long, and you were always inclined to see things. If all this had happened now and not six months ago you'd never have seen Evan Owen going into that wood up on Pen Gof.'

'You think I imagined it all, Mr Jones?'

'Knowing you as I do, I'm sure you did. You probably had a bad conscience about those anonymous letters and feeling the way you did about Mrs Owen. Things began to get on your nerves. In the end you saw things that weren't there. People do.'

'They never found the body, did they, Mr Jones?'

'No, they never found it and I don't suppose they ever will. But for all that Bron Owen admitted to the murder. That was a ghost you saw in the oak forest up on Pen Gof, Beynon lad.'

Jones went back to the station and spent an hour of his own time composing a report about this episode. He handed it in in the morning and the next day passed in expectation of being called in for an interview with the Inspector.

That evening just as he was going off duty the Station Sergeant handed the report back to him. The Inspector had scrawled across it in blue pencil 'No further action, please'. The, please, had been underlined three times.

20

The first year at Northfields passed easily enough. Bron was a quiet patient; the kind approved of by the staff. He gave no trouble of any kind, complained of nothing, wrote no inflammatory letters, requested no special interviews with the Superintendent, did the work he was given to do. He was soon issued a parole card and transferred to the privileged Block A.

Northfields was officially not a prison but a hospital for men and women driven by mental illness to commit crimes, but Bron soon found that even here it was a bad thing to be obviously mad. He discovered a class structure too, closely resembling the one the patients had suffered from or enjoyed in the outside world: a social pyramid with men who had always been relatively affluent, calm and well organized at the top, and the weak, the poor and the hopelessly foolish at its base. There was little mixing of the classes. The noisy, maniacal or 'difficult' patients of the inferior blocks lived comfortless, barrack-room existences, while their superiors of the parole block occupied bed-sitters surrounded by their personal property. From below there was proletarian envy and from above aristocratic fear and distaste.

But they were all there under Her Majesty's Pleasure, and the one punishment in common for all was celibacy. Males and females (pleasure men and pleasure women) met only under the closest segregation for concerts, or in the case of the top class for the Christmas dance. Here constancy was expressed in glances and gestures in the direction of an unchanged love object, and fickleness in their transfer to another – and in these nods and smiles the whole gamut of the relationship between the sexes was contained. At the Christmas dance of the apparently sane, bodies could be pressed discreetly together, and notes exchanged. Thus was the butterfly of love firmly pressed back into its chrysallis.

Bron, successfully sedated in accordance with Dallas's recommendation, lived coherently once again and avoided what was officially described as 'the period of adjustment' passed by so many new arrivals in a hospital bed, unable for weeks and months to face the brutal cropping of the dimensions of their lives. One of the first books he borrowed from the excellent library was Aubrey's *Brief Lives* and opening this by accident at a passage describing John Hoskins's experiences in close confinement in the Tower of London, he read, '. . . through a small chink he saw once a crowe, and another time a kite, the sight whereof was a great pleasure to him.' Bron found this in no way remarkable. He understood that the human capacity for joy could be cramped into any space and forced into any shape. He was able to divide his time between work in the library and in the garden, both of which gave him as much quiet pleasure as he was capable of feeling.

The main thing in Block A was to demonstrate one's normality and for this reason many of the pleasure men claimed that they were where they were only as the result of a successful counterfeit of madness at their trial. A man who could convince the Superintendent that he had feigned insanity was thought to have a better chance of eventual release than a sincere madman, however evident his cure. Bron admitted believing himself to have been the victim of complex delusions, and to have had no memory whatever of the murder he agreed that he had probably committed.

The admission cost him some loss of status, and two well-wishers, one of whom had strangled a mistress and the other who had pushed a complete stranger over a cliff, recommended him to change his mind as soon as possible and leak the information to the Superintendent through a sympathetic staff-member that he had in reality hoodwinked justice.

Despite all treatment, aspects of his delusions persisted. He was continually amazed at the detailed records preserved in his memory of the phantasmagoric affair with Wendy. Dallas had remained unimpressed. 'The brain's capable of inventing a whole lifetime of fictitious experience in a matter of seconds. You're the victim of a self-imposed emotional swindle.'

'She had a black mole on the inside of the thigh, just above the knee. Wouldn't it be possible for the Police Surgeon to examine her?'

'It would be quite out of the question. After all, she hasn't committed any offence.'

'Sorry, you're quite right. It would have put my mind at rest, that's all. It doesn't matter.'

'You'd better take my word for it that that mole doesn't exist.'

Dallas visited Bron in Northfields.

'Well what do you think of it after all?'

'We tame birds, sow seeds, play chess, write letters to M.P.s. I'm on the sports committee. There's just enough small worries to keep you happy.'

'Dr Simpson says you've made remarkable progress.'

'Things begin to add up.'

'That mole still there?'

'So far.' Bron laughed. 'It may vanish any minute now.'

'Don't let yourself be carried away on the tide,' Dallas said. 'Hang on. Don't go under.'

'I'm still afloat,' Bron said. 'It's a very insidious business though. Five years in here seems to be about the limit before you start softening up. The way I cope is to get interested in people's problems. Don't believe that story they tell you that you only have to cut out money and sex and everything straightens itself out. They still worry about how their kids are doing at their O levels.'

'Is there anything I can do for you?'

'As a matter of fact there is. I often wonder what became of Cathy. Sent her a letter but she never replied. She's a nice girl. I've a soft spot for her. I'd like to think she'd got over this business and looked like making some sort of life for herself.'

A few days later an attendant came to Bron's room to tell him he had a lady visitor.

'You mean the Official Visitor?' Bron asked, preparing his excuse.

'I imagine it's a friend, Mr Owen. Like to see her on the terrace?'

Bron followed him and found Cathy waiting, a slim shape in a dark dress, half-obscured by a gaunt potted shrub.

He took her hands. 'I've thought a lot about you, Cathy.' Bron was on good terms with the attendant, who decided to overlook the rule which prohibited any physical contact with a visitor.

'Dr Dallas came to see me,' Cathy said. 'I got your letter, and I've written three or four times and torn the letters up. I didn't know what to say.'

She seemed to be shrinking, becoming smaller in these surroundings which apart from the presence of the attendant, his head thoughtfully averted, resembled the palm lounge out of season in a second-rate seaside hotel, and smelt of Flit.

'Let me get you some tea,' Bron said. 'The canteen's just round the corner.'

She shook her head. 'I don't want anything,' she said in a whisper.

'I do,' Bron said cheerfully. 'I haven't had tea for months. Can't be bothered when I'm by myself.'

The attendant had come up. 'Anything I can get you, Mr Owen?'

'Some tea and cakes would be very nice, Peter,' Bron said.

The man gave a smile and something like a wink and went off to the canteen.

'Are they treating you well, Bron?'

'You can see for yourself. Peter's supposed to be on the spot keeping a look-out all the time, but he's quite prepared to stretch a point for a friend.'

Steam fizzled round the corner in the canteen as boiling water spurted into a teapot. A tall thin man came into sight wearing a sports coat and trousers identical with Bron's but with the additional sporting touch of a muffler wound round his neck. He went treading softly to a corner where he sat down with his back to the wall and took a small book from his pocket. His name was Burroughs and Bron knew that the book was a Bible he preferred to read where no-one but the benevolent Peter was likely to look over his shoulder. A-Block patients were careful to avoid any possibility of the stigma of religious mania.

Cathy was still inclined to glance round nervously as if afraid that some homicidal maniac might burst in upon them in these sedate surroundings. Peter shuffled back on his flat feet, carrying the tray. He recognized the superior intelligence of patients in A Block, and liked nothing better than the chance to serve these men he admired, and their visitors, with tea and rock cakes. He put down the tray and backed away before turning as if from the presence of Royalty.

She found it hard to speak. 'It's very quiet here, isn't it?' she said. Peter had picked up the Flit spray and wandered away to squirt at the high fronds of a rusted palm. In the corner the man in the muffler read contentedly of the begettings of the Book of Genesis, a forefinger passing from name to name.

Bron agreed. 'It's quiet enough most of time.' Like an iceberg, he thought, a fifth of its freezing mass showing above the surface in placid, arctic sunshine. 'Sometimes it reminds me of Mother's notion of heaven,' he said. 'Or at least the idea of it she managed to pass on to us. In the part where we are now, anyway. There's no marrying, or giving in marriage. You cease to want anything very much.' As he spoke Peter had put down the Flit spray and reached for a switch which flooded the space around them with a woolly rendition of Mendelssohn. 'And music all the time,' Bron said. 'Heaven plus barbiturates and regular meals, you might say.'

There was an expression of pain and wonder on her face. 'Is it as bad as prison was, Bron?'

'No,' he said. 'Not really. It's a different thing altogether. Prison's more like real life. It hasn't got much of Mother's idea of heaven about it.'

In his corner Bron noticed that Burroughs had got up, straightened himself carefully joint by joint, removed his ear-plugs, and was making for them. It was a sauntering, pseudo-nonchalant black-marketeer's approach.

He reached them, bowed to Cathy and smiled, then glanced away after Peter prowling distantly among the palms with his spray.

'Owen, so sorry to be a bore. Could I possibly have a word with you?'

238

'Of course you can, Eric. Excuse me a second,' Bron said to Cathy and got up.

'Don't come any closer,' Burroughs whispered. 'I think Peter's in a suspicious mood today. I can rely on you, Owen? You won't let me down, will you?'

'I won't let you down, Eric.'

'I know that my Redeemer liveth,' Burroughs whispered. Bron nodded agreement, and he smiled with relief.

'It's most kind of you, Owen. I knew you wouldn't mind. Do forgive me, won't you?'

He bowed again to Cathy, went back to his corner, found his ear-plugs, put them in his ears and went on reading. The music changed from Mendelssohn to Debussy.

'How's New Mill, Cathy?' Bron asked.

'I sold it to Roberts as soon as I got probate. I'm working in a shop in Brynaron now.'

'I'm glad of that. I used to worry, thinking about you alone in that place.'

'There's some money in the bank for you,' Cathy said.

'For me?' he said. 'Why?'

'I gave some of the money I got from the farm to my sisters and the rest is yours.'

'Money's no use to me here, Cathy. It's a generous thought, but all our wants are taken care of. There's nothing to buy but odds and ends from the canteen. Money hasn't any meaning any longer. You're allowed to earn a few shillings a week pocket money and that's all that's necessary. Really, Cathy, I don't need the money.'

'What can I do with it? I couldn't bear to touch it.'

'There's no shortage of charities,' he said. 'Hundreds of them. You could make out a list from the newspaper ads, shut your eyes and stick a pin in it.'

'I wanted so much to be able to do something for you.'

'I know you did, Cathy. And as a matter of fact there is

239

something you can do. One of my friends was given the bad news today and I'd like to give him a little present from the canteen. A pot of jam or some hair-oil.'

'The bad news – what's the bad news?'

'His wife won't be coming any more. The Superintendent had to break it to him. If you left ten shillings at the gate I could buy him something to cheer him up. I'm the luckiest man in A Block because I'm never going to be called up for one of the famous interviews.'

'The wife couldn't wait for him?'

'She waited three years. That's about the limit. People set out with the best of intentions, but a husband in North-fields is a hard thing for a woman to take. It's not a good idea to be a married man in Northfields, waiting for the blow to fall.'

'I'd wait for you for ever, Bron.'

He didn't understand. 'I think you probably would, Cathy. But you're one in a thousand.'

'And I will wait for you if you'll let me.' Her eyes were brimming with tears. This time there was no mistaking what she meant. There was a chink of alarm in his huge astonishment. He was not in a position to allow anything to threaten this unique tranquillity of mind.

He got up and took her hands again, and Peter, scenting tension in the air, moved closer to them.

'I'm lonely,' she said. 'Oh Bron.'

'You're going to be the loneliest girl in the world if you meant that.'

'Will you let me come and see you again?'

'I'd like to hear news of you.'

'And you won't let me come?'

'I can't stop you, Cathy, but it's better not to. I don't know how to explain,' he said. 'It's all very complicated. But hope is poison. So many people here are dying of it. We're all

240

going to die in this place anyway, but it's an easier death when you can get rid of hope. That's why I know I'll feel better if I don't see you again.'

Another spring and summer passed and Bron became more and more a part of his background. He read most of the books on historical subjects in the library and then stopped reading altogether. Having discovered a flair for the kind of macabre-facetious writing appreciated by the readers of the Northfields *Argus*, he took over the paper's gossip column. His daily newspaper had been discontinued back in the winter. Now he told the Welfare Officer he wouldn't be wanting his radio set any longer. He kept the relayed gramophone music switched on while in his room and every day for hours on end the soothing and persuasive waves of the music, so intelligently chosen by the Medical Superintendent, lapped softly on the beaches of his mind.

By the Superintendent he was regarded as the perfect patient. Above all, one who had a calming influence on the others. He was polite but inaccessible to the Church of England chaplain, and after two of her friendly and invigorating chats the Official Visitor quietly dropped him.

That winter the major topic in Block A was the relapse of a patient who had once been a personality of some stature in the City of London. It was the happening that created time in timelessness. This man had been released after fifteen years only to be brought back some six weeks later and thrust into the outer darkness of Block C. Bron obtained permission to visit him and offered many hours of solace in the form of close attention to the man's heartbroken outpourings of stock-exchange jargon. Bron found at about this time that he had lost his taste for smoking, and was happy to be able to give his cigarette ration away.

In the late spring the flower show was held, and in summer, sports day came and went. Four months ahead the Annual Dance and the Dramatic Society's play loomed like the pinnacles of Everest.

At the beginning of September Dallas called on Bron in his room. He immediately noticed the increasing bareness and above all the absence of the small, creased photograph of Bron's mother in its imitation tortoise-shell frame bought at the canteen.

'Still keeping afloat?'

'Swimming vigorously,' Bron said.

'You're looking very well, I must say. How's that mole these days?'

'The mole's gone,' Bron said. He smiled. He was correcting the proofs of his column in the *Argus*, and a sparrow hopped in through the bars of the open window and dipped its rump to let fall a small, glistening deposit on the top sheet.

He's humouring me, Dallas thought.

'I saw Cathy.'

'I know you did, thanks.'

'Anything you need at all – books or anything like that?'

'Absolutely nothing, thanks. Everything's fine.'

Dallas, who had intended to stay a half-hour, left Bron after ten minutes and called on Dr Simpson.

'Owen seems to have broken the cycle, as you predicted,' Simpson said. 'It's a remarkable recovery. Unique if the diagnosis was correct.'

'What now?'

'Just the usual convalescent period.'

'How long's it likely to be?'

'Allowing for the slow process of liberalization, I'd say ten years. It's fourteen at present.'

Dallas took a quick breath. 'Eric, when Owen came here I

had very definite reasons for believing that strings could be pulled.'

'Strings, James?' Simpson looked at him with curiosity.

'Haven't there been cases of certain patients being given – well, special consideration? I mean where positive guarantees were forthcoming.'

'I wouldn't know about that. Certainly not recently. Not in my time.'

It's too late, he's changed, Dallas thought. Two or three years ago he'd have done it. He'd have found some way. Now he's got his position to think about. Probably got his eye on the Super's job when he goes. He plunged in desperately.

'You're a very old friend, Eric. This is of great importance to me –' He stopped.

'Go on,' Simpson said.

'For the first time in my life I want to get on the Old Boy network. Can you arrange for me to meet the Superintendent socially?'

'It wouldn't do the slightest good, James. You'd be letting yourself in for a great deal of embarrassment, that's all.'

Dallas floundered on. 'There must be some way. I'd be prepared to take the man into my personal charge. Never let him out of my sight.'

Simpson shook his head. 'It's out of the question. Might have been possible to do something with the last Super, but not this one. In any case you're forgetting the Home Office. Things got a lot tougher after Randell went over the wall and strangled that girl. Pressure of public opinion.'

'He'll deteriorate,' Dallas said.

'They usually do.'

'The thing defeats its object, doesn't it?'

'Inevitably. It's all punishment under a different name. A superstition we inherit.'

243

'Wouldn't a recommendation from you to the Super do any good?'

'I'm afraid not, James. Let's face it, I'm not much more than a machine-minder here.'

'I see,' Dallas said. 'So there's nothing to be done. I'm sorry to have been a nuisance.'

'Not at all. I only wish I could have done something to help. Do forgive me for asking you this, though – but why do you believe, as you obviously do, that Owen is worth going to all this trouble about?'

'He's a good man,' Dallas said. 'One of the few really good men I've run into in my life. I seem to have let him down rather badly. Even a life sentence would have been better than this, because at the end of it there would still have been life.'

Dr Gooddy, a man affected by worry all his life, had become a psychiatrist because it upset him to lose his patients through death, and psychiatric patients rarely died of their complaint except by suicide. Beneath a façade of almost graven composure the Medical Superintendent's nerves twitched and crackled. He had three years to go to retirement, the C.B.E. and the shattering anti-climax of all the straining machinery of his small taut body and brain thrown out of gear, racing aimlessly in neutral until stopped by the breakage of a component. Only the immediate members of his staff could recognize the agitation of the moment by small unlikely symptoms – the sleepy narrowing of the eyes, an occasional attempt to yawn unobserved behind a raised palm.

'Tell him now,' Dr Simpson suggested.

'Wait for the order,' was the advice of Bennett, the psychotherapist.

244

'I must say that this is one time when I feel the Home Office might do its own dirty work,' Dr Gooddy said.

'Is there any drill at all laid down?'

'Absolutely nothing. That's just the trouble. There's no guidance of any kind. Nothing like this has ever happened before.'

Life in Northfields was conditioned and protected for staff and patients alike by the rules. There was an answer in the book to every question and a precedent to turn to in coping with every emergency. They lived in a cavern of petrified shapes which the drip of water altered so slowly that the change was never noticed. Once in ten, twenty, thirty years something like this happened, calling for agonized improvization, and then the improvization, too, became encrusted with its limestone. There was no hint in any of the rules and regulations, most of which Gooddy knew by heart, of what was to be done in a case like this.

'What *does* one do?' the Superintendent asked again.

'Would you like me to be there, sir?' Dr Simpson asked.

Gooddy had been hoping that Simpson would have offered himself as a volunteer for a preliminary chat with the man – a few considered words to prepare him for the official shock.

'If you'd care for me to be present –' Simpson said.

'Oh, I don't think so, Dr Simpson. Perhaps one should aim at as informal an atmosphere as possible. I was merely wondering about the possibility of breaking the news in some less brutal fashion.'

'Is it really a matter of breaking news at all, sir? Especially when you're dealing with a patient who's basically a very reasonable man.'

'I confess I hardly know what to expect. How *can* a man be expected to react to this kind of bombshell?'

.   .   .   .   .

The Superintendent compromised by sending for Bron outside his normal interview hours at a time just after lunch when a double brandy worked its short-lived daily miracle on the flattened perspectives of his life.

Normally the attendant who had come up with Bron would have stood behind his chair during the interview but Gooddy told him to go.

'Sit down, Owen. I've remarkable news for you. I won't keep you in suspense. I've just received a telephone message that the body of a man has been found that has been identified as your brother's.'

Bron nodded, accepting the inevitable. He was mildly surprised that they should have gone on looking so long.

'Death took place two or three days ago, and the cause was coronary thrombosis. My information is that your brother was working as a farm labourer, under an assumed name, about twenty miles from the place where he disappeared. A letter was found making it appear that the disappearance was elaborately planned as an act of vengeance. I've no doubt whatever that the balance of his mind was disturbed. Only the victim of paranoid delusions could have conceived such an extraordinary plan.'

Gooddy had keyed himself up for something that didn't come. What, he didn't know. A-Block patients were incapable of outbursts, but surely some outward evidence was to be expected of the huge chain reaction of emotion that such news must set off?

'I was going to say I can imagine what you must be feeling, but I simply can't. It's a situation that beggars the imagination. Really I'm at a loss for words.' A slight quiver of agitation had started in his hands and he thrust them away out of sight, under the table.

Bron said, 'I've learned here to accept everything, sir. Almost.'

246

'Whether the question of compensation will come up or not, I can't say. We've nothing to go by. I imagine something will be done.'

Having said this, Gooddy felt in some way demeaned.

'Is there anything else you'd like to know at this stage, Owen?'

'I don't think there is, sir.'

'As a matter of fact I must admit you know as much about what has happened as I do myself. I expect we'll receive an official release order from the Home Office tomorrow or the next day at latest. What are you doing this afternoon?'

'Correcting the proofs of my column in the *Argus*, sir.'

'Well, I'd give that a miss in the circumstances. There's a town shopping party going out in about half an hour and I think you'd better go with it. I leave it to you though. Do whatever you think you'd like to do.'

Inclusion in shopping parties to the town was the ultimate reward of the virtue of sanity, the summit of privilege to be reached only by a handful of A-Block patients in the last years of their official convalescence. They had come through every test of normality and their EEGs would have been more totally devoid of suspicion than nine samples out of ten taken at random of men and women in the street. Dr Simpson, in putting forward his list of names of candidates, had once said, 'These men are saner than I am.' He would have liked to add, 'And you too, sir.'

The eight men went down to Stoke Benham in the minibus, escorted by an attendant similarly dressed in a sports jacket and grey flannel trousers, and carrying a greenish light-weight raincoat. Bron, included in the party for the first time, sat in the back next to Burroughs, who as usual had slipped his Bible into his pocket before leaving. These

247

days it was respectably disguised under the dust cover of *From Russia with Love*. Twenty-two years before Burroughs had shot his wife and children. 'You seem on the quiet side today. Not enjoying yourself?' Burroughs said.

I must accept this too. I must accept this too. In a hundred wordless forms the thought had insisted itself in his mind. 'I expect it's my piece in the *Argus*,' he said. 'I seem to be running out of steam in the way of ideas.'

'More likely to be the time of the year,' Burroughs said. 'The atmosphere of stagnation. Nothing happening till Christmas. Find it will be all right when you've something to write about.' Burroughs had a secret motive for going on these parties, otherwise far preferring to remain undisturbed in his corner of the terrace reading in peace.

At Stoke Benham they put the car in the park and, to avoid being conspicuous, split into two groups of four, each group separated from the other by three or four paces, and made their way to Woolworths. Each man had been given 3s. 6d. to spend out of the 10s. he earned weekly.

Once in Woolworths Burroughs awaited his moment before quietly slipping away to spend his money as usual on a child's bracelet of coloured glass. This he would sleep with under his pillow for a night, sometimes dreaming, and in the morning he would put it down the lavatory.

Bron had placed himself alone to face a display of greenhouse equipment, but saw nothing. I must accept this too. Hatred he had never been able to understand. Why hatred?

One of the patients came up quietly.

'Owen, aren't you going to spend your money?'

'Nothing I want.'

'Could I borrow it then?'

'All right with me if you feel like taking the risk.'

'It's my passion for sweets. I'm so tired of all the canteen varieties. Are you all right by the way?'

Bron's lips had been moving.

'I'm fine. Wondering if it isn't too late to make a few changes in that *Argus* piece I just did.'

'Wouldn't bother, old boy, if I were you. You're too critical by half. Doing a wonderful job.'

From Woolworth's they moved on to Birdie Bride's tea-shop for tea and biscuits, paid for by the attendant and deducted from their credits. They sat at the two tables reserved for them at the back of the room and were served instantly and with superabundant friendliness by the waitress who, like all the other townspeople, knew who they were. This terrible isolating consideration with which they were treated was always a major grievance with the patients – in so far as they dared allow themselves a grievance.

Tea finished, Burroughs took out his Bible and read for a few minutes, with the pretence of an occasional chuckle at the exploits of James Bond. The heavy ticking of the grandfather clock in the corner called the attendant's attention. 'No hurry, gentlemen, but when you're ready.'

'I'll follow you,' Bron said. He went to the wash place, washed his hands, ran a comb through his hair and stared at himself in the mirror. I have to accept this.

By the time he reached the street the party, exhausted already by liberty, was straggling away in the direction of the car park, only three of them still in sight. Security on these outings was always very relaxed. As the Superintendent had decided, pleasure men who had worked their passages as far as this were amply guarded by the fear of forfeiting any part of their huge privileges.

It was a late autumn day in which summer had been called miraculously from its grave; a day with keen edges, its sounds chiming in the cool clean air, and the sunshine still bright and yellow, drawn up to the top windows, across slated roofs and into the treetops. The town was full of sharp movements, bicycle bells, and the laughter of people hurrying home.

Within seconds the last of his friends had been drawn away into the crowd and out of sight, and he turned away. The town was small and compact and he was soon outside it and at a crossroads where a signpost pointed in one direction to Bristol and the West. It seemed almost a command, and hardly had he made up his mind when a car stopped for him.

Bron got in.

'Where are you making for?'

'South Wales, by stages,' Bron said. 'Anywhere in that direction.'

He sat back in silence as the fields and the villages went past.

Brynaron. I'll get there by morning with luck. I wonder where I'll find Cathy?